RED TEARS

A Novel

Richard G. Higgins

RED TEARS

Available from Amazon.com, CreateSpace.com, and other related outlets.

ISBN-10: 099051840X
ISBN-13: 978-0-9905184-0-2

First Edition: June 2014
Printed in the United States of America.

Cover Design: Emily J. Brown

The poster used on the front cover can be found by going to www.allworldwars.com and then clicking on the Russian WWII Propaganda Posters link. The Cyrillic translates to: "Red Army soldier, save us!"

To my dearest fellow traveler, my wife Jean.

Acknowledgments

The subject of World War II in the Soviet Union has often been a journey in a dark tunnel for those of us in the West. However there have been significant explorers along the way who have enlightened our search.

The British writer John Erickson was one of the first and his work is still a great foundation. In more modern times fellow Brits Simon Montefiore and Orlando Figes have shed light on the Communist system and its wars. There are many others and their work deserves your attention. Earl Ziemke, Anthony Beevor, Stephen Fritz, David Stahel, Dennis Showalter, and Richard Overy are just a few.

It is my opinion that all of the German or Russian military memoirs such as those written after the war by Manstein, Guderian, Zhukov, and Rokossovsky are worth a read but should be taken with a mountain of salt. The war was still being fought in those writings.

To investigate the Soviet soldier, *The Damned and the Dead* by Frank Ellis, *Ivan's War* by Catherine Merridale, *Why Stalin's Soldiers' Fought* by Roger Reese, and Vasily Grossman's fiction epic *Life and Fate* are all must reads.

There is much more!

Those who inspired my effort deserve special recognition. Certainly at the top of the list are David Glantz, and his partner of several books, Jon Houston. Their spectacular search for the truth and brilliant writing, and their personal encouragement were so greatly appreciated. The noted historians Flint Whitlock, Don Miller, Carlo D'Este, and Rick Atkinson all added their encouragement. Flint Whitlock, my editor for *WWII Quarterly*, is also a technical inspiration.

Finally my close friend, Major Adam Morgan, my brother Mark, my life partner, Jean, and my daughter Colleen made everything possible. Thank you!

Table of Contents

Characters

Historical:

Stalin, Supreme dictator of the Soviet Union

Beria, Head of the NKVD (secret police), Stalin's chief executioner and GULAG commander

Molotov, Politburo member and Stalin confidant

Mekhlis, Chief political officer (Commissar) of the Red Army, Beria's right hand man

Marshal Zhukov, the equivalent of Eisenhower later in the war and Dmitry's "uncle" after the death of his parents

General Rokossovskii, later Marshal, brilliant Soviet war leader, also half-Polish like Dmitry

Various Soviet generals and marshals, including Tukhachevskii, Boldin, Kachalov, Pavlov, Timoshenko, Voroshilov, Budyenny, Konev, Shaposhnikov

Various German Generals, including Guderian, Bock, Model, Von Rundstedt

Fictional:

Dmitry Zhankovskii, Colonel in Soviet Military Intelligence (GRU) and Hero of the Soviet Union

Sergeant-Major Vladimir Rasilev, aka The Bear, Dmitry's friend and comrade

Major Irina Petrova, Red Army surgeon and Dmitry's long-time lover

Taka and Sachino Sharadze, Georgian brothers in the Red Army, serving with Dmitry

Felix Vasilev, seasoned *razvedchik* and member of Dmitry's command

Lev Nitkin, ditto

Piotr Shanislav, Red Air Force pilot assigned to Dmitry

Lucy Masterson, a lover of Dmitry's later during the war in Washington, DC

Thomas Masterson, Dmitry and Lucy's son

Yedved, Commissar and executioner for Beria and Mekhlis

Alexander and Maria Zhankovskii, Dmitry's parents, killed in the Bolshevik war with Poland, 1920

Natasha Zhankovskii, Dmitry's sister

Glossary

cucumber - Russian slang for a soldier, similar to GI

front - Group of Soviet armies, no US equivalent

Einzgruppen – German *SS* Death Squads operating in the Soviet Union

GKO – Political committee running the Soviet war effort, headed by Stalin

GRU – Soviet Military Intelligence

GULAG – The system of prison and death camps run by the NKVD.

HOSU – Hero of the Soviet Union, the highest Soviet civilian and military award.

Lubyanka – Headquarters building of the NKVD, the Soviet secret police.

Kremlin – Ancient Tsarist fortress in Moscow, center of the Soviet Government.

NKVD – Soviet secret police in charge of internal security, the prison camps, and special units designed to police the Red Army.

OSS – Office of Strategic Services. US spy network headed by 'Wild' Bill Donovan.

Politburo – Ruling committee of the Soviet Union.

Razvedka – Russian term for reconnaissance.

Razvedchik(i) – Specialized GRU troops for actions behind enemy lines. Arguably the world's first special forces.

SS – German special units derived from Hitler's body guards. Responsible for both battle troops and death squads.

Stavka– Soviet high command composed of political and military members, headed by Stalin.

Vozdh – Russian for the boss. Commonly used to refer to Stalin.

Wehrmacht – German armed forces.

Prologue

Dmitry Zhankovskii prepared himself for the drop. Agent exchanges at his age were something you must be totally prepared to execute flawlessly. At the same time he allowed his gaze to wander. The autumn weather was brilliant with change and warmth. A golden haze of leaves embraced the green expanse and contrasted with the white marble of the edifices. He always enjoyed the enemy's capital. It was more open and less dominating than the maze of the Kremlin.

Staring down the Mall to the Washington Monument he reflected on the change from wartime. Back then the Mall had been thick with temporary housing for various military and civilian war agencies, a hive of activity. However, on this September Sunday it was tranquil. The miracle of the transformation to a quiet contemplative landscape amazed him and brought back memories.

The OSS office had stood nearby where he worked with General "Wild Bill" Donovan, head of America's spy service during the war. The various Lend-Lease offices were also near here, where he had arranged for the shipments to Russia via the terrible winter convoy routes into Murmansk. He still recalled the stoic American acceptance of the losses in men, ships, and materiel to deliver the trucks and aircraft to the desperate Soviets. At the time it had taught him a lesson about the soft capitalists. He never underestimated them again.

But most of all he remembered Lucy. He had never seen her again after leaving Washington in 1943.

Memories of a hand on his knee, sending a message of caution at a meeting, the same hand welcoming his advances and cherishing his battle scars, the same woman in so many roles. Most bitter was the memory of how he had betrayed her and all those he had worked with in the US. All for the greater good of the Soviet Union! He smiled, at how he had actually believed that! So naïve, the Hero of the Soviet Union, the great general, the secret agent!

Now the physical vista was wiped clear of the past and Lucy was long married. His short grey hair provided a great scrubbing board as his hand swept over his head, seemingly to erase the mental vista he had been visiting. His stature, while he sat, improved and resumed that of the general, the experienced military man. The tautness in the jaw relaxed as he began to prepare for the short meeting.

She had described the agent to him. Eighteen years old, tall, blonde, lean. An athlete and avid student at his high school, he was already slated for Yale University. Smart and agile like his father; actually like both of them, Dmitry smiled. This was his only chance to meet his son of long ago. His son, Lucy's son, accepted by her husband who had been at military training in the Western US when Thomas was conceived but was fortunately confused by a Christmas leave. A boy they were all proud of. This was Dmitry's one chance at seeing him, arranged by Lucy. He had sent her a message using their old lover's code. She had responded immediately, yes. The tourist map he would exchange with Thomas was the mechanism for changing his life, as they say, forever.

The bench and the sun were warm so he removed his sport coat but kept the sweater on. The eyes which had seen much of war and subterfuge scanned the area and saw nothing remotely representing a threat. While staying at the Embassy he had talked of memories and the Mall and the likelihood of dropping by to examine the past. The KGB had probably made a mental note and followed him from his quarters this morning and were lounging somewhere near, but a chance thirty second meeting with a young runner could easily be dismissed.

At that moment Thomas rounded the corner onto the Mall's dirt walkway and Dmitry rose as he got closer. "Excuse me young man! I am visiting but lost, could you point to my location on the map?" Thomas slowed and stopped and took the offered map. "Here," he said, "you are here." "Thank you and have a good run," Dmitry concluded. Dmitry's map had slipped very quickly into Thomas's shorts and been replaced with a duplicate. Thomas waved and was off. His mother had coached him well and clearly the courage of deception ran in his veins.

Dmitry rose to walk and as always was reminded by protesting joints of his many adventures both on the battlefield and in clandestine corridors. He looked ever so tenderly at the rapidly disappearing figure and his hand moved as if stroking him, longing for a touch that was not to be. More important things than feelings were being played out on this fall day in 1962. The photos he sent with Thomas would shake the world awake. As he walked back in time he remembered when it all began to unravel, June 21, 1941.

Chapter 1

Dmitry stepped into the chaotic office where General Zhukov was bent over his cowering secretary, shouting into a phone, "No, do not fire on the German aircraft. Comrade Stalin has expressly forbidden it. Continue to report but no shooting or you will be on the receiving end of shooting. Do it!" The office's normal sense of organized purpose was buried in a wild symphony of shouts and gestures.

The phone slammed into the receiver and the bulldog General, Chief of Staff of the Red Army, looked up as he released his secretary. "Dima," Zhukov smiled and moved to hug Dmitry. "So good to see you, looking very smart in your new Colonel's insignia. However, in any uniform of the Workers and Peasants Army your parent's eyes would swell with pride. But enough pleasantries, tonight we have a tough nut to crack. The Politburo and Stalin are still hamstringing our efforts to prepare for a German attack. You must convince them! Timoshenko and I are halfway to Siberia on this topic but you are respected and remembered as the savior of Lenin. They will listen. Are you ready?"

"Always ready, Comrade General," Dmitry replied. They both shared a grin at this overzealous expression but a trusted glance exchanged between them conveyed the true urgency of the situation. Dmitry had been orphaned when his fervently Bolshevik parents were killed in the 1920 invasion by the Soviets of Poland. Lenin had been close to his parents and personally selected Zhukov to raise him. Their relationship was as strong as the stoutest oak.

"Fine," Zhukov responded, "Let's go, get the lead out." They walked down the long Kremlin corridors to the meeting room for the night and entered as Stalin was berating Chief of the Army Timoshenko for war scares. Zhukov looked to his boss for a signal but Timoshenko was at attention and silent as the scathing tirade continued. Finally when he paused for breath, Stalin said, "What lamb for the slaughter is this, Zhukov? It is our young Red hero, Dmitry Zhankovskii. Welcome to our party, young comrade. What do you have for us?"

Zhukov replied for Dmitry. "Comrades, I have asked comrade Colonel Zhankovskii here to demonstrate the latest advances in aerial reconnaissance. His techniques have given us powerful sky-borne eyes with which to defend the Motherland. He will demonstrate and explain his findings."

Dmitry scanned the room but other than the military present he saw little support. Ah, the state has asked much but this might be the last stop before Siberia, he thought. He especially watched Marshal Budyenny and Stalin's chief of the secret police, the NKVD, Beria, where the opening attacks would likely come from. Give me a battlefield and no hope any day over this bunch, he reflected.

Stiffening to attention he opened, "Comrade Stalin, members of the Politburo, and fellow members of the Red Army and Fleet, I have the latest aerial photos from our borders to show to you. I will pass them around and explain what you are looking at. Comrade

Stalin, please examine the first photo." He waited as an aide delivered the photo to Stalin who squinted at the image. "Comrade, the dark blotches in the center have been revealed to be tanks in camouflage. Further we have identified them as the *Das Reich* and *Grosse Deutschland* elite *SS* divisions under General Heinz Guderian. He is the German expert on tank warfare and after Poland and France has earned himself the nickname 'Hurrying Heinz'. This was not given to him by the ladies of the aforementioned countries but by the *Wehrmacht* who could barely keep up with him. We at the GRU believe he will be the spearhead for the German attack, and here he is a few miles from our border near Brest on the River Bug."

Stalin passed the photo on and in a very soft tone said, "Enough, Zhukov, we have been through this and little shit marks on a photo do not change anything. There will not be a German attack. Germany is busy up to its neck with the war in the West, and I am certain that Hitler will not risk creating a second front by attacking the Soviet Union. He has assured me of this time and again. I am tired of this discussion and we are wasting our young hero's time. By the way, rather than sitting at a desk looking at pretty pictures why is he not in the field with Budyenny? Get him there and we will not discuss photos anymore."

Zhukov visibly swelled and muttered as if being strangled. Finally he exploded, "*Vozdh*, we will be attacked and within days. You must listen to us military men. We are sworn to protect you and our Red Motherland. The Germans will come and we must be ready. We have *razvedchiki* behind German lines and also overseas agents, such as RAMSAY (Richard Sorge of the GRU), in Tokyo telling us daily to expect an attack. Even Churchill tells us to be ready. *Vozdh*, we must improve our readiness!"

Stalin's eyes turned black and opaque as he shouted at the General, "No, no, and no, Zhukov! And for the last time. This discussion is over and perhaps you need a visit to Comrade Beria's fine accommodations to think this over? This discussion is finished."

While Beria smirked at Stalin's comments, Marshal Timoshenko rose very slowly and with the demeanor of a man walking his last steps said, "Comrades, can we not agree to issue orders for higher vigilance and further reconnaissance? These can be issued within hours and provide good guidance to our field armies." Timoshenko stood waiting for the human hurricane to end his tenure as military chief. Instead, Stalin looked at Beria who nodded ever so tightly. "All right," Stalin declared. "But I must personally approve the orders. We will stay in session until they are drafted. Comrade Zhukov, leave the room and draft the order now. Don't waste my time with military fluff and hidden meanings, keep it simple."

Zhukov stood, nodded his assent and barely able to navigate, grabbed Dmitry and headed for the door. Once on the other side and with no witnesses, he whispered to Dmitry. "I felt the damp of the Lubyanka on my face, I tell you Dima, and you were almost training ponies in Siberia. We will work out this business with Budyenny; give me a day or two. Let's write these goddamn orders and do the work we are best at, fighting fascists."

Zhukov rapidly dictated the orders which stated that Red Army elements on the border and NKVD Border troops should move to a higher level of readiness and recon their front for signs of German forces. Additionally, as steady streams of German deserters had been warning the Red Army of an upcoming attack, these reports were to be immediately forwarded to Army HQ. Zhukov scanned Dmitry, "You are a tough old dog to have walked into that trap. Leave for tonight while you can, but come see me first thing tomorrow. We need to talk." Dmitry saluted the General and with the words, "I am honored to stand beside you, Comrade General," spun on his heel and walked erect and smoothly out of the Kremlin office.

Dmitry headed for his flat in Government House on the Moscow River, not far from Red Square. As he walked to cross at the *Bolshoi Kamenny Most* (Great Stone Bridge) his thoughts almost overwhelmed his exterior poise. He was no foolish young officer. He was a seasoned Colonel of the GRU, the most secret and effective military intelligence unit in the world. Therefore, he knew how to interpret what had just happened and his finely trained mind sifted and turned evidence into conclusions.

He recognized that there were at least two messages being sent in that meeting. One was for him personally. Stalin and Beria had their eye on him and that was not a good feeling. Sending him to Budyenny effectively got him out of the intelligence loop and under Budyenny's observation which would be passed directly to Stalin through Beria. An inadvertent shudder accompanied the thought of how he would be portrayed in those sessions.

He had no desire to return to the Lubyanka basement. He remembered 1938 after the deaths of many in the Red Army officer corps, how the knock had eventually come to his door. There were many 2 AM noises in Government House as party members and military officers were taken, with few returning. His turn came on a night when, thank God, Irina was not with him. The NKVD loved that type of double capture and personal pressure. They had not yet attacked one of the most prominent female physicians in the capitol but who knew what schemes they were hatching. At any rate, they had torn his apartment apart looking for evidence of association with 'right-wing Bonapartist' factions in the Red Army.   His mentor, General Rokossovskii, half-Polish like Dmitry, had gone to the camps under this charge and had just recently been released as the need for proven officers overcame political judgments. After hours of wrecking his small and meagerly furnished flat they had taken him, in one of the bread trucks used so as not to alarm the good citizens of Moscow, the few blocks to the Lubyanka.

The interrogation was somewhat light by their standards with just body punches and kicking but it hurt nevertheless. His old teacher, now purged and shot, Marshal Tukhachevskii, featured prominently in the "conversation." He admitted studying with him and later working on tank tactics with him as they both rose in the Red establishment until that day in June 1937 when the Army purge began and the Marshal and a number of others of high rank were executed. Just as

Tukhachevskii and Rokossovskii did before him, Dmitry took the beating and rolled with the questions. "I lost two fingers and many teeth due to my insolent attitude. It doesn't pay. Don't confess to their absurd charges but don't taunt them either," Rokossovskii had advised.

Well, as usual the General had been correct. When the chief torturer for the NKVD, Yedved, had come to his cell to conduct the formal interrogation Dmitry was bloody and bruised but had not lost any extremities or critical body parts, yet. Yedved said, "Comrade, what have you done to be in such a fix? You must have committed an awful sin against the Motherland or Stalin to be visiting with us here." Having expected a torrent of charges and falsified evidence, Dmitry was surprised and somewhat encouraged by this opening. Maybe they don't have even the foundation of a false case and they are fishing, he thought.

"Comrade, I have no idea why I am in this place. I am loyal. I have always been stalwart in the service of my country!" Well, that doesn't mean much these days," Yedved smirked. "You were too close to Tukhachevskii and his Bonapartist plans to assassinate Comrade Stalin and also with the conspirator Rokossovskii! So don't play innocent. I can only imagine the crimes perpetrated when you were hanging about in that company, not to mention your time in Berlin with the fascists. Tell me comrade, what was the plan?"

Dmitry decided to play his only card. "You know I saved Comrade Lenin in 1918 and at a young age proved my worth to the state. Comrade Stalin has awarded me the Hero of the Soviet Union for this action. He has praised me as the ideal Bolshevik soldier. How can he be wrong?" The smallest of uncertainties hatched in Yedved's eyes and he in turn shrugged. "People change and they always hide many things," he said."Will you tell me what you and the others were plotting? Perhaps a word with comrade Beria would keep you alive, so many have died."

Dmitry shook his head and said "I have no knowledge of any plot by the Red Army against our Motherland and I proclaim my loyalty to Comrade Stalin!" Yedved sighed and nodded to the two brutes standing beside him. As he left he said, "Please think about your situation and we will talk again."

But they didn't, and after another somewhat cursory beating, Dmitry was taken to a bread truck and driven home. More or less dumped on the street in front of Government House, he counted himself very fortunate.

As he continued his walk home he recounted that memory and decided that a fragment of a threat to mind his opinions had come from Stalin tonight. The second message from Stalin was for the Red Army. They did not know their job and he would tell them how to do it. Perhaps after the miserable debacle in Finland there was some truth in this, but with the promotion of Zhukov and Timoshenko things had all changed. The new orders and army regulations which instilled rigid discipline and required more training had improved the Army's skills, but the *Vozdh* had a long memory. This message had been received by Timoshenko and Zhukov and they had to live with its consequences. Little did any of them know what the consequences of that memory were for the future.

Chapter 2

Rising early with the Russian summer sun, Dmitry moved into his routine but a knock on the door shattered that morning and many to come. His heart raced at the early morning knock but thankfully it was followed by shouting. "Comrade Colonel, you must come to HQ at once. Comrade General Zhukov orders this." As he moved for the door Dmitry thought perhaps this was a trick and grabbed his TT-33 revolver, even though a fight was suicide. He opened the door and recognized Sergeant-Major Rasilev and said, "Holy Mother, Bear, what are you doing, auditioning for Beria's greeters?" The somewhat large and disheveled sergeant looked first hurt, then sly, and replied, "If I were, you are a fine catch in your shorts, Comrade Colonel!" As they embraced he exclaimed, "The Germans have attacked. The front is a mess; the Comrade General needs you now, Dima!" Dmitry was the picture of disbelief as he absorbed the intelligence. "Are we fighting? Where are they attacking? How are we doing? Are we driving them back?"

The look in the Bear's eyes said it all. "It's total shit, Dima. Nobody knows anything except that we are running out of our pants to get away from the fucking panzers. We are overrun and nothing is known of the actual situation. That is why Comrade Zhukov wants you, a decorated Hero of the Soviet Union, to fly to the front and figure out where Comrade Stalin's front yard now ends! God and St. George will bless you for your bravery and the mighty state will sing your praises! I am to get you to the airfield and, with a tear in my soldierly eye, salute you as you take off on your brave but suicidal mission."

This was quite a long speech for the Bear but he clearly relished making it and smartly, in direct contrast to his embarrassing uniform, he threw a very British style salute at Dmitry, who just shrugged and observed, "All in a day's work.," he said as he pulled on the uniform. "Come on Bear; let's visit Uncle and then do some flying!"

Red Army HQ at the Kremlin was chaos. Even to find Zhukov was difficult, but find him they did. Zhukov eyed Bear's uniform with a look that said later for you, my friend. The Bear stood at enormous attention hoping the thrust of his chest hid the stains on his tunic and his slightly off center Order of the Red Banner, Order of the Red Star, and Order of Bravery, plus his Lake Kazan medal earned while fighting with Zhukov in Mongolia. No Marshal could match the military splendor of his chest, he thought. However, Zhukov was too distracted to even notice. "Dima, get a plane from Monino and fly west down the Minsk highway until you locate the fighting. Sort out the troop positions and land in Minsk where you can call me with the information. Do not tell anyone, but we have no idea where any of our troops are and the orders being issued do not reflect the reality of the situation. Casualty reports are either nil or ludicrously low and I am worried about our real capabilities. Get going and do this well for the Motherland or we will be fucked! I need intelligence! Get it! Bless you and luck!"

With that the General plunged back into the chaos and Dmitry took off at a run. The Bear huffed along beside him and said, "I have a car at the Watch-tower Gate and I'll drive you to Monino." Dmitry risked a side long glance as he plunged down the Pal-ace stairs since he didn't know Bear could drive. It was obviously a newly acquired skill as gears clashed and tires slipped and grabbed, protesting with their screams as the vehicle careened through Moscow's streets. There was panic in the crowds and air raid si-rens blared but Dmitry dismissed this. The *Luftwaffe* came by night, not by day.

At 0300 on June 22, 1941, Hitler launched an overwhelming force at the unready Soviet border. From the Baltic to the Black Sea, a front of over 1500 kilometers, the *Wehrmacht* and *Luftwaffe* went for the throat of the Russian bear. The massive attacking forc-es included four million men, 3350 tanks, and 2000 aircraft. The Nazi forces attacked in three major groups: North, Center, and South. The surprise and initial success was complete. The German Field Mar-shals were confident it would all be over in three months. Dmitry was heading for the initial attack by the German Center Group focused on the city of Minsk.

Dmitry and Bear both survived the drive and a plane was waiting. Dmitry shook his head in wonder at yet another miracle pulled off by the Bear. As he got his gear from the aviation officer including a camera and a newly issued PPsh submachine gun, a pilot stepped forward. "Lieutenant Pilot Shanislav to fly you, sir!" Dmitry slowed and eyed the young pilot, his immaculate uniform, Order of the Red Star badge and sized him up as a good man. "Comrade, today I fly myself; there is no need for two to take the risk." The pilot snapped, "I have orders, sir." "I'm a GRU colonel, young aviator, and I give you new orders, go kill some fascists, I fly alone." The aviator snapped a salute and said, "If I can be of use to the Colonel in the future please do not hesitate to order me."

With that Dmitry got into the two-seater open cockpit Polikarpov R-5 biplane and radioed for clearance. The tower warned him that many Red Air Force planes were taking ground fire from friendly but nervous troops and to gain altitude quickly after takeoff. They wished him luck and the soft lift of the tiny aircraft sent him straight skyward and west. He did notice the massive bulk of a certain sergeant at rigid attention and saluting on the airfield, as he increased throttle.

He overflew Minsk about three hours later after a refueling stop and observed that the streets were clogged with troops, civilians, and livestock. He continued west and listened for artillery but the airplane noise was just too much. Suddenly about 60 kilometers west of Minsk the road became completely clogged with Red Army troops, heading east! What the shit, he thought as he flew lower, but soon he began receiving rifle fire, wild but dangerously close. He rocked his wings to show the Red Star with mixed results and decided to gain altitude and keep an eye out for the aircraft causing the troops to be so trigger happy. What he didn't know was that by the evening on the first day of the fascist attack the Red Army air force in this region lost over seven hundred planes, mostly on the ground, and the colonel commanding the force had committed suicide. The fascists owned the skies over the retreating Soviets.

Just ahead the smoke was cripplingly black obscuring his view of the ground action. He tried flying low but even within one hundred feet of the ground it was too dense to see in the smoke, and the smell! It was hell itself, a combination of burning grain, fuel, and bodies. He choked and tried to breathe shallowly but the toxic cloud was too much. Dmitry winged north to get a different view and broke into the clear. Here he saw Red Army troops engaged with panzers, falling back. The armor's advance was relentless and the grey of the *Wehrmacht* infantry was right behind the tanks. As he watched, a *Stuka* broke off from ground attacks to target him. He could not outrun the fighter so he headed for the suffocating smoke where he could at least hide. He circled for a while and finally headed east, having seen both too much and not enough. He landed in Minsk's main square to avoid the burning airfield and ran for the familiar Party HQ building.

He ordered some guards to refuel the R-5. It was bedlam inside with someone screaming on the phone with the Kremlin, "We are under massive attack; the Army is fighting but cannot hold. We need assistance." Dmitry grabbed the phone and the burly Georgian accent on the other end could only be Beria. "Comrade Beria, this is Colonel Zhankovskii, is comrade General Zhukov there?" The phone almost froze in his hand as the breathing on the other end heightened and quickened. "What? What are you doing in Minsk?" "Scouting for the General, is he there?" The phone was handed over and Zhukov came on the line.

"What the fuck is going on, Dima? Where is the army? Are we holding? What forces are we facing? "Comrade General, it is difficult to know anything here but I overflew the battlefield and saw panzers pushing our lads back. They are only 50 kilometers from Minsk and the fight is desperate. We must have reinforcements and organization. We also have no air cover. The fascist *Stukas* are everywhere."

"Dima, get back here and try to map the situation. Bring a Party official or Army officer with you to assist. We need information!" "Yes, Comrade General, I will land in Red Square with the information in three hours." Dmitry handed the phone back to the cowering official and looked around for someone who looked calm. He spotted an evident leader giving evacuation orders and approached him. "Comrade, you are to accompany me to Moscow by order of General Zhukov." As the man turned white and passed a hand in front of his face, Dmitry realized what he had triggered. "Not for questioning but to help build a picture of the situation for Red Army HQ." The man assented and introduced himself as Nikolai Translet, Deputy Party Leader in Minsk, and they headed for the plane.

The guards were pushing crowds back from the plane and told Dmitry they could not hold for long. "Fire some shots in the air and I will throttle out of here!" he ordered. They complied and some taxi space opened for Dmitry. He shouted, "Good luck and kill some Germans for me!" as they got airborne and turned east for Moscow.

Returning to Army HQ via a landing in Red Square that fortunately Bear supervised to prevent a

---

bad reception from the Kremlin Guard, who by this time were shooting at anything unfamiliar, Dmitry and his passenger made their way once again into the furor of Zhukov's office. On the way Dmitry deposited his film with the developing room and after a few encouraging orders of *Bustro! Bustro!* (Hurry, Hurry) they agreed to a one hour developing process.

Back in Zhukov's office Dmitry began his report. "Comrade General, if we can have some maps, I can give you an idea of the Minsk situation. By the way, this is the Minsk Deputy Party leader, comrade Nikolai Translet, and he will assist." Maps were brought and spread on tables in the meeting room adjacent to Zhukov's office. Soon other staff officers arrived including Dmitry's boss, GRU Chief Golikov, who reported directly to Stalin.

"Comrades," Dmitry began, "Our forces are under extreme pressure and appear to be losing ground quickly to a combined air, ground, and armor attack. Just west of Minsk I identified the forces of our 3rd and 4th armies. Opposing them is the *Das Reich* combined infantry and tank force. From the air, the failure of our counterattacks was apparent. They are too widespread to counter the German armor advantage and consequently once they reach their exhaustion point the fascists counterattack from the flanks and our men are forced to retreat. I saw this happen twice in 30 minutes. We will likely lose Minsk if things are not shored up. We should establish a heavily fortified fall back line in front of the city and await the fascist attack there."

As he spoke Dmitry was aware of the disbelieving looks being cast at him from around the room. His own boss seemed to wear the sourest expression. When he paused to let Translet discuss the civilian and resource situation, the room literally lifted in reaction to the negative comments being voiced. "How can this be?" Where is our armor?" "What of the established defensive positions?" They should stop the fascist dogs in their tracks!" "Our brave men never retreat and a major Soviet city cannot be allowed to be captured!"

Zhukov intervened, "Comrades, Colonel Zhankovskii and Party Leader Translet have provided us with vital information. What is to be done? First, the air force, what are you doing?" The staff liaison shook his head and stated with gravity that they had launched waves of fighters which never returned and had also taken severe losses of aircraft on the ground. Additionally, their bombers had been wiped out to the last machine due to a lack of fighter support in their daytime raids to assist the ground forces. "I am sorry to report, Comrade General, that the air force can provide only minimal ground support until our losses are replaced, which will take weeks."

Zhukov stared at the maps and swept his hand across the Minsk area. "Then the cucumbers are on their own. Contact General Pavlov and find out his plans and let me know. We need to slow this wave down before we are overwhelmed. Comrade Colonel, further develop the positions on the map and then report to me soonest." Zhukov stomped from the room and a heavy door slam was followed by a heavy thud as his fist crashed into his office wall. The assembled staff all quietly slipped out to fulfill their assignments.

Dmitry looked at Nikolai and said, "Welcome to the Workers and Peasants Army. You see us at our worst." He hastened to add, "Things will get better as we regain our poise. The Red Army will not allow the fascists a free walk into Minsk!"

With that he told Nikolai to plot the civilian routes out of Minsk so the military could avoid them. He arranged for food for Nikolai, begged some tea from the office personnel and headed for Zhukov's office with a heavy step. His razor blue eyes betrayed nothing but his heart was heavy and to get his thoughts in order, his right hand scrubbed at the short regulation style dirty blond hair until some badly needed ideas began to flow.

He entered Zhukov's private office and was signaled to close the door. Zhukov gave a sour look and stated, "We have cleaned the NKVD bugs from this office five times in six weeks, so we should be free to speak our minds. First, good job in Minsk. Believe it or not that is the only information I have. We have been unable to reach the *front* commander, Pavlov, by phone, so I am blind as a pig in the trough. As always, Dima, you did a good job, and by the way we need to talk about Sergeant-Major Rasilev's appearance especially when he is in the Kremlin, someday. However, he escapes for another time as the *Vozdh* and the Politburo have ordered me to meet with Khrushchev in Kiev to ascertain the situation there. Vatutin will act in my place. A good man and capable. I have told him to use you in any capacity and if there is any issue with that skulking Golikov I will straighten it out on my return."

"Dima, things are clearly very bad and the fact that we have no information says they are probably worse. I am putting you in charge of the Minsk plan as you have been on the scene. The plan is to abandon Minsk, but no one can know this for now. Work with your Party Leader to develop an effective evacuation plan for both the army and civilians. Then recommend where we can make a stand in front of Smolensk to stop this fascist barbarian horde. All in secrecy, Dima! It could kill morale if it became common knowledge, use Bear as an orderly but clean him up! Take whatever support personnel you need and lock them in my conference room. No one is to know, not even the *Vozdh*. I will tell him when I return."

"Got it? Go with God! I need you, Dima, to make this happen. Now get something to eat and get to work, you have two to three days! Out!" "Comrade Marshal, uncle, I will do this but I urge great care on your journey. The fascist aircraft are everywhere and our flyboys are not to be found. Journey quietly and quickly. Until your return, Sir!" As Dmitry turned and left, Zhukov shouted at his back, "And get the goddamn wall fixed!"

Dima went through the door more stunned then he had been at the first knowledge of war. War he had expected, but to abandon Minsk, as historic as any city in the Soviet Union, to the fascists was staggering. My God! The knowledge stunned and humbled him but his resolve climbed as he thought of the Germans in Minsk. No more! Not again, he resolved.

The next few days were a swarm of activities, planning, and trying to understand dispositions and the status of armies. The news was universally bad as troops were cut off and masses of equipment lost. The only hope was to bring up reserves and troops based in the Far East. Dmitry drew up the orders and submitted them to Vatutin for review, and when Zhukov returned the plan was ready.

Finally Timoshenko and Zhukov met with the Politburo to explain the plan. The meeting was again contentious and instead of letting the army fall back from Minsk as recommended, they insisted on another counterattack. The military resisted but the political wing was adamant. Orders were drafted for the *front* commander, Pavlov, to send General Boldin and his tank army on the attack. Dmitry was designated to carry the orders to Pavlov and to stay and witness the results.

Again, a plane was arranged and with Nikolai, the Party executive accompanying him, they flew to Pavlov's HQ, now found near Baranovichi, just outside of Minsk. "Comrade General, I am Colonel Zhankovskii of the GRU," announced Dmitry at Pavlov's HQ. The staff and the general all looked downcast and sour, expecting the worst. "I am carrying orders to have General Boldin attack the Hitlerites and stop their advance," Dmitry continued. At this most of the group either looked sullen or stared at their boots. There was no sense of energy or defiance in the room and Dmitry felt his own self-confidence disappearing. If this is how we act in private, how can we muster the men to fight! Where can we get the strength to resist and throw back the Nazi horde?

Pavlov spoke up, "Where is this order? Who

issued it? Why should we listen to you? Perhaps you are a German agent provocateur." "Comrade General, Comrade Marshals Timoshenko and Zhukov send me with Comrade Stalin's personal order!" The personnel in the room universally turned pale as snow. They understood the implications of this type of order and the level of interest in the room was elevated by a factor of ten. "What? Why were you hiding this?" Pavlov screamed and grabbed at the paperwork. "It is encoded, Comrade General, and your staff has the cipher," Dmitry stated simply.

Soon the room had taken on a more business-like atmosphere. Orders were given to Boldin's large tank forces and infantry support to move up and position themselves for the attack. Dmitry requested over and over that reconnaissance data on the forces facing Boldin be shown, but was pushed aside. He finally grabbed the GRU Major assigned to Pavlov and moved into a small room with him. "Comrade Major, what are the enemy's dispositions of artillery and tanks? Have we positioned our thrust where they are weakest? The barely shaven Major stood at attention but his eyes would not meet Dmitry's. "Comrade Colonel, we have been greatly confused by enemy movements and restricted by General Pavlov to only short *razvedka* missions. Therefore, I have been unable to advise him or tell you any of these things."

Dmitry was astonished at this information. "But the attack is scheduled for dawn tomorrow. How can we attack if we don't know where the enemy is, or in what force?" The Major slumped and looked at the floor and tears came. "Comrade Colonel, I have been on the front since the attack and we have done nothing useful for the Motherland. We should be shot and the boys going in tomorrow will have to follow their noses for all the good we can do. I am ashamed and only want to be given a rifle and allowed to fight with the men."

Dmitry was not just staff, as they say; he had fought in Mongolia and Finland and conducted numerous secret missions. In his entire career he had never let his commander attack blind, even when he insisted on it! He had always closely followed the now dead Marshal Tukhachevskii's motto regarding speed and secrecy supported by absolutely thorough reconnaissance. The Red Army was now deploying its largest regional tank force of over one thousand machines with no idea of what was in front of them! He went to Pavlov, leaving the humiliated Major behind with orders to personally begin *razvedka* missions and find out what was in front of the tank army.

"Comrade General," he addressed Pavlov, "I am most disturbed at our lack of information concerning the enemy positions. I request permission to launch aircraft to pinpoint strong points and panzer forces." Pavlov eyed Dmitry with distrust. "You are here to provide Comrade Stalin with the information required to shoot me! I am here to lead the forces of the Motherland against the fascist invader! Leave me to my job and tell the Politburo whatever you please but leave me alone."

Dmitry could not help but turn red in the face of this tirade. His first reaction was to argue but he decided to do his job and work with General Boldin and other army commanders to convey any intelligence he could. They were probably too late to support Boldin's attack but he would organize GRU forces into *razvedka* ground and aerial units to obtain desperately needed intelligence.

He saluted Pavlov, begged his leave, and departed. Three days into the war, on June 25th, over 1300 tanks of Boldin's shock army hit the German line. General Khatskilevich's Red Army 6th Corps fought like demons, as opposed to the demoralized and weak defense seen up until that point. At first there was some success as the *Luftwaffe* had failed to warn the *Wehrmacht* of the advancing force. However, once the force was identified a deadly trap was laid for the Soviets. As the tanks rolled forward without air cover or intelligence, Guderian pulled his lead elements back, as if they were retreating. The blind tankers of the Red Army drove forward into a murderous trap of anti-tank guns and aerial death from the *Stukas*.

The Soviets were simply annihilated. They fought, often to the last man, and in many cases they did not leave the field until they were out of ammunition. The pride of the Red Army, the 6th Mechanized Corps, disappeared on the battlefield. The lack of air cover and of any intelligence regarding the enemy position doomed them. Pavlov and his staff had no idea where they were or even if they had attacked! The catastrophe was so complete that Boldin and a remnant of his forces would not surface to the Soviet High Command for another month!

Many of the new T-34 tanks were destroyed because their crews were not familiar with the new equipment, even though they outgunned the German panzers. Even worse, the lack of radios in the tanks made them islands in a sea of slaughter so that no coordinated action was possible. The embattled 11th Mechanized Corps came out of the storm with only 30 out of 300 tanks left. The massacre from the air by the *Stukas* and twin-engine Bf 110's was of unbelievable proportions as von Richthofen's *Luftwaffe* forces singled out tanks from the air and destroyed the defenseless ground machines in droves. Russian valor was no match for planning, overwhelming force, and air power. Dmitry observed much of this from the air and flew back to Moscow with tears streaming from his eye. The smoke laden airstream had nothing to do with the tears.

Chapter 3

Both Zhukov and Dmitry soon arrived back in Moscow. In Kiev Zhukov had launched a terribly expensive counterattack against Guderian, which temporarily slowed him down, giving the Red Army some breathing space. Dmitry had reported to Marshal Vatutin, and the GRU boss, Golikov. He had detailed the leadership failures in the Minsk defense. This had caused Stalin to order Marshal Kulik to Minsk to "stiffen" General Pavlov. However, Kulik was almost captured when his plane landed in a German encirclement and he was not very effective since he couldn't find Pavlov!

Stalin then sent former Army Chief and long-time crony, Voroshilov, to find them both. He had some success but due to the failure of Boldin's attack, nothing useful was accomplished. Voroshilov reported back to Stalin and the stage was set for the next act of the farcical drama of the direction and command of the Red Army by Stalin.

Dmitry hurried over to the Kremlin to see Zhukov after washing and changing. He was allowed into Stalin's ante-office in time to hear the classic sarcasm ripping Timoshenko and Vatutin to shreds. As the two officers left the office, Vatutin grabbed Dmitry. "Comrade Colonel, report to General's Zhukov's office immediately. We have forty minutes to get back to Comrade Stalin with a new plan to halt and crush the Hitlerites. As you have been to the front we need you there and we will need a complete reconnaissance plan. For God's sake, Pavlov has no idea where his troops are. Go and prepare the room for the conference; we will talk with Comrade General Zhukov."

What they discussed behind closed doors was not pretty. On his return Voroshilov had not only questioned Pavlov's tactics but attacked the meal he was served, described how he reminded Pavlov of how Pavlov had once denounced him to Stalin, and of Pavlov literally kissing his boots and begging for mercy as the grand finale. It was not to be. On hearing the report of the disasters outside of Minsk, Stalin had choked out, "This is a monstrous crime. Those responsible must lose their heads." It was clear that Pavlov's days were numbered.

Word came down that due to the riot of business the new plan had a day or two in which to be done; the Marshals, Dmitry, and other staff labored hard on how to save Minsk. With no information from Pavlov, it was impossible to plan and in reality the exercise had been passed over by the war. On the 28th of June, one week after the invasion began; Minsk fell with the loss of over 400,000 men.

Stalin, Beria, and Molotov drove over to the Defense building and burst into Timoshenko's office. "What has happened in Minsk?" Stalin cried. Timoshenko said, "We don't know yet!" Stalin eyed him and Zhukov, "What kind of Army is it where the commanders don't know what's going on!" "Do you need our help?," Beria insinuated. Zhukov replied to them both tenaciously, "Let us get on with our work to defend the Motherland!"

At this Stalin exploded with a list of invectives

and criticism that lasted a full five minutes on how the military had failed the Politburo and the Motherland. The tough and ruthless Zhukov burst into tears and fled the room, leaving Timoshenko to bear the brunt of the rest of the assault. When the tirade stopped, Zhukov reappeared under enormous self-control, and Stalin said, "Enough, let us work together to save the Motherland, political and military together. Work on your plans but we must stop the bastards soon! Beria and Molotov, with me!" They exited at speed and got into Stalin's sedan to drop him at his *dacha* at Kuntsevo. "God in heaven," Stalin muttered, "Lenin founded our state and we've fucked it up."

"Now children the greatest mystery of the early war days commenced," Dmitry began. He was often asked in the 1950's by his nieces and nephews to tell his stories of battles and Kremlin conferences. Whenever he told this particular story his shoulders hunched forward, his expression darkened, and his breathing slowed. "Children, when Comrade Stalin left for his *dacha* this was the last time that he appeared for 48 hours. He did not summon the military or his political henchmen, Molotov and Beria; he just sat in his *dacha* and brooded. Some say he was hiding because of the disaster of the defense against the fascists. Others thought that he was summoning his strength. No one knows. What we know is that after two days Beria and Molotov vowed to break his solitude and intruded on him."

"As they entered his study his expression was one of fear and Beria, the priest of fear, thought, perhaps he thinks we are here to arrest him! Such were those days that this seemed possible. But they implored Comrade Stalin to lead them and the nation and with this he seemed to revive. He got cleaned up and with them headed for the Kremlin. Young ones, when he reappeared he was a man reborn and the commands flew. Never again during the war were we so leaderless, but what Beria saw frightened him." "Molotov, we have seen Joseph V at his worst and we will live to regret it," he said.

"However darlings, with energy, brilliance did not follow. Another flawed attack was launched and again failed with heavy losses. I felt my parent's tears falling like rain as they watched their beloved Red nation dying. But we reorganized to try and save Smolensk." "Uncle, what did the people think?" his nephew Konstantin asked.

Dmitry nodded and replied, "Both Stalin and Molotov made radio speeches and especially Stalin's helped. He was not totally honest but he did tell a version of the truth. He admitted to losses and to terrible casualties but this was hardly news as refugees from the West flooded into Moscow with horrible tales of the Germans. Their stories more than anything else made everyone realize that we had to fight and win or die. The fascists murdered whole villages and burnt everything. Some of our people panicked and ran from Moscow but others resolved to defend Moscow to the death. I was chosen to help in that effort but that is another story. Children, the Soviet Union must never again let an invader cross its doorstep, it must always be protected."

With this, his sister Natasha stepped in and

said," Enough." At this point Konstantin always begged to hold the gold star of the Hero of the Soviet Union which Dmitry wore on his lapel and to read for the thousandth time it's very low issue number. "Tell me Comrade General, how did you save Vladimir Il-lyich's life?" Konstantin would listen, sigh, and dream, but as Dmitry remembered, his sorrow welled.

Back in charge, Stalin initiated many changes which affected the war effort. The good part was the forming of the *GKO* and the *Stavka*. The former was a political committee to lead the war effort. The *Stavka* was a mix of political and military leaders designed to provide a coherent military response to the German invasion. On the not so good side, Timoshenko was replaced by the inept and submissive Voroshilov as Army Chief and sent to command the Western *Front,* where the hapless Pavlov was arrested. Zhukov was relieved as Chief of Staff by the very ill Shaposhnikov after another violent confrontation with Stalin over surrendering Kiev, and he was sent to command the Reserve *Front* which would be deployed at Kiev. The order placing the Communist Party Commissars back in dual command with military commanders was rein-stituted and young risers like Khrushchev and Brezh-nev became *front* level commissars to control the mili-tary decision making.

Marshal Budyenny, a Stalin toady, was sent to oversee all of the Southern *Fronts,* with Khrushchev in political command. But worst of all was the institution of Orders 270 and 246 which called for the use of blocking troops to fire on retreating soldiers and the organization of penal battalions where those who had been captured or had run would be sent to atone with their own blood. Other penalties included imprisoning the families of captured Red Army and Fleet personnel.

The crushing grip of terror was fully unleashed on a population being invaded by the grimmest army since the Mongols. The enemy offered only death or slavery while their own government seemed to be only slightly better. The population groaned under the weight of this horror and Dmitry wondered whether they would fight for the regime or fold. But the Germans themselves eliminated this choice with their murderous plans for civilians and captured troops. As the death toll from the *Einzgruppen* and deliberate starvation mounted there was no choice but to fight for the Motherland, no matter what their own leadership did to them!

Throughout this period Dmitry worked tirelessly at *Stavka* HQ trying to build a comprehensive picture from the limited intelligence available. General Golikov dropped by periodically to review his work but showed more interest in having tea with Stalin and generally stayed out of the way.

Before leaving for Reserve *Front* headquarters, Zhukov came by, "Comrade Colonel, please attend me in my former office." After they entered Zhukov turned to Dmitry. "Close the door and please sit, Dima. This talk is long overdue. First to duty, you are to report to Comrade Timoshenko on the Western *front* and be his intelligence Chief. You will have command of several GRU units, all good men with the possible exception of the Bear. Give Timoshenko every assistance and strike ruthless blows for the Motherland. We must try and save Smolensk. It is one of our largest and most important cities. Be Timoshenko's eyes and ears, help him kill the fascist dogs and drive them back. As you well know, after Smolensk is Moscow. I can smell the panic at the top. We are soldiers, we fight, and we do not panic. Save Smolensk, Dima! Any questions?"

A small lowering of his eyes signaled his understanding to his Uncle, who continued. "Listen Dima, all of our heads are on the block. I know you are aware of this but you need to know more and time is very short so listen with attention." The tough soldier hesitated and his expression was sorrowful and his heart floated on his face. Dmitry had only seen Zhukov like this with his daughters and he decided that perhaps their relationship was deeper than he realized.

"Dima," the Marshal continued, "Beware Beria, Stalin, and Budyenny. But especially Beria, he will do anything to please the *Vozdh*. Dima, bad things happened in Poland before the death of your parents. Even I do not know exactly what happened but I do know there was a break between your parents and Dzerzhinsky, the head of the NKVD, and Stalin. I don't know why but it was serious. Since then you have been on Stalin's list and hence also Beria's. As a Hero of the Soviet Union and savior of Lenin they are hamstrung in their attacks on you. Know that it was Timoshenko and I who had you retrieved from your short stay in the Lubyanka. Timoshenko went out on a long limb for you, so protect him now. Also, stay close to your Polish "cousin," Rokossovskii. He is a fighter and tough as nails. Learn from him and help him as well. There is no more time for now; they will begin to wonder what we discuss. That is all I can say except God bless you and St. George watch over you. Be a hero, make your parents smile, and save our Motherland. When you open the door to leave do not embrace me but look like you have been terribly reprimanded. Go!"

Dmitry stepped out of the office with a carefully constructed downcast look and slouched down the hall. He sensed the NKVD eyes on him but paid no attention. At the same time his mind was racing. A break between his parents and Stalin! Also, a break with Dzerzhinsky, head of the infant CHEKA, and parent of the NKVD? What could it have been? How could it have happened? Why had no one ever breathed a word to him about it? He felt as if he had stepped in some of the animal offal left in Moscow gutters, soiled and rank. The past was now not a window to his parents but a fog of deception. Zhukov must have thought it was of critical importance to pass this information along before he left. Why? Dmitry realized the questions were many and vowed to turn his formidable intelligence skills to unraveling this mystery; but first to Smolensk and war.

Chapter 4

"Bear," Dmitry whispered, "Take two scouts and move down the road. I see German lorries loaded with petrol cans. I want their source. Return by morning if you are unsuccessful. They are likely to be near or on the road because they are using captured French lorries which cannot get off a prepared road surface. If you find them, post a man to maintain watch and get back here as fast as your paws will carry you. Clear?"

In his week at Smolensk Dmitry had seen enough to know that the Red Army couldn't hold, but they could buy time. If they could find a major German fuel depot and blow it, precious time would be bought as the panzers were slowed in their breakneck thrust towards the city. Ten miles behind German lines with his squad of six, he had already provided valuable intelligence to Marshal Timoshenko and General Rokossovskii. But he wanted a more direct revenge on the fascists and he was determined to get it.

Sergeant-Major Rasilev understood all this and as he nodded and signaled for the two experienced scouts to follow him, he reflected on Dima's appearance in the field. His two-piece camouflage overalls were properly mud smeared to enhance invisibility and his German BP38 sub-machine gun would be dismissed if fired behind the lines. All of them had German weapons except the Georgian brothers, Taka and Sachino, who carried the PTRS anti-tank rifle and ammunition. The Bear still pondered why Dima was making them lug that thing around behind the lines. Any panzer back here was already disabled, but he had learned in Mongolia that Dima always had a reason. When he took in Dmitry's three-day beard and the now deeply tanned face with the fierce blue eyed battle countenance, he knew the fascists would be surprised at some point.

At any rate this was safer for Dima than the Kremlin halls and they both excelled in true *razvedka* far behind enemy lines. They had even seen and almost taken a shot at "Hurrying Heinz" Guderian himself the day before and only the total absence of any chance of escape had stayed his finger on the trigger. It was much too early in the war to be trading deaths one for one. The Red Army needed every fighter at this moment and the Bear stilled his finger from delivering a shot that would have dropped Guderian in his tracks. Oh well! Life in the army always had surprises.

"Come on you malingerers, we are going for a nice stroll down the lane and if any of you makes a sound I'll sit on you until you're flat as a potato pancake. Move!" Dmitry shrugged at Bear's tender words to his partners but knew that these men were skilled and close. They would do what he required. Now they had to wait. He called Taka over and spoke to him about the PTRS. "Comrade Taka, are you and your brother ready to carry out great service to the Motherland with the anti-tank rifle? Have you both studied the weapon and read the manual?" Taka considered, "Comrade Platoon leader, as you know our great and wonderful Georgian, now Supremo of the Soviet Union, Comrade Stalin, has announced that all Georgians can read. Therefore we can read but unfortunately cannot study. We are endeavoring to learn this manual with comrade Sergeant-Major Rasilev reading it to us. I hope this is satisfactory. It is only a big gun and as to its use, Comrade Stalin has declared all Georgian soldiers are brave and skilled and therefore we are! We stand ready for your orders!"

Dmitry scanned the night sky for inspiration on how to respond to this seemingly nonsensical response to a simple question. The Georgians, he reminded himself, were never simple and never willing to give a direct answer. Somewhere the truth was buried in these statements, but for right now he was hungry and tired. They had enough food as the German larders provided for any want, but sleep was dear. He decided an hour would have to suffice and settled with Taka. "All right, comrade, why don't you and your skilled and courageous Georgian brother take the watch and wake me in one hour." Yes, Comrade Colonel," Taka responded and was there the smallest of twinkles in his eye? Dmitry pulled more leaf and pine boughs to cover himself up, and slept.

The gentlest of whispers woke him. "Comrade Colonel, we found it, not too far down the road, probably five kilometers west of here. There are all types of vehicles carrying fuel and troops are loading the lorries in a large clearing. A regular bee hive which we bears do enjoy," Bear stated. Dmitry was driving sleep away and looked at his American phosphorescent watch. He had slept over two hours and eyed Taka, but decided to hold a private discussion about the vaunted Georgian ability to tell time at a later date. "Right, let's move. What is between us and the depot? Troops and type?" Bear responded that the guard was light.

The bigger worry was that the infantry was struggling to keep up with the tanks and periodically files of troops came through which might surprise them.

"We can handle that," Dmitry stated. "We move in ten minutes." Not that there was much to move, but a few minutes to get ready was best for the men. "Unload weapons," he declared. "Keep ammo in your pockets for immediate use. Is the PTRS ready for use?" he queried the Georgians. Taka started to remark on the battle readiness of Georgians as professed by Comrade Stalin but shortened it to a "Yes, comrade Colonel," when a questioning glance came from Bear.

The six of them silently glided through the Belarus forest on the far side of a small ridge above the main Minsk-Smolensk highway. Bear led and Dmitry was last. He observed his other three companions, the Georgians, Taka and Sachino, and the GRU scout Felix whose partner Lev was keeping watch on the depot. He had handpicked them all and was so far satisfied with both their morale and skill level. Except for the Georgians, they were all experienced *razvedchiki* and knew their business. They were also all loyal and fiercely aggressive towards killing Germans, characteristics much required right now. Tracking the road was easy but he halted long enough to query Bear on the distance they had yet to travel. "We are about one-third of the way," Bear stated and they kept gliding forward.

Finally, after having seen what appeared to be half of the invading army pass by, blacked out on the road below, they arrived at the dump area and Lev greeted them. "As always comrade Private, you are lucky," commented Dmitry. "It looks like we have a full house tonight." Indeed they did. Every type of lorry from Western Europe was assembled in front of them, all captured in last year's Blitzkrieg. "How do they keep so much mixed up equipment running?" Bear asked. "Probably very slowly," Dmitry replied. "Too many parts and too many vehicles to keep track of, so they just fix what they can. Well, we will relieve them of their headache tonight. Listen up and you will all get to sleep tomorrow if this goes well." Dmitry took them through the plan and the smiles grew as he elaborated on why the PTRS was with them and why they were equipped with German weapons.

"I want to get us out of here alive," Dmitry counseled. "Therefore, we will break up into an attacking Red Army unit and a defending German unit." This brought quizzical looks. He continued, "The fascists are using good procedure and have spaced the vehicles so that an explosion from one is not likely to set off another. However, if Bear and Lev act as "defending" ground forces guarding the depot and accidentally hit several trucks and tankers so that the fuel sprays outward…and if at the same time our Georgian brothers fire incendiary armor piercing ammo into the tankers, I think there will be a very satisfying explosion of many vehicles which will likely continue until all are gone!"

The men smiled at each other with confidence and the excitement sparked between them. "Felix, you stay with me for coordination and we will be the attacking unit. We will fire randomly at the troops scattered amongst the tankers to distract them. After Taka and Sachino have done their job we will all form up on that knoll west of here. Yes, deeper into German lines. They will not look there first. Once together we will head south and get back to Smolensk through Orsha and get a cup of tea, or perhaps some honey of the vodka variety for the Bear and his cubs. Questions?"

"One question, Comrade Colonel, can we kill Germans while the fires rage?" "Good question, Taka, use your shoulder arms and target officers and drivers. Forget combat troops. They will be running around and searching for us. Randomly target drivers to stall the convoy and always target the officers." Anything else? No, OK, let's go."

The Bear and Lev headed for the road and proceeded to make a silent crossing. Felix and Dmitry would fire the first rounds of the attack; the two men posted on the opposite side would respond as German defenders but shoot wildly and hit a number of tankers and lorries. Finally, the Georgian brothers would wait as the fuel shot out of the bullet holes and spread and then target several carriers. As soon as the fires started, they were to pack up.

"Comrade General Rokossovskii, it went like a dream." Dmitry related back in Smolensk the next day. "The fuel must have been overloaded and the interior pressures very high as it flew out of the bullet holes. The Georgians put three incendiaries into as many trucks very quickly and the explosions might have been heard in Berlin. Confusion was total in the blackness and we slipped away easily. I sent Comrade Pilot Shanislav out to take a look and he reported that the fuel is still burning and the smoke column is several miles high. That should take the "Hurry" out of Heinz Guderian for a while."

Rokossovskii, tall, handsome, and always as smart in appearance as in his intellect, surveyed the mature colonel before him and remembered him as a young cadet; all the training they had invested in him had paid off and more. He smiled and as he did, the steel teeth which replaced those broken out by the NKVD shone in all their brilliance as he said, "Well I'm glad you got that out of your system. Maybe now you can focus on the *razvedka* required for our counterattack. Give the men a break, but I want to know what's in my front and what to expect on the soon-to-be-famous death charge. Write up a short report on all aspects of your mission and I'll send it to Timoshenko and Zhukov. Anything you think is important to our understanding of the enemy or our own faults should be remarked upon." "At once, comrade General!"

"Dima," Rokossovskii inserted, "We need you and your skills desperately in this next phase. We must slow the fascists down to permit defenses to be established on the road to Moscow. We will lose Smolensk but the fascist bastards must pay. Look what they have already done to our beloved Poland! They plan as bad or worse here. They must not get Moscow. The Red Army must fight and fight well. Help us get ready!" Dmitry came to attention, "My very best, comrade General!" Rokossovskii almost smiled, but that would be unfair to this Red soldier.

"Dima, I talked to Bear. You risk yourself too much. Bear and the men could have carried out the mission and you could have returned. Why didn't you?" "Comrade General, we *razvedchiki* are all one when behind the lines. We share all risks and always sustain each other. I could no more leave it to them alone than you leave this post. I plead insubordination and it will likely be repeated, but it is how I can help, sir."

Again Rokossovskii submerged a smile; he had known the answer before it was delivered. He got up from his desk and took Dima's shoulder in his hand. "I know, but remember I am your "godfather" in the Army and I rely on you. Take more care and for Lenin's sake get the Bear cleaned up! He left stains on my office floor from God knows what! Also, I know you do not like to, but please wear your Hero of the Soviet Union decoration when in field dress. The men love to see it and it gives them great hope. Combined with true Red leadership like yours it is worth a Division. Dismissed, comrade Colonel, good job."

Dmitry resolved to keep better track of Bear, who perhaps even now was hobnobbing over tea with Marshal Timoshenko! The picture was frightening for the whole Soviet war effort, he thought as he headed for a wash and a shave.

Chapter 5

Comrade *Razvedchik*, comrade *Razvedchik*!" A female voice called to Dmitry as he walked briskly through the main plaza of the Smolensk Kremlin, Western *front* Army HQ. He turned to respond and a petite, dark haired, intensely blue-eyed Red Army medical staffer stood in front of him, pulled him behind a truck and kissed him long and hard. With his breath returning he replied, "Irina, Irina, I was going to look for you. Are you OK? Where are you stationed?" Irina Petrova stared at him like he had just landed from outer space and said, "Dmitry Alexanderovich, what a sight you are! There is a war on and a colonel should be at the front not lazing around the rear rolling in mud and out of uniform!"

He stammered to reply but she beat him to it. "Oh my dear, we all heard what you and Bear have done. It gives us great heart and I think it is my duty to personally thank you." She again drew him in and gently smiling, let a longer, more tender kiss linger. By now Dmitry was wildly scanning the plaza and trying to enjoy the kiss, but not present a non-military front. Shit, he thought, I'll probably be dead in a week. He plunged into the kiss with gusto and Irina responded. They had spent much time together, on and off as lovers, but were now separated by career. Any moment they had together was precious. He finally broke off and asked, "Well, comrade Major," her rank as a surgeon in the Red Army, "when do you intend to salute, tomorrow?"

She threw a very thorough and proper salute

and hugged him again. "Oh Dima, Bear has gotten enough vodka telling your story that he could float to Moscow. Is it all true? Did you really singe Guderian's gold braid? Were they all running back to Berlin and squealing like pigs?" Tell me it was so!" Her eyes were twinkling but there was an element of pleading in them also. Dmitry sighed. "Who am I to disagree with the great and courageous Bear? Like Comrade Stalin he only speaks the truth!" She laughed and grabbed his arm affectionately. "Oh Dima, this is stupid of me but do be careful. How can we succeed without men like you leading? But our boys are dying in droves, and the wounded! God and St. George, I cannot do enough, we are here to pick up supplies because all the orderlies I sent deserted after working with the wounded."

"It is as if a huge beast is mauling and teething on our men. And the stories, my god, they are charging the Germans without cover or maneuver. They say their officers only want to die. The wounds are terrible and I must get back, but to see you is to see the sun in July instead of this horrid smoke filled sky." Dmitry responded by hugging her and saying, "Irina what do you intend if we fail to save the city?" "Why, stay with the men," she quickly replied. "*Mon cher*," Dmitry said, "The Germans are killing the wounded and sending the prisoners to camps. They kill the doctors too, this must not happen."

The familiar chin thrust forward in defiance and eyes changing from a lustrous blue to a hard winter gray signaled her response. "Never. I will not leave the wounded." Dmitry knew from experience that further pleading was hopeless so he threw in the towel with a 'Be careful!' which sounded totally inadequate even to him. The orderlies decided that enough time had elapsed and came round the truck and saluted, "Comrade Surgeon Major, we are ready to depart!" Irina returned the salute and waved Dmitry off. She said, "Thank you, comrade Colonel, for your report; it gives us much valuable information. Good luck and may we meet in Berlin!" With that she climbed into the truck, which moved out of the plaza towards the hospital site in the city even as German shells began to fall on the fortress.

How could someone named 'peace' be such a whirlwind, he wondered? They had met in their twenties when he was at the Military Academy and she was one of the few females studying medicine at the Science Academy. The small Gorky Street café they frequented soon became their meeting place as both lived in multi-family one room apartments with absolutely no privacy. Somehow the love affair had thrived and lasted years before their first separation. That was followed by the realization that her total devotion to medicine and the hours she drove herself combined with his always being gone on strange or overseas assignments, prevented a normal life.

Yet now they still loved each other and once in a great while she would stay at his apartment at the Embankment and share a true moment of peace. That was clearly gone now with the war and she had handed him another problem. There was no way that he would let her fall into German hands, he knew the fate in store for a Red Army female officer, and death would be a release. He had to find a way to get her out as the city fell, even against her will. A partisan kidnapping might work, as might a fake German capture. Nothing was beyond the resources of the GRU and he would apply them all to not letting the Germans capture this incredible Russian spirit.

He stomped off in deep thought as he again headed for a personal cleaning. As he walked on, in a window above the plaza, Yedved smirked at the scene he had just witnessed and speculated on how he might carry out Comrade Beria's wishes regarding the female surgeon. In his newly minted Commissar's uniform with the Red Star and Hammer and Sickle on his sleeve and his new Nagant pistol at his waist, he had the power to summarily execute any soldier not doing his duty, and to submit Marshals and Generals to the Politburo for "justice." This was immense power and he relished every bit of it. His brow creased as a plan began to form and a wider smile broke out on his face. Surely, eliminating the female would hurt and render vulnerable the great "neighbor" colonel at a vital moment, exposing his true weakness and making an arrest possible. The thought was warm and satisfying for Yedved, who stepped out of the window to make some calls.

Finally shaved and washed, Dmitry changed into field dress and as requested pinned on the gold star of a Hero of the Soviet Union. As he did so the scene in 1918 when he won the medal rolled back into his mind.

It was warm in August in Moscow. Lenin was addressing the workers assembled in the city's Corn Exchange on the southern end of the city. He had just finished speaking. Dmitry's parents, Alexander and Maria, were congratulating Lenin on a rousing call to arms for the workers as they exited for the car. Lenin had left his bodyguards behind due to the overwhelming Bolshevik commitment of the crowd. As they got outside Lenin unexpectedly went around the vehicle to climb into the seat on the other side of the vehicle to let Maria enter directly from the curb. Dmitry followed his hero and was to ride a running board the short way to the Kremlin, Bolshevik Headquarters.

As Lenin and Dmitry rounded the car, a woman rushed at Lenin shouting, "Traitor, Traitor, Traitor to the Revolution!" Lenin turned at the sound and as she raised a revolver, Dmitry jumped toward her with his fourteen year old lack of protective instinct and launched himself airborne to grab the weapon. Not quite succeeding in grabbing the gun, he did succeed in spoiling her aim and a bullet struck Lenin in the neck while another lodged in his collarbone. Lenin slumped. Dmitry's father hustled Lenin into the car as others wrestled the woman to the ground. His mother grabbed Dmitry and threw him into the vehicle crying, "Get them to the Kremlin and a doctor!"

The vehicle sped off and it was a few blocks later before Dmitry realized that the bullet which had missed Lenin's head and hit his neck had deflected from the large metal Bolshevik star Dmitry always wore but had also caused a flesh wound to him. His blood flowed copiously from the wound and he fainted. He awoke to his mother bathing his forehead and singing quietly a favorite Polish melody. He opened his eyes and asked, "Does he live? "Oh yes, my hero," she replied with glistening eyes and a simple kiss which sent him back to sleep. During the weeks of his recovery it seemed every top Bolshevik in the nation came to see him to shower praises and flowers on him.

His most wondrous moment occurred when Lenin and his wife, Krupskaya, came and sat on his bed and told him of their gratitude and admiration for his bravery. He smiled and blushed and as he did Lenin exclaimed, "You see my dear, he is my dashing young red hero!" Dmitry remembered that moment all his life and the scar always itched with intensity on the anniversary of his saving the leader of the Reds. Years later Stalin included him in the first issue of the Hero of the Soviet Union and Order of Lenin awards. That was never as much a reward as his mother's soft kiss.

Dmitry shrugged off the nostalgia and went in search of tea, the Bear, and the squad, in that order.

Chapter 6

Bear was regaling a troop of admirers with his tenth retelling, or so, of the blowing of the fuel dump episode when Dmitry found him. Vocal chords well lubricated by the admirers' liquid generosity, he was recounting their exploits in full and colorful detail. "Comrade Sergeant-Major Rasilev," Dmitry barked, "What are you doing still in *razvedchiki* dress and covered with filth? You should be setting an example. Retire immediately and get into field dress and meet me in the map room to go over what we saw! Now!"

Bear realized he had pushed Dmitry too far but always looking to the future said, "Comrade Colonel, I will be ready in five minutes but I was just helping to brief these troops on German procedures. They have just arrived from the reserve with Marshal Zhukov and appreciated the information." "What, comrade Marshal Zhukov is here!" Dmitry almost yelled. "Yes, comrade Colonel, the *Stavka* has sent him with new orders for comrade Marshal Timoshenko." His posture and expression seemed to say that a good intelligence man is always ahead of the leadership. "Fine," said Dmitry, "Five minutes." With that the Bear ran towards a communal shower and grabbed his pack containing his uniform.

Dmitry headed for the informal map room he had established for Timoshenko and Rokossovskii, hoping that neither Zhukov nor the other commanders were there. He had to put his thoughts in order but first was the plan for Irina, and that would be the Bear's assignment. He checked the calendar for the first time in days; it was July 12, only three weeks since the beginning of the invasion. As he headed for the map room the shouting started. Curious, he went into a room to ascertain the reason. "What is happening, comrade?" he asked the first uniformed soldier he saw. "We are evacuating the city; only a small obstructing force is to be left. We are all to be out by tomorrow morning, including the civilians. The roads are already clogged and NKVD troops are forcing civilians to abandon all of their belongings and head for Moscow. They can only take livestock as we might need it. The damn Party officials have already left! Sorry, comrade Colonel, that is all I know!"

Dmitry staggered with the news. The defenders were leaving already? He had fully expected it but this was an enormous blow. So soon! Did Stalin know? The thoughts were burning through his mind when the Bear appeared and with a clean shave and haircut! Amazing, Dmitry thought. The man can accomplish anything even in the face of a major retreat.

"Bear, how was your tea with General Rokossovskii?" Dmitry inquired. "Oh, I had a grand time with the two comrade Generals and the comrade Marshal. They loved to hear about our small adventure and insisted that I have a field ration of vodka to recover. They also consumed several field rations to relieve the burdens of command. It was a grand time!" Dmitry didn't know whether to be stunned, laugh, or cry. The thought of the three leaders of the Soviet forces on this front chatting about Bear's exploits brought tears to his eyes. "Well, I am glad you enjoyed your time with them. We have work to do, old friend."

This seldom used salutation brought the Bear to attention. "Comrade Colonel Zhankovskii, name the mission and it is done." Dmitry smiled again because this was truth. He looked at Bear a bit upwards as it had to be and started. "As I'm sure you know we are evacuating the city and will likely reform behind Smolensk to launch counterattacks against the fascists. We will help our leaders develop the plan and location of the attacks. Before I send you out on scout again there is one other task." "The Bear jumped in, "Comrade Major Petrova." He stated. As usual Dmitry could only shrug or smile. "Yes, you are correct. Do bears also read minds?" "Oh yes," was the innocent reply. "It was simple, Dima. Everyone in the compound saw you two together and they spread the news of the gallant Hero of the Soviet Union making an instant score on a doctor! I knew better. She won't leave, will she?"

Dmitry sighed, "Right. She has her hard attitude on like a shawl. Nothing will penetrate it. We must act. You know the fascist bastards and their treatment of women, and think, a woman officer!" The Bear virtually snarled at this and turned a shade of black and seemed to swell in size. "Easy, my friend." Dmitry said. "We will not let that happen."

"I think that she will be knocked unconscious by a piece of building as the shelling increases and will have to be removed to our lines. What do you think?" "Oh that is good, Dima. A soft touch of my blackjack will do the trick with a rigged explosion at that moment. She will never know!" "OK," replied Dmitry. "This becomes your most important job, and thank you, old friend. She will never agree to evacuation and she is too valuable to lose."

The Bear came to attention, saluted and asked, "When?" "I'm not sure. Let's give it a day or so, and thanks again." The Bear looked his most open and simply said, "She is so much to so many. She has the true Russian heart. Have no fear she will arrive at HQ in my arms." The last was accompanied by a shy smile and Dmitry laughed and clapped him on the shoulder. "Watch out, this she-bear has thoughts of her own. Careful, my Bear! Now to work. I want to organize our thoughts for the Marshals."

Several hours later the room was filled to capacity by Dmitry, several other GRU officers, and Marshal Timoshenko, commander of the *front*. While bowing under the pressure, his tall cavalryman's posture grounded in his riding boots and topped by his Hero of the Soviet Union combined with severe eyes to establish his authority in the room. Marshal Zhukov and the generals Rokossovskii, Kachalov, and Khomonov rounded out the command leadership. The newly minted commissars were there to watch over them. Beria's man, Mekhlis, was as always dark and threatening, and Yedved was armed with his perpetual smirk. Also in attendance were numerous staff officers. Dmitry had also added his pilot, Shanislav, who had been over-flying the region for intelligence purposes for the last two weeks.

"Comrades," Zhukov announced. "The *Stavka* has ordered me here to convey their order for a new series of counterattacks against the fascists. You know that we are falling back from the city and that Comrade General Lukin will lead the fighting in the city to slow up the bastards. Meanwhile we are establishing a new defensive front on the Dneipr and running south to Bryansk. From that line we are ordered to counterattack. I have brought forward Reserve units to be split among you and some tanks, but really not enough of the newer T-34's."

"It will be desperate but we must break the speed of the Hitlerites. Moscow is next. The city cannot fall! Comrade Colonel Zhankovskii has been personally conducting *razvedka* in the German rear and surveying attack and defensive sites. He will brief us on the plan as it now stands. Comrade Colonel!"

Dmitry moved to his photo board and map display. "Comrades, please advance and study the photos before you. Comrade Pilot Shanislav has become our eyes over the German forces in his Polikarpov." At this point Shanislav blushed but stiffened to display his new Order of the Red Banner pinned on him by Zhukov for these efforts. Dmitry continued, "He will fill in my descriptions. I remind you that *razvedchiki* have verified the positions of all units on these photos so that there is no question of their accuracy. First, the bad news. Note that a number of Guderian's Second Panzer and Hoth's Third Panzer have crossed the Dnieper north and south of the city, seeking to envelop us. That is why we must abandon the city. However, also note that are troops are holding well in the immediate front of the city but that the fascists have spread towards our rear from our flanks."

"Clearly encirclement is planned. Also, clearly we must counterattack and keep open a small funnel area for troops trapped in the unfinished encirclement to make their way to the rear. Our forces are only marginally large enough to accomplish this but we must attack or suffer another Minsk." All in the room stared at the floor at this mention, as General Pavlov, the commander at Minsk, had been shot at Stalin's order along with a number of Air Force generals just the day before.

Dmitry scanned the group. "The good news. Our air force has returned to the fight and just yesterday dealt a smashing blow to Von Richthofen's fliers with minimal losses. This helps our ground troops immensely. Also, our men trapped behind the German lines are forming with loyal Communists into partisan groups that are beginning to significantly hurt the rear echelon forces of the Germans and draw on their front line troops for support. Also, note the large separation on the map between the fascist Panzer and infantry forces. Heinz is again hurrying forward ahead of the main body and this time we will make him pay. Comrades, this is the moment to deal a significant blow for Stalin and the Motherland. Let us now go through the plan in detail."

The conference moved on as Dmitry and other staff officers briefed the others on targets and organization for the attacks which would begin from the new lines in a week. Rokossovskii would organize broken units and hold the road to Moscow. Generals Kachalov, Khomenko, Kalinin, and Maslinnikov would lead counterattacks in various sectors seeking to encircle German units and hold the escape route open for encircled Red Army forces. As Dmitry, Zhukov, and Timoshenko knew, the plan had three major flaws.

First, the Red Army would be significantly outnumbered, in some cases three to one. As if that was not
bad enough they were tremendously outnumbered in
tanks and this was especially critical since the new T-
34's, which were death on Panzers, had mostly untrained crews and no radios for inter-tank communication. Finally, air cover and ground support were going
to be minimal due to losses in the Red Air Force. This
was indeed a death ride but a necessary one to save
Moscow and perhaps the war.

For the next several days Dmitry was out of
touch with the Bear and had appointed Felix the head
of the now beefed up *razvedchiki* squad. Every day
they were out on patrol, establishing German troop and
mechanized unit locations for the upcoming attack.
Aerial reconnaissance and ground reconnaissance supported each other with the result that this would be the
best informed Soviet attack of the war. Dmitry argued
in vain for a greater amount of deception to fool the
Germans about the attack but the army commanders
did not agree. They were too distracted just organizing
the attack. As foreseen the German's of Guderian's
Second Panzer Army entered the city on the 16th of
July and the house to house fighting began. This was
the signal for the Bear to move forward with the plan
for Irina.

The shelling and now even mortaring had gotten much fiercer in the last day as the Germans entered
the city. The old fortress city was quickly becoming a
ruin as Bear made his way forward. He had quietly
scouted the hospital during the last few days and knew
how to enter without Irina sighting him. His

razvedchik uniform gave him carte blanche to go wherever he cared to with no questions regarding his presence. Negotiating the streets leading to the medical station he noted the new sandbags and anti-tank defences manned by very grim looking Red soldiers. Also, the bridges across the river were being blown as he watched. Truly, except for the blood and death, the end was near for Smolensk.

As he neared the hospital site the stream of walking wounded heading for the trains and safety became a flood. It seemed that half of the Red Army had been wounded in the recent battles. The defense of Mogilev to the south, was now called "Red Madrid" in honor of the fighting done there, being compared to the Spanish loyalists who fought to the last man against the Germans in the Spanish Civil War. The casualties were rumored to be in the tens of thousands. Here he surveyed the human results of the fighting around Smolensk and noted the severity of the wounds on those who were still walking. Missing limbs and blinded eyes did not slow them. No one wanted to be left behind. They all knew the fate of captured wounded, murdered in their beds or never seen again. Every individual had but one thought, not me! Bear could feel the desperation of these wounded and it deepened his hatred of the Germans. He held that thought for his next action.

Reaching the hospital proper, he knew he couldn't ask about Irina since he wanted to leave no trace of his actions. He had established his own general reconnaissance and narrowed her location down to a couple of possibilities. She was most certainly asso-

ciated with surgery and there were a number of theaters where she might be. By sweet talking a nurse, he
knew the one where she was most frequently at work.
He made his way through the wards of suffering, pain,
courage, and cowardice. Amid the constant rumble of
shelling and prayer he made out individual messages
for mothers, wives, and God.

The effort required to march through this land
of the dying and soon to be dead almost dropped him
to his knees. How could a true Communist like him be
concerned with only one life and not try to save all?
Yet he knew that saving all was impossible and it felt
right somehow to save one so dedicated. Bear was a
pine shedding its winter snow as he shook himself to
better focus on the mission. He had to get this right.
There was no room for error. Dima needed Irina and
Irina needed Dima. It was that simple. Like the stories
of old, he, the Russian bear, would save the knight and
his lady in their time of need. He smiled and climbed
the stairs and became very light-footed and silent as he
drew near her likely location.

The hall was filled with wounded, with a few
nurses trying to ease them. In his *razvedchiki* uniform
he would be accepted as coming from the field to see a
comrade. No one questioned the GRU. He made his
way down the hall and kept a sharp eye swiveling to
make sure that he was not overly noticed. The sensa-
tion of walking through ghosts was almost too much to
take but he stayed focused. He felt the new plastique
explosive and its small timer in his pocket. He intended to locate Irina at work, plant the charge near her
and when it went off, blackjack her from behind .He

had added smoke generators to the plastique to both cause confusion and hide his identity. It was amazing how a bit of training could make a giant almost invisible and Rasilev had practiced it on many occasions.

He was in her ward. He heard her clear commanding voice! Ever so silently he sought out the location of her voice. Down the hall and to the right there was a small office. Perfect! He could plant the charge near the door and blow it as he moved into the room and capture her unaware. All was ready and he drew himself inward for the effort.

At that moment several shells landed in the building and courtyard. At the same moment a massive explosion, likely demolition, was heard from in front of the fortress. Probably a bridge being blown, he thought. The whole building rocked from these explosions and the screams of the frightened and trapped rose to intolerable levels. Irina came out of the office and turned away from Bear. Ah, well, improvisation is the heart of the *razvedchik,* he thought. He moved forward to hit her from behind. Even though the hall was crowded with beds and wounded he was convinced he could do it so no one would notice. As she worked her way down the ward, like a raptor swooping in for an attack, a German grenade came rolling down the hall. In a split second the Bear lunged forward to do what, he didn't know. In his eye and mind he registered a running soldier in a non-descript uniform. All of this happened in an instant. At the same time Irina spotted the grenade and threw herself on a wounded officer in a bed near the explosive. It went off and the explosion threw shrapnel throughout the ward.

Bear was superficially wounded as he had instinctively balled up when unable to reach the weapon and had sheltered against the wall. Irina, the soldier, and the bed were thrown through the air and sprayed with hot metal from the grenade. They came down hard. The smoke covered all and Bear moved forward quickly and silently. The screams were awful and help nowhere to be seen, but he had only one target: Irina. He found the shredded bedding and the nearly shredded officer who had ended up sheltering his protector. She was lightly wounded but nothing too serious. She was also out like a light. He picked her up and headed for the stairs and the exit. It was like swimming against the current as doctors and nurses raced for the scene but his size and authority brooked no interruption.

He reached the plaza and Felix came forward with the stolen truck and GRU driver. They all bundled in and headed out of the burning, tortured city. The only sounds inside the truck were in Bear's head. "Who did this, who, who?" became a troubled mantra.

Chapter 7

The truck drove the 30 or so miles to the new *front* HQ. As Irina remained unconscious, they checked her breathing and decided to get her to a major field hospital. Bear and Felix left the GRU scout/driver with instructions to head for the hospital, identify her as Major Petrova, and without mention of them, the driver was to maintain that she had been thrown into his truck and evacuated. Finally, he was to inform Colonel Zhankovskii of her whereabouts and then return to his unit.

They hitched a ride to HQ where they hoped to find Dmitry and resume the fight. They were successful after some searching when overhearing a lecture on Georgian military prowess. They grinned at each other and headed for the raucous laughter greeting the speaker's remarks. Of course, Taka was at the center of a crowd regaling them with great Georgian victories from the past. "Comrade Private!" the Bear roared and Taka froze. "Comrade Sergeant-Major Rasilev, we are most pleased to see you in one piece! Your cubs welcome you back." Rasilev smiled at that and almost preened as if he truly had fur. Any allusion to him as a real bear always pleased him. "Where is the comrade Colonel?" the Bear asked and Taka pointed him to a small building in the village.

"Comrade Colonel, we report from our mission." Bear stated as he surveyed who was in the building. Dmitry looked up from his surrounding coterie of GRU and staff officers all examining maps mounted on planks and improvised saw horses. "Were you successful, Sergeant-Major?" he asked. The Bear replied in the affirmative but hesitated to make any further remarks. Dmitry picked up on this and dismissed the group with a curt, "Figure out the best approaches and timing and report back to me in two hours. Thank you, comrades."

He and Bear drew aside. "Dima, first, we got her out and her location will be coming in soon." "Location?" Dima asked. "What do you mean?" "She is in hospital, comrade Colonel, but not seriously hurt." At this Dmitry bristled, "Did you hit her too hard?" Bear returned the bristle with a curt, "*Nyet!*" "So what happened?" The Bear looked hard at Dmitry. "Someone tried to kill her and make it look like a German sneak attack." "What!" Dmitry shouted. The Bear explained what happened as the furrows on Dmitry's brows deepened. "My god, what is going on?" "Realize only Soviets were in the area, Dima. Someone wants her dead and my guess is that it's because of you. Is anyone after you?" Dmitry grabbed Rasilev, "She is OK?" "Yes, she was just wounded superficially but remained unconscious so I had the scout take her to a hospital. We will hear from him soon."

Dmitry looked stunned and nodded. "I will go to her when I can. I must think about this. Again my deepest thanks, Bear. Catch a break and report back in several hours. I have work for the squad."

Dmitry shook off the news to clear his head. Timoshenko and Zhukov had been summoned to Moscow. God knows why, he thought, at a time like this. He had strict orders to get all possible intelligence to the various army staffs as they planned the counterat-

---

tack against the fascists. They would punish the "villain" Guderian as he was now called and hurt him deeply but there was still much not known about German positions. The Germans, however, knew the Soviet positions because of their air force's ability to fly over Soviet positions with impunity. Air cover was critical to the upcoming battle but so far only a hundred or so aircraft had been patched together from the *front's* devastated air forces. These planes would have to do for this job.

He groaned at the thought but kept himself optimistic due to the capabilities of Rokossovskii and Kachalov. The attacks were to begin in only two days and they were nowhere near ready. He waited for the staff officers to return and passed the time by studying Shanislav's aerial photos for further clues.

Following another session with the staff officers, where they demonstrated their complete ignorance of the need for *razvedka* (deep reconnaissance) prior to an attack and the use of deception to hide the forming up for the coming attack from the enemy, Dmitry dismissed them back to their units. He informed Timoshenko's staff that under previous orders he was heading to Rokossovskii HQ's to assist him with the upcoming offensive. He gave orders to the GRU staff but felt somewhat hopeless about it. The purges had weakened these functions tremendously as the NKVD took out its hatred on its intelligence "neighbors," the GRU, during the bloodletting under their direction. Unfortunately for them in the final act of that round of purges Stalin had turned his monstrous fist on the NKVD and eliminated many who had murdered others in the belief that they were somehow protected.

Dmitry had never come to terms with this, only focused on his own survival, but now with the country under attack, for some reason the these crimes came to the surface of his thoughts. Rubbing his stubble-covered head, he sought to clear these thoughts which did not help the current situation. He was anxious about Irina but that would have to wait for the briefing with the squad and Shanislav.

He met the men in a field outside the immediate HQ area where they could not be heard or observed as anything more than a group of men and an officer taking a break before moving out. "Comrades," Dmitry began, "We have spent several weeks together and I admire all of your skill and bravery. You have provided much needed intelligence to our leaders and in no small way carried the fight to the enemy yourselves. I know that you do not value tin soldiers but you all wear medals of distinction won in recent weeks when significant portions of the army were collapsing. More important you have stood for each other and with socialist brotherly concern helped and supported each other. I salute you!"

Dmitry paused as they variously slapped each other on the back or poked at their medals in fun. "We now enter a new phase of the war. We will take the fight directly to the Germans in four major attacks. I have decided to split the squad to best assist two of the armies with the most need. They are comrade Generals Kachalov and Rokossovskii. Sergeant-Major Rasilev will take Felix and Lev and I will have the honor of serving with the Georgian brigade, Taka and Sachino.

Comrade pilot Shanislav will accompany me with his now much holed Polikarpov. How many holes at last count, Piotr?" The pilot blushed as always and the men kidded him about needing even more ventilation than an open cockpit can provide.

"The attacks are to begin soon but we will be forward of the lines to help provide direction and prevent Hitlerite surprises. These will be desperate efforts but they are necessary, not only to kill Germans, but to provide time for Moscow's defenses to be strengthened and valuable industry moved east. The bombing of Moscow has begun and our pilots are fighting with great glory. Indeed, after using all of their ammo at least two pilots have been made Heroes of the Soviet Union after ramming and destroying fascist bombers."

At this the men cheered. "That is how Russians fight!" escaped the lips of Taka who retreated when he realized he had said Russian instead of Georgian. The mood continued, serious but light hearted, and they all threw sticks or dirt clods at the brothers. Dmitry signaled for attention. "We move right now. Report with all your gear and kiss your girl in the next fifteen minutes. Bear, with me. The luck of Lenin to you, comrades!"

"Bear, report directly to Kachalov and his GRU staff Officer, Major Suvorov. They are expecting you and need you. Take the men as far forward as you can and take some experienced runners with you. Keep the generals informed of German movements and force concentrations, just like we did in Mongolia! Remember that bears own the woods and use that strength to watch for any sign of German awareness of our plan.

Now old friend, take care and spit in their eye for me! We form after the battle in Vyazma with the grace of god." The Bear gave one of his rare salutes and with a, "Right, comrade Colonel," was on his way.

"Comrade Pilot Shanislav, fly the men to comrade General Rokossovskii's HQ. You can sit one on each wing for the short flight. I know you will treat our Georgian aviators with great care." Shanislav smiled at the thought and couldn't contain his mirth. "It will be a great pleasure, comrade Colonel. Do you have a suggested altitude?" Dmitry only smiled and said, "Don't kill them. Believe it or not they are good fighters and born *razvedchiki*. I'm counting on you. I'll meet you in six hours at the HQ." They saluted and parted.

Dmitry could now open the note from the scout regarding Irina's location. With a relieved sigh, he noted that it was the main hospital and a short ride from his location. He gathered his gear and gave the borrowed motorcycle a rolling start and headed for the hospital and Irina. He arrived and was shown to her bed. "Comrade Major, how are you?" he asked the lightly bandaged woman. She glared as she responded. "Fine, but not allowed to work as they are insisting on 48 hours bed rest because of my concussion!" "Why comrade Major, you should never question medical instructions. I believe I learned that from you." She only grimaced and grabbed his hand. "Dima, I saw the grenade and the next thing I know I'm here. Some personnel put me in a truck and the driver brought me in. How did it all happen? It was a German grenade. How did it get thrown into our ward? Is there a fascist conspiracy to kill the wounded?" "I'm sure that's the case Irina Nataloivich, but don't worry about what happens in war. It is full of randomness and chance. At least you are not badly hurt and soon will be back mending our men."

For a moment they just stared at each other in the wonder at the realization that they both lived. As long as that was the case what else mattered? Well, for the both of them much mattered. They dearly loved their country and socialism and were dedicated to this fight of fights. All this passed unsaid in an instant. Dmitry leaned forward, "Dearest comrade, I must leave. Yes, there will be fighting but you know me, a nice safe staff job awaits this desk-bound Colonel with comrade General Rokossovskii's army." "Oh Dima, you are full of the bear's last lunch. I know where you will be and bless you for it but please, please, I beg of you be careful. I have prayed to your mother to protect you. Your parents are as proud of you as I am, but we need you. Do not be foolish!"

"I completely agree, Irina, the thought that our officers seek death in battle is repugnant to me. This is to be a long war and we need to make the Germans suffer, not us. I will do my best and my duty." She smiled, "You are such a boy in a man's body, Dima. Don't be too gallant and please seek me out when you are done. Tell Rokossovskii that I hold him responsible for you!" The softest, gentlest kiss followed and he slowly left, never looking back.

Chapter 8

The Bear, Felix, Lev, and a small following of runners were dug in behind German lines on the axis of Kachalov's upcoming attack. They had been feeding his staff information from the Germans' midst for three days due to continued delays, and awaited the Red forces. Bear was buried under dirt and grasses with a small window of visibility. Currently he was scanning the Russian front for signs of activity. He smiled to himself when he refocused his beautiful Nikon binoculars. They had been retrieved from the desk of a Japanese general just prior to the battle of Khalkin-Gol when Zhukov had sent him and Dima to ascertain Japanese plans.

They had done that flawlessly and Bear couldn't help but relieve the general of his binoculars. He didn't need them the next day to see the Red Army tanks bearing down on his position. Oh those days were fun, he remembered. He shook himself alert and continued the scan. As requested they had identified the seam between German units where the attack had the best chance of succeeding and they were buried in position right there. It will be tricky, he thought, to not get shot by the trigger-happy cucumbers as they came forward. No one knew they were there and recognition was going to be a challenge with everyone's nerves strung thin.

He motioned Felix forward. "Well, my pet cat, how are your many lives today? Does a stroll to HQ and fresh tea sound good?" Felix was almost indistinguishable from the ground but his smile was still visible. "Ah, we cats don't like the day time but throw something stronger than tea into the bargain and away I go!" Bear smiled. He truly loved Felix and they both knew their days were numbered in the *razvedka*, but they loved it and were the best. The war would demand their use in staff positions. Bear unwillingly let himself see the void without Felix as his mate and his heart missed. He had to stop thinking this way. It was next to death itself.

"All right, comrade cat. Tell them at HQ that we risked sending you in daylight because the fascists are changing formation. They are bringing armor forward and also that the air cover has thinned a bit. Show them the map coordinates for the attack but indicate that the troops need forward armor in order to penetrate the German lines. Then grab some fresh refreshment and don't return until night fall. OK?" Felix just smiled and started rearranging his camouflage for movement. "Wait for some more fascist fly boys heading over and begin your run when everyone is staring skyward and admiring the gallant knights of the air.

Blessings on you, my friend. Straight to comrade General Kachalov and no one else. Push the staffers out of the way if they object. Do you have officer's pins with you? Use them to get to HQ. I promote you captain." The ability of the GRU to be any service and any rank at will drove the rest of the army crazy but was a very valuable tool as Bear knew from experience. At that moment the overhead drone of a flight of Stukas was heard and the Bear even saw the flash of German binoculars pointed skyward. "Off you go, my cat! No hunting and luck be with you!"

Felix moved out at a crouch as Lev and the other runners stared at him. His field camouflage blended perfectly with the tall grasses as he crawled and stumbled forward. He had over ten miles to go and he knew speed was critical. Only the best *razvedchiki* could move the way he was, an easy but deceptively quick zigzagging low crouch to preserve field cover, interspersed with gliding, crawling, and freezing. As Bear watched, he thought, poetry, that is Red Army poetry.

Felix finally hit a tree line, dropped his grass cover and trusted his field camouflage uniform and began to really move. The Bear sighed and continued to scan all sides. Where were they? The attack had been scheduled for 24 hours ago. What was the holdup? Be patient Bear, he reminded himself. This is the first time we have a real chance of hitting the bastards hard. Let's do it right. Just settle in and be a bear in his cave.

Almost 60 kilometers to the north, Dmitry was reporting to General Rokossovskii's HQ and asking where he could be of the most use. "I need reliable eyes and ears near the front. Take a radio operator and keep your motorcycle and get one for the radio man. In the next day I'll tell you where to head and when our attack begins I'll need reports from you. Can you do this?" "Yes, comrade General," Dmitry replied. "It's a good idea but as you know the radio will have to be in clear air. I'll arrange a simple code with your staff to prevent the bastards from getting what we send." "Good," Rokossovskii replied. "We'll need every bit of information. I wish I had some planes but we are not equipped with fighters to escort reconnaissance flights so everyone I send up is shot down."

Dmitry jumped in, "We can help, comrade General. I have brought the best recon pilot in the Red Air Force with me. He and his little Po-2 can go anywhere and the Poli is so slow the Stukas and FW's fly right by him. At that point he either hugs the ground or heads for the clouds. He's brilliant! Comrade General Zhukov just gave him an Order of the Red Banner for his work in the first few weeks of the war. I'll get him sorted out on some missions."

"By the Black Madonna, you are very good, Dima. This is the best news I've had in days. I also have news for you, Dima. After Zhukov and Timoshenko left Smolensk for Moscow, they met with Stalin and the Politburo. In front of everyone the *Vozdh* asked Zhukov if he should replace Timoshenko. Zhukov said no and the game began. Beria and that scum Mekhlis were all over Timoshenko but our grand old soldier just stood there and said not a word. Some Politburo members came to the defense of Timoshenko and no changes are planned for this minute but they are coming. I feel it on the wind from Moscow."

"Also, they have reinstated the Commissars as you have probably seen and we are all being watched and reported on constantly. I can't ignore it but I'll not let it take away my initiative. I have to discuss everything I do with the one assigned to me, Novarov. Frankly, he's not too bad but would sell me out in a minute if it gets him Generals' tabs. So watch yourself."

"On top of this Stalin and the Supreme Council have issued orders purging army units of politically unreliable men. I thought we needed men? And more dangerous, anyone escaping from German capture or encirclement is to be interrogated by the NKVD and have to prove that they are not traitors. These are dangerous times, my friend. The battlefield might just be the safest place."

Rokossovskii sighed, "Well, we are red soldiers and must do our duty. Talk to my staff to get the details but the general plan is to counterattack against the fascists in two days to prevent the complete encirclement of the Smolensk pocket. We have hundreds of thousands of troops trapped there and we cannot lose them. Also, we need time for "Uncle" Zhukov to bring up the Reserves on the road to Moscow so when we do fall back a new line is ready. At any rate we must keep a corridor open for our boys. Get your flier up and tell him enough so he understands, but no capture for him. He must die rather than be interrogated if forced down."

"Find me the place where they are weakest at their front so I can cause a breakthrough that will draw in their other forces and relieve pressure on Smolensk. Got that? OK, get going and requisition whatever you need in my name. Wear that HOSU and your Colonel's tabs to keep these lazy bastards hopping! Thanks! Dismissed."

What is happening, Dmitry thought as he left Rokossovskii's temporary HQ to find Shanislav and a motorcycle-riding radio operator. Jesus, where do I find one of those? But his thoughts returned to the political stories and new directives the General had related to him. Discipline needed toughening but these rules seemed desperate. Probably over a million men had escaped encirclements and capture. What would they do with them? Damn, we need everyone one of them right now. Yet we are warring on ourselves and that bastard Beria and his NKVD seem to be enjoying it and growing every day. At the same time we have no air force and our tanks are being destroyed faster than the replacements can arrive.

What is going on back in Moscow? Do they want us to win or not? They'll all be shot if the fascists break through, so what are they thinking? Ah well, some head scrubbing followed. I have my orders and I better get organized and get them done, he thought resolutely.

It was some hours later at dawn that the Bear in his position far to the south saw the snouts of the first Soviet tanks rolling forward. Good, good, he thought. They are leading with the tanks. Felix must have gotten through. "Heads up, my pirates. It looks like the glorious 28th Army is coming to our rescue. Lev, get the flag ready but no one break cover or fire till I give the word. Got it?" They all nodded grimly and began to appreciate the position they occupied in the midst of the German line. Any false move and they'd be shot by their own comrades. A three tank force came through the same tree line that Felix had used for cover. Just behind them the Bear heard the whine of the IL-2's, the Red Army's new ground support aircraft. Thank god we have some air cover, he thought. Maybe we do have a chance to give the bastards some red hell!

The Germans were silent and waiting. The line

was strong but not invincible. There was too little artillery and the tanks were dug in, making maneuver difficult. The three T-34'S came on. They should know right where the line was and make maximum use of aggressive maneuver. As he watched he started to squirm. God, they are heading right for the bog in front of the German line! A very clever piece of fascist planning but they had sketched the bog on the map. Didn't they know? Were they overconfident? Maybe the T-34 could cross this type of ground? Well, we are going to find out very soon.

The tanks were in open echelon to prevent concentrated fire on them so one was slightly ahead of the others. As it entered the bog it slowly ground to a halt but having no radio could not warn the others in time. They too entered the wet ground and were stopped. The Germans waited, as did Bear. The hatches clanged open and like a dream he watched as all twelve men of the three crews were machine gunned down coming out of their hatch. Not one shot fired in return!

Bear groaned in fury and as the Red Army troops broke cover he ordered his men to fire on the machine gun posts and break out their mortar. At least the surprise of the automatic fire from the PPsh's directed on the machine gun nests surprised the Germans. However, even more spectacularly the presighted mortar delivered on target and blew the fascist gunners to hell before their surprise registered. A deep hurrah surfaced from the Russian line and the men surged forward towards the Germans who began to retreat.

Knowing what was next the Bear grabbed Lev

and turned to the runners. "Keep the heat on. Lev and I are going to become tankers." One of the tanks was burning but as far as they could tell the other two were undamaged. They should be able to use them briefly as gun platforms before the Panzers blasted the attacking troops. Bear and Lev seemed to rise out of the ground and shouting "For the Motherland and Stalin!" to catch the attention of the attacking troops, made for one of the undamaged tanks. An officer spotted them for what they were and shouted, "Don't shoot, *razvedchiki*! Keep moving. Forward, forward!"

German mortar and machine gun fire became intense and dozens of Red soldiers toppled over but the blessed IL-2's came in blazing and added aerial death and chaos to the scene. Climbing into the tank Lev and the Bear found a round already loaded. "We must get those dug in Panzers!" the Bear shouted. Lev was already ahead of him as he rotated the turret to where he knew a Panzer was hidden. 'Ready to fire, comrade Sergeant-Major!" he calmly mouthed with a fierce light was in his eye. The Bear punched the fire control and the tank recoiled. "Load!" They fired on top of the first round and a satisfying explosion of flame rewarded them. Bear started screaming at the burning tank while loading another round. "Find the next one, Lev!" They moved the turret to the right and saw the telltale gleam of machine gun fire. "The bastards don't see us yet! Fire!" They saw the shell burst just feet from the tank, and reloaded and fired after correcting. Another fireball was their reward.

However, the commander must have been in the third tank because he now figured out that his companions were dead not from air support but from one of the stranded tanks. The Germans fired a near miss and Lev looked at the Bear. "One more shot down his muzzle and we return to our proper station! Let's get the bastard!" Racing they shoved the shell home and fired. The German fired at the same moment and secured a direct hit on their forward armor. The almost two inches of good Communist steel held but they were catapulted up and over. Without waiting to see how their shot had done, they tumbled out of the tank and crawled away.

They saw their mortar shells bursting around the men in their hidden position and Bear signaled for the runners to break out before the fascists scored a direct hit on them. They fell back inside the Soviet lines to regroup. Bear pounded the runners on the back. "Good men! You can fight with the Bear any day!" They in turn looked like that might not be the best idea for longevity, but smiled at the praise. Not true *razvedchiki,* they held these men in awe for their invisibility and fighting legend. However, joining the club was a different manner.

The corporal spoke up, "Comrade Sergeant, my god, you two took out the Panzers and look at our boys pour through. Our "Flying Infantrymen," the IL-2's, are hitting them hard. The goddamned Hitlerites are running!" The Bear smiled and said, "Yes, they are. Come on, we have more to do to make sure they stay in that condition.'

However, the Germans were the first rate *SS Grosse Deutschland* division and they didn't run far. Regrouping in their improvised second line of defense they began to hurt the Soviets badly. The frontal assault techniques of the Red Army eschewed by Stalin and his yes men, like Budyenny and Voroshilov, not only got the men slaughtered but the tank lanes were predictable and the Soviet tanks were quickly destroyed as German artillery was called in. Bear knew how this story would end but also knew further gains were possible from the information they had gathered and hastened to find a command station.

Meanwhile, pilot Piotr Shanislav banked over the River Vop on the Rokossovskii front for what seemed the one hundredth time. Even at 1000 feet he had trouble locating camouflaged German forces. Damn, they are better at that than our boys, he reflected as he overflew the lines and snapped more photos. The Polikarpov glided silently with its engine switched off and he had plenty of time to survey for tank and infantry forces. The plane had a new camouflage paint scheme recommended by Dmitry and the new camera mount and auto shutter were working fine.

Shanislav enjoyed the work which allowed him almost complete independence and great flying time. The hitch was that one missed sighting of a Hitlerite plane and he was likely dead. As long as he maneuvered them into having to make turning passes they always overshot. His other main defensive tactic was diving for the clouds or like today, climbing into them. All in all he was quite happy having met Dmitry and his "interesting" squad. His thinking refocused as he shot more photos of the same German group in the open near the village of Yartsevo.

This was the point of the northern claw of the

German pincher movement and if they could break this one the encircled troops around Smolensk could continue to pour through the unclosed German pincher. This was the spot! He knew Dmitry and comrade General Rokossovskii would both agree. With that he headed for home and a hot drink. Although still summer the year seemed to be moving towards fall very early. He drew his leathers and scarf tighter and restarted the engine for a burst of speed towards home.

When Shanislav landed, Dmitry came down to the improvised airfield. "Well, my young knight of the air, did you find it?" "Just as you described, comrade Colonel, the fascists are in the open with tanks and men but very little artillery. They are massed in clumps. Oh! If we only had some IL-2's I'd make a pie out of them!" Dmitry sighed and slapped Shanislav on the shoulder. "Good job, Captain. Let's get the photos developed and we'll meet with the General as quickly as we can. Get the lab moving and I'll see you in an hour or so. Again, well done!" Shanislav saluted, gave the ground crew some points to tune on the Po-2, and ran for the Photo Lab.

"Comrade General, observe the fascist formations and their lack of march discipline. They are feeling the exhaustion of constant campaigning for the last month. Look at the string of broken down tanks and trucks. We can hurt them here. Surprise and above all effective artillery will hold them even if we are severely outnumbered, which will likely be the case." Dmitry glanced up at Rokossovskii as he studied the photos. "I agree, comrade Colonel. For once we have them. Clearly there is confusion on their next step and they have been told to hold for supply or orders or both. Now is the time. Orderly, get the staff assembled. Get comrade General Kazakov on the line. I want his artillery moving forward within the hour which should put it past dusk. Here are his location coordinates, targeting will follow. Move!"

"Young pilot, you have done great service to the Motherland today. As a groundhog, I thank you and salute you!" Rokossovskii's words brought tears to Shanislav's eyes. "Comrade General, it was only my duty. I have come to love cucumbers and am glad to help." "All right, my son. Get some rest. We will not need you tonight. Comrade Colonel, with me."

Rokossovskii drew Dmitry aside. "I want him spotting for us when we attack. How is your radio plan coming?" "I'm ready, comrade General. As it turns out I can use my own men and three will be better than two in this case. Where do you want us and when?" Rokossovskii pursed in thought and moved back to the map. "Get yourselves set up near Yartsevo; it will be our initial focus. See this wooded ridge here? It looks perfect for you, but you decide. I have to move everything at night so as to remain unobserved. Therefore we attack in approximately 36 hours. Dawn on July 28th. Kachalov has already gone in and the fighting is brutal. He is dreadfully outnumbered."

"With all that, he is giving some of their best a very bloody nose. That is drawing them off of our trapped forces. We must hold the corridor open for our men to escape. Dima, our men, I dreamt of them last night. I saw them drowning in the fear and chaos of being caught behind the lines, fighting to get home.

We must save as many as possible! You know the plan. Get yourself in place and establish communications with the staff quietly and then wait for hell on earth. We may be the biggest collection of survivors in the Red Army with hardly an organization but we are going to hurt the Hitlerites like nothing they have yet seen. God bless and luck!"

Dmitry snapped to attention and threw a salute and moved in to hug Rokossovskii. "You too, Uncle. The Black Madonna is watching over you. Good hunting!" A quick exit was best as they were both forming Polish tears.

Sixty miles to the south of Rokossovskii's forces, back with the Kachalov force, Bear was at Kachalov's field Headquarters pleading for a change of course. After two days of brutal fighting it was clear that the mass of the southern portion of the German Army Group Center was on their flank. Some success had been achieved by the partial isolation of the *SS* units *Grosse Deutschland* and *Das Reich* but the Bear and his scouts had traversed most of the German rear to their immediate west and saw the build-up that was heading for Kachalov and his now exhausted forces.

"Comrade General," Bear tried again, "We must either establish a strong defensive perimeter or withdraw. The fascists are massing on the flank with much more armor and will hit us soon." Kachalov wondered how a sergeant could interpret so much but the Bear was something of a legend after Khalkin-Gol so he listened. He listened, though he knew he could do nothing about the situation. He had radioed and begged the *Stavka* for just such new orders but the reply always came back, "Attack! Attack! Do not fall back."

Kachalov knew his army was dead and he himself either would die in the next attack or be shot by Moscow, and damn that happening! He would never give them the satisfaction. He straightened and addressed Bear and his staff. "Comrades, we have our orders to attack northwesterly towards Smolensk and we will follow them." He stared straight at the Bear as he spoke and the Bear nodded. "We will launch another all-out frontal assault centered here at Starinka. We can possibly break their lines and defeat them in detail for the glory of the Motherland." The staff stared and then nodded, all knew what was expected and the plans were drawn up.

Bear asked the general for orders. "Return to GRU command at Comrade Marshal Timoshenko's Headquarters and tell them what we intend. We will attack tomorrow at dawn. You are very famous for a sergeant, comrade, so I know your reputation. I count on you to tell the truth to HQ about what happened here. We are outnumbered three or four to one. The axis of attack they have ordered sends us straight into the heart of the beast with an exposed flank. The orders are crazy but they will not back down. I never thought a bear would tell the story; the stories are always about bears. In this case you tell the story so that the Motherland will remember us for patriots and Bolsheviks to the end. Dismissed, comrade Sergeant!" Bear saluted and with a single motion and no words put out his hand to the General. They exchanged a strong grasp and parted.

Bear gathered up his men. "We head for HQ, wine, women, and song," he declared to the smiles of Lev and Felix. "Find us some transport with the wounded or staff so we don't have to walk. I'm going to try and find the comrade Colonel's whereabouts because either his location or Vyazma will be our next stop. See you in an hour or sooner if transport is ready. Thank you, comrades. You have done good duty."

Group Kachalov rode into history the next morning. Fantastically outnumbered and battling Guderian's best, they drove deeper into the German forces and their flank became longer and more exposed as Kachalov knew it would. The vultures of the *Wehrmacht* wasted no time in picking away at the edges and eating their way into the Russian center. The fighting was desperate, hand to hand, and tank to tank. Most of the Soviet pilots and aircraft had been killed and destroyed in the last two days and the Germans took advantage of this.

Without air cover the Reds were doomed but fought on. The *Stukas* were everywhere, strafing troops, bombing tanks into flaming pyres to Soviet glory or some such. Kachalov led from just behind the front line. He had a radio hooked into a T-34 and directed his tankers from the turret. Eventually his wish was granted and a German 88 used as an anti-tank gun scored a direct hit on his tank and the General simply vanished. The attack faltered and failed, and those who could fled for the rear as the Panzers moved in to mop up with machine guns fired into the retreating masses.

Very few surrendered or were allowed to as the Russian war moved into higher and higher levels of death and brutality. A week later some small groups surfaced behind the then new Soviet lines to tell their story. Of course, they were arrested and interrogated by the NKVD according to the new regulations. To hide the magnitude of the inept leadership of Stalin and the *Stavka*, the Army's chief Commissar and Stalin's butcher, Mekhlis, personally had the word spread that Kachalov had gone over to the Germans. In Stalin's Order No. 270 it stated, "Lieutenant-General Kachalov, the commander of the 28th Army, displayed cowardice and fell captive to the German Fascists while encircled with a group from his force's staff." Anyone who disagreed with this statement, because they knew the truth, was shot.

Back in the North with Rokossovskii's Army, Dmitry and the Georgians were hidden in a wood near the center line of the coming Soviet attack north of Yartsevo. In deep camouflage they observed the German line and saw that while a bit stronger than on the previous day it was still strung out in advance formation and not well positioned for defense. They sent this information to Rokossovskii but kept a sharp eye out for German spotters. They knew that their messages were being read but the crude code they were using should last for a day or two. They were more concerned with German radio direction finding and being spotted. The messages were kept to the shortest possible length to prevent this for Dmitry knew their time was short.

Then they heard the scream of diving aircraft. The few remaining IL-2's came screeching in and hit the German front hard. They came back and back, strafing and bombing until everything was black with oily smoke. Good, good, Dmitry thought. The comrade General knows his business. What the Germans can't see they can't shoot. He turned to Taka and Sachino, "The tanks are next. We move ahead with the line. We are to keep HQ informed on progress and threats. I may send one of you back if required but otherwise we rely on the radio. Any questions or Georgian war proverbs I should know?" Used by now to the kidding, Taka just sighed and said, "We Georgians always respect the ability of the Russians but we will point out any shortcomings, comrade Colonel." Dmitry smiled and nodded, "*Spasibo* (thank you)," he said quietly. 'Get ready to move on my word. Sachino, your job is to keep our trigger happy comrades from shooting us. When they come forward, you will fall back and establish contact with the lead elements and let them know we will be in their front." "Yes, comrade Colonel, done!" Sachino slid off to await the lead tanks and special troops.

The crashing of trees and clanking of gears was numbing as the T-34's came forward. Sachino waved and was gone and Dmitry signaled, "Enemy force in sight" to HQ. He watched as Sachino climbed on the lead tank and almost caused a heart attack to the tank commander standing in the hatch as he thumped him from behind. Dmitry smiled grimly. These men were getting better and better, silent, invisible, and fearless to friend and foe alike. He felt his heart swell with pride for being allowed to lead them.

However, another surprise soon enveloped the battlefield. Still in the forest, as if by a silent hand, the

Soviet tanks came to a halt. Dmitry used his field glasses to try and see the reason but it was not apparent. At the same time the IL-2's broke off and headed east to re-arm. Dmitry was surprised by the pause in the action. Hadn't comrade Rokossovskii learnt the lesson of speed while studying with Tuchachesvkii and his team? But that was soon answered as the scream of 150mm shells arced over the front lines. This was followed by an almost hellish screeching as hundreds of the new *Katyusha* rockets slammed into the lead German positions while the shells headed miles into the German rear.

Taka glanced at his Colonel. "Send brilliant!" Dmitry ordered. As Taka sent the one word he looked again at his commander. "Where are the shells going, comrade Colonel?" "To the bastard's rear," replied Dmitry. "How could I have doubted our brilliant comrade General? He has taken a page from Marshal Tukhachevskii. To prepare for a penetration he is hitting the enemy in depth. The rear is where the German staff, reserves, and supplies are. With the artillery fire he is devastating their support and reinforcements. Therefore, when the attack comes, which mark my words will be with tanks and aircraft supported by some of our tough cucumbers, the Germans will not be able to plug the gap but will have to fall back. This is Red Army fighting! The Marshal (Tukhachevskii) would be proud and damn the NKVD for putting a bullet in his head in '38."

Dmitry knew that while the strategy was brilliant, they were still too far outnumbered to be completely successful, but the return to strategy rather than mindless frontal assaults caused his hopes to soar.

The heavy artillery and rocket fire went on for 45 minutes with changes in targets and pace. The earth was bucking and rearing like a cavalry steed. The fountains of earth, trees, body parts, and equipment were frighteningly hellish. Finally, the whine of T-34 engines could be heard again as the tanks rolled forward. In magnificent but coincidental precision, the IL-2's showed up at the same time. The combined forces smashed the German line and kept going. The infantry was fighting with vengeance for the weeks of slaughter and no prisoners came out of the smoke.

Dmitry hand signaled Sachino to return and as soon as they were all together said, "We are moving forward and will hitch a ride on a tank to stay in the van. The comrade General will need information now more than ever." They approached one of the command tanks and hopped on. Banging on the hatch Dmitry explained their mission and they were reluctantly welcomed aboard. The ride was exhilarating. Clinging to handles and ropes on the tank exterior they traveled through the now open fields at over 30 KPH, seemingly masters of all they saw. The tactics had worked brilliantly and there were very few other than dead fascists in sight.

Dmitry grabbed Sachino and shouted, "Grab a prisoner. I need more information." Sachino obediently jumped off the tank and circled back to the front line of German entrenchments where he grabbed a shell shocked young Grenadier. "Here's a fish, comrade Colonel, fresh from the stream" "OK men, off the tank and thank you comrades!" Dmitry shouted to the crew as they moved away. A few quick questions and assessment of his uniform informed Dmitry that they had routed members of Guderian's Fourteenth Panzer Army.

Good show, he thought. That means that per our intelligence, reinforcements will not be arriving for a day or two. This outfit was large enough to operate independently so other units will have to be diverted to this area. Finished with the young shaking soldier, Taka asked, "What do we do with him, comrade Colonel?" Dmitry realized he didn't know. Behind the advance there was only a death sentence for him but Dmitry was not keen on individual killing. But they couldn't let him go. If by a miracle he made it back, German staff could piece together valuable info. Oh damn, Dmitry thought.

He looked at Taka and Sachino, "Shoot him" They nodded and took the young German to the trench, pushed him in and two quick shots followed. They returned and stood near the brooding Colonel. "This is war, men, and we cannot show any mercy. There was no one to guard him and that fixed my decision. Let's go."

Once behind Soviet lines Dmitry felt more confident about sending a detailed message to Rokossovskii. He outlined the battle so far and the details of enemy reaction to the initial operation. He asked for more air support but knew that was likely in vain and urged the artillery forward as well as more troops and armor. Now that the penetration was achieved, keeping maximum momentum and mass was the key.

All this Rokossovskii knew on the other end of

the radio and was already implementing. He smiled at Dmitry's very correct analysis and asked him to move forward and report the enemy's actions. They had struck a solid blow to keep the northern pincer from closing. Rokossovskii was aware of the destruction of Kachalov's force so he understood that this was the one life line for the encircled Soviets and the longer it stayed open the more men would make it to the Soviet lines. He also knew that Guderian knew the same and now that the southern forces were destroyed, he would turn his full group on Rokossovskii's force. Hell and more was on the way. He ordered every reserve forward, every plane into the air, and every tank to roll. There was no reason for reserves any longer. They must hold as long as they could and trust that the *Stavka* was moving quickly to establish a new line in their rear.

After the brief radio conference Dmitry, Taka, and Sachino hitched a ride on another tank. Pulling rank Dmitry ordered the five tank unit to make all speed forward where he heard intense sounds of multiple arms firing. In the melee, organization was no longer a factor for the tanks so Dmitry had no doubts about this action. He also knew they were moving too far ahead of the infantry and soon would have only the Hitlerites for company. The moment of truth for this attack was close at hand and he wanted to be at the front for that moment.

They passed through an abandoned German artillery position and Dmitry's heart soared. He halted the tanks and told two crews to debark, turn the artillery and set fuse and range for three or more miles and start dropping shells in the new German rear. This would prevent reorganization and keep the attack moving. When they reached the third line of German defenses the Soviets should occupy them and prepare for the counterattack. He radioed Rokossovskii and got the OK for the plan.

He left the tankers behind as their few remaining assault tanks continued forward and as the now grounded tankers gleefully manned the deserted artillery and started hurling shells into the German rear. Dmitry pulled out his intelligence map and saw that in just a few miles they would be at the third German line. He started drafting orders from his notebook for Taka and Sachino to distribute to the infantry as they came up.

As he had expected, just behind a ridge and beyond the last main German line, the Soviet tanks were halted and grouped together. He signaled for the unit commanders to come to him and the word spread as they converged on his tank. "Comrades, Colonel Zhankovskii operating for comrade General Rokossovskii. I have been in radio contact with the comrade General and he wants a defensive line established here." "What!" they cried as one. "We are beating the Fritzes and they are running. Let's roll them under our treads and pay them back for the last weeks of murder."

"Comrades, that is also how I feel, but we know that just several miles ahead they will form up and eventually be joined by reinforcements. Running into them piecemeal, they will have us for lunch. If we await them here, we will be in force and ready. By the way, jackrabbits, where are your cucumbers? Who will fight the fascist infantry?"

At this the tankers looked somewhat surprised and glanced around and realized they were all alone on the forward point of a very long spear. "OK, comrade Colonel. Where do you want us?" "Just behind and among these trenches. We will fill in with infantry and anti-tank forces. Spread out and do not bunch up. We will take the bastards apart when they come. OK. Questions? No? Move out."

Some lead elements of infantry had ridden the tanks forward and Dmitry now explained the task to them. They were all short of officers due to casualties in the last weeks so he appointed sergeants to platoon command and formed up stray units. Taka and Sachino pointed him out to advancing officers for orders. Soon the lines started to look like a force to be reckoned with. He called to Taka, "Comrade Private, we desperately need anti-tank forces. Go to the rear and find them and hurry them forward. Find a horse to move faster and get them back here. Time is everything." Taka visibly grew in stature, "Comrade Colonel, Georgian horsemanship is world famous. I will fly like the Georgian wind and get what you need." Snapping a salute he was gone and grinning from ear to ear, sought out the German supply horses.

All day the line was lengthened, strengthened, and deepened at Dmitry's direction, assisted by two other colonels. Tank and infantry support was as good as they could hope for but Dmitry anguished over the still absent anti-tank guns and artillery. To compensate he positioned squads of men forward with mortars pre-sighted on likely attack lines and with orders to fire five shots and retreat. It would help break up the German foot soldiers but the tanks would shrug off mortars. Damn, where was Taka. He also prayed for night to fall as von Richthofen's fliers were beginning to swarm around the line. Their hastily improvised camouflage would not fool these experienced pilots and he dreaded the damage they would receive from the air. Oh, for fighter cover! He knew none was coming and that alone spelled their doom, but doom would also visit the lead German elements and they would pay!

As he reflected on the likely German attack plan he realized that he was building a trap for his own forces. Idiot! He had not applied what he had learned on maneuver in the 1930's and seen in action at Khalkin-Gol and the last few weeks. His line would hold for a while but when its flanks were peeled back and things got bad in the center it would rapidly collapse and the men encircled. He needed deeper lines and more surprises for the Hitlerites. He called together the officers and some of the engineers.

"Comrades, I am failing you. The plan will not hold against the villain Guderian. He will slowly eat us alive with his larger forces and creep around our edges." They looked stunned that a senior officer would admit to a mistake and all hastened to support him as they didn't know what else to do. Dmitry continued, "Here is the new plan and dispositions. Listen carefully and criticize what won't work. Then take this back to your men. This is going to be complicated and tough but it will hurt the fascist bastards more and maybe we'll even live. Attend!"

As Dmitry sketched and described the new plan, grunts of assent were heard amid gasps of surprise. As he observed their reactions, he realized this might just work. When complete with the briefing and with everyone given new orders, Dmitry had Sachino raise HQ. He discussed, via radio, the outline of the plan with Rokossovskii, who approved and told him that he would find Dmitry that evening to review dispositions and plans.

Chapter 9

That night under a blanket to shield their light, Dmitry and the lanky General discussed and improved the plan. Arriving only with guards and no staff, Rokossovskii had immediately scrutinized Dmitry's lines. "Comrade General, who is my relief, sir?" Dmitry asked, expecting a General to take over the defense. "Sorry, comrade GRU, but you are caught in your own trap. For once you staff types will have to lead. The general officers are all occupied." Dmitry was a bit surprised by this but decided this was a compliment from the tough Rokossovskii and said a quick, "Yes, sir!" "Let's look at this plan of yours," and for the next 90 minutes the two were huddled over maps and notes.

Finally satisfied, Rokossovskii asked, "How long can you hold against Heinz and his bandits?" Dmitry thought for a moment and said, "A day, with great luck two. It will be the air cover that kills us. Any hope of air support?" "I wish I could grant you that wish, but no, we have nothing left." Dmitry absorbed these words and grimly nodded. "We will hold for two days, comrade General!" Rokossovskii took his shoulder and quickly squeezed it. "See you in hell, comrade!" was all he said as he turned, climbed into the jeep and left with his heart full of the certain fate awaiting Dima and his command.

There was plenty of night left so, bolstered by some tea, Dmitry continued to place the various commands. Almost forgotten, Taka and Sachino dogged his steps silently in case of need until finally he pulled them over. 'My Georgian friends, let's talk about tanks

and dragon killers!" At this allusion to their patron
saint their eyes lit up and Taka intoned, "Comrade
Colonel, we Georgians have killed many dragons, the
most famous being Comrade Stalin killing the tsarist
capitalist dragon choking the life from Mother Russia!" Dmitry just thought, Lenin had something to do
with that, but moved on. "Comrade Private Taka, those
tank killers you found will do good duty. You are in
charge of their field deployment." At this Taka almost
fainted. Dmitry continued, "I hereby appoint you Mas-
ter Sergeant, collar tabs to come later!" Now Taka almost keeled over and Sachino grabbed his sleeve to
hold him up. "Have you got all that, my Georgian warrior?" Taka could only squeeze out a "Sir!" Dmitry
brought them closer and said, "Here is your assignment and may St. George keep you safe.'

As expected the *SS* division came forward at
dawn. The question was, "Panzers, troops, or both?"
They had not even deigned to have an opening artillery
bombardment. Dmitry's net of *razvedchiki* had not had
a reconnaissance hit all night. These bastards are arrogant, Dmitry thought. Well, we are not the fucking
French and will show them some fighting, 48 hours,
God, can we do it? Then peering through the glasses
his heart sang, oh yes my Germanic friends, welcome
to Russia!

The bastards had only sent tanks with no infantry support. This was the best of all possibilities. One
of his fellow commanders rushed up and slapped him
on the back. "Perfection, comrade Colonel! Just like
you predicted, not only have they outrun their troops
but maybe the artillery also! God, we have them."

Dmitry allowed himself a confident grin to help the spirits of the men observing this meeting. "Your orders, Comrade?" "Kill the bastards! But wait for my signal." The red tabbed infantry Colonel threw a massive salute and said "Yes, sir!" and bounded back to his men.

Soon, soon, Dmitry thought. The noise was becoming all encompassing. The clanking treads and roaring exhausts invited the strongest heart to run from these monsters. Dmitry saw a few men break but the sergeants rounded them up and threw them back into line. Most held but fidgeted and twisted at the wait. If only the NKVD could hear the noise of the prayers being spoken out loud, he reflected, they might question their anti-religion campaign's effectiveness.

Now, he hoped and indeed, in the rear of the first tank echelon something went wrong. Two of them ground to a halt, hit by Taka's anti-tank fire. Their crews cautiously exited the wounded beasts. Wait, my children, wait, Dmitry again hoped. They did. Taka had iron discipline on his men. Per orders they were dispersed right in the tank paths, slightly to their projected flank. The orders were to pick off the rear tanks and as the men came out wait till they bunched up and then hit them with withering PPsh sub-machine gun fire. The lead tanks rolled on oblivious. Their rear force was being taken out and without them and infantry the front elements were easy prey. As he finished the thought, lightening bursts of PPsh fire at 900 rounds per minute of 30 caliber lead tore through the exposed tankers. Five more rear tanks went down as the anti-tank rifle PTRS teams fought from cover and round after incendiary round penetrated into the Panzers and either ricocheted through the interior, turning human flesh into meat chunks or finding some exposed ammo, turned the tank into an inferno. The slaughter was immense and satisfying as Dmitry punched his fist up in the signal for the trench troops to join the fight.

In response to his signal, designated troops along the whole line either rose up from hidden positions or came out of the trenches with Molotov cocktails flaming. The attacks were spectacular on the lead tanks. To a tank they were aflame with the screams of the crews echoing across the line or the burp-burp sound of the sub-machine guns annihilating them as they tried to escape. A deep satisfying 'hurrah' arose from the Russian ranks.

The field was littered with a dozen dead panzers with minimal casualties on the Soviets. Nearby officers came saluted and congratulated Dmitry. "Now we attack!" was their cry. Dmitry made sure the forward units were returning and told the officers. "We fall back to the second trench line!" They were stunned, "But comrade Colonel, we have them on the run!" Dmitry drew himself up, "Yes, we do but they will be back with troops and air cover. If you rush out now you will be slaughtered like sturgeon on harvesting day. We go to the next line of trenches according to the plan. We must camouflage better. The bastard Stukas will soon be here. Move! If I can see one sign of that line, I will break the officer responsible. Go, go! *Bustro, bustro!* (Hurry, hurry!).

They saluted and moved. At least they are taking orders, Dmitry reflected. Taka and Sachino reported in. "Georgians, brilliant work. Comrade Stalin will pin your Orders of Glory on you. I promise! All we have to do is live to see Moscow. Get your PTRS squads in standard formation with the anti-tank artillery and then head back out in front. I want warning when the ground forces come in. Stay well hidden as the air pirates will be everywhere! Thank you, Comrades!" The last was said with a smile but Dmitry had really begun to love these crazy Georgians. Their fighting was courageous and disciplined. I wish I had more, he thought. He fell back to critique the camouflaging of the line.

The Stukas and Heinkels were not long in coming. They buzzed and machined gunned the forward line, even hitting the disabled tanks with bombs as Dmitry had hoped. From the air it would appear, not as an abandoned Soviet line but as a disorganized one. God knows he had seen many of them the last 8 weeks. His men had turned some of the German tanks around and put out the fires to simulate Soviet tanks in position. Soon afterward the German artillery must have arrived because random shells began to fall but with no real idea where the Soviet lines were, very little damage was done. The individual shots from the snipers' Nagodev rifles let Dmitry know that German forward observers were being picked off. As night fell he thought, Comrade General, there is half of our bargain. We live to see another dawn.

The night did not bring a complete respite. The Germans probed and sought prisoners. The *razvedchiki* held solid and made sure none could penetrate to the Soviet line. In the morning the attack would be blind for a short while until the Soviet fire was spotted by air support. This would expose their location, and the dying would begin in earnest. The Soviets had to last until nightfall so the survivors could escape. No blind cattle to an encirclement here, Dmitry thought. He had arranged his lines carefully. In each case resistance increased as they fell back. If they could break a few panzers early they had a small chance of living until nightfall.

Dmitry assigned another Colonel to assume command as he tried to sleep. He was out in a minute and awoke with a start as Taka said, "Comrade Colonel, I can hear tanks. It is 0330; they will be on our lines soon." Dmitry nodded and willed himself awake. "OK, Comrade Sergeant. You know what to do." Taka nodded and jogged down the line alerting the men with Molotov cocktails to get ready. They would lead this time. However, with ground troops likely in the tank formation, few would live, but the chance of an early victory was too critical for Dmitry's small force.

The men moved into the field beyond the trench line into shell holes and other cover to await the tanks. Once again the pre-dawn echoed with the sounds of the mechanical monsters inexorably approaching. But now they faced a blooded victorious Red Army, not the panic stricken units they were used to fighting. At the moment the lead tanks with their infantry support left the tree line, the first cocktails flew through the brightening summer sky. A few of the courageous men lived to break away but as foreseen most died. Each one would be awarded an Order of the Red Star if Dmitry could convince Zhukov.

Several tanks were hit and the line of armor degenerated into confusion as burning tanks were steered around or pushed out of the way. The German troops started to fire forward at their unseen attackers but with little effect. About 300 yards from the line Dmitry shouted, "Fire!" The anti-tank artillery, pre-targeted at the likely approach lanes, let loose with immediate results. The Maxim heavy machine gunners dropped troops in their first steps of the day. Dmitry's heavy artillery hit their rear to slow down reinforcements and things looked good for a moment. But with increasing daylight came the Stukas and the Heinkels. Without Soviet air support the results were horrendous. Once the line was recognized from the air they were all over it with machine gun fire and bombs. Dmitry waited for the first attacks and then ordered the fall back to the next line while the German tanks and artillery fire was still halted.

The German artillery was mainly silent for fear of hitting their own troops. The lead officers saw the maneuver of the Soviets and thought, ah, the cowards are running again. As soon as they could they leaped forward at the second line which they could not see in the smoke and they fell in droves to machine gun and howitzer and mortar fire. This confused them again and while more armor was ordered forward the air forces continued to hammer Dmitry and his men.

The slaughter from the air was truly terrible. With the Soviets well dug in and camouflaged, identification from the air was difficult. The more experienced pilots just waited for the Soviets to fire and then dove on the positions. The heavy machine guns and cannons ripped through the ranks and blood was a fog above the trenches and gun emplacements. Dmitry knew the next move was critical. He called up his captain of engineers, "Comrade Captain on my mark, the time is 1412. Mark!" The engineer adjusted his watch. "Your orders, Comrade Colonel?" Dmitry sized up the youngish captain. "Have you placed both sets of charges on the river?" "Yes, Comrade Colonel," was the quick reply.

"At the start of the next German attack blow the first set fifteen minutes from the first salvo from the anti-tank guns and for Lenin's sake, hold on the second set for my direct order. Clear?" "Yes, sir. You need not worry. We are now well experienced in demolition since that is all we have done since June 22." Dmitry liked his attitude and responded when asked about the two sets of charges. The answer brought a broad smile and a fist driven into his hand from the Engineering captain. "Comrade Colonel, it is a privilege to die with you for the Motherland!" Dmitry shook his head in wonder at the charge and die Russian attitude. How long would it take for them to learn? "Comrade Captain, you are a good man and I mean no criticism. But let us not die for the Motherland but allow the Germans the privilege!" This brought a sharp salute and a "Good luck!" as the Captain headed for the river.

As the German's reorganized for their third try against the Soviet line, Dmitry went down the line, briefing officers on the plan and resetting positions. He finally came to the tank and artillery officers clustered behind his makeshift bunker. "Comrades, we are near the end of our efforts. But our role is not to die here but to kill Germans. Is that clear?" Nods followed his statement. "Artillery, as the Hitlerites advance you will gradually shorten your range until you are right in front of our own trenches. When you have five rounds left, you will mount up and cross the river. Tanks, as the bastards move in, wait till the artillery is silent to cross our line and take out as many tanks as you can. When you deplete your ammo head for the flanks, *razvedchiki* will lead you to the rear. Finally, you cucumbers watch all this and when I give the signal pour everything you have into the lead troops. Then have your men use the narrow trench system to head for the bridges. Is all that clear? Questions?"

There was some stirring amongst the group and an older Major spoke up. "Sir, should we not stay and fight to the death? Will the Commissars not have us shot for desertion?" 'These are my orders and only I can be shot for them," said Dmitry. The skepticism was open. "Comrades, we must live to fight. We have held the fucking *SS* for 48 hours. The men deserve to live and use their new found strength to fight another day. General Rokossovskii has personally approved the plan." Dmitry waited.

This was the moment for this leadership group to either commit suicide or kill a bunch of Germans and live to tell about it. A Colonel spoke up, "Boys, the comrade Colonel is right. Do you want to die on a fascist bayonet or under a tank tread, or show this army how to win? We will do this to the man, comrade Colonel, and we need no note from you to show the NKVD." In disbelief Dmitry listened in stunned silence as the officers broke into "The Red Army is Invincible." The troops around them gazed in wonder at their officers singing and soon the words of triumph were echoing along the line. What will Heinz make of that? Dmitry wondered. He broke in with tears streaming, "Comrades, I can think of no one better to fight with. Death to the Hitlerites! For the Motherland!" They echoed his cheer and went to their units to prepare. As Dmitry had hoped, the Germans would make one more try before dusk and it came very soon.

The Red artillery opened as the tanks and troops advanced from the trees. The German artillery and air attacks slowed. As planned, again there were anti-tank rifle squads who scored a few successes and Molotov cocktails were thrown with good effect. It was not enough and the gray line moved forward, crushing all before it. Finally, fifteen minutes into the attack with several hundred yards still separating the groups, the river erupted into geysers near the bridges giving the effect of the bridges being blown. The Soviet officers calmed their troops. 'The bridges live, comrades, but now watch the German reaction."

The German line leaped forward at the sight and that of a number of well-rehearsed Red soldiers breaking for the rear. The Germans almost jumped forward in their haste to close for the kill with the cut off troops. As they did the artillery and anti-tank guns hit them hard and scored hits. However, they also took many hits from the tanks and gradually their fire diminished. The Soviet tanks closed with the Panzers and individual jousts that could only end in death for either party began across the field. This completely negated the German artillery but some pilots were still able to close for kills. On schedule, the infantry laid massive small arms and mortar fire into the advancing troops, and the German line halted and began to retreat. The artillery (Soviet) fired their last volleys and limbered up and retreated over the river. After the smoke from the tank fight obscured all, Dmitry ordered, "Retreat! Retreat!"

The men headed for the slit trenches and the bridges. The German air forces kept up a furious fire but also began to slow as darkness and fuel consumption forced them to leave the scene. Finally, with the survivors across, Dmitry grabbed the Engineer Captain and shouted, "NOW!" The bridges were spectacularly blown and Rokossovskii had his complete 48 hours. Dmitry organized the march and figured he had sustained about 50 percent casualties but the fascists had paid and would not cross the River Vop for at least a day. He sighed and fell into the back of the truck Taka had commandeered and joined the retreat, fast asleep.

Chapter 10

Rokossovskii was standing and looking at maps when Dmitry was shown through into the general's newest temporary HQ. Rokossovskii was as transfixed as a believer at a miracle. He looked in wonder and extended his arms. "Nephew, I could only hope and gods, four days, you gave me four days. I have tried to honor you by using them well!" Dmitry moved into the hug of the tall, impeccable general and only said, "We were fortunate. Heinz was at his worst and his troops and supplies exhausted." The General stepped back and expanding to his full height said, "That's not what I heard. I heard you were the Siberian fox surprising them at every turn. The fake blowing of the bridges was brilliant. I must remember that one. Once you left we gave them a day to get their pontoons in place and then Shanislav led his beloved Il-2's in and took out every single boat. Hence we got four days!

Gods, the *Vozdh* was pleased! We are to retreat and reform behind the new line at Briansk, in front of Moscow. But first, a toast to your miracle and return. Sergeant!" In walked the Bear with a bottle of the standard field issue vodka. But at the sight of him Dmitry broke his stance and was enveloped by Bear's grasp. "Sir, I am reporting back," said Bear. Dmitry pulled back and eyed his neat appearance. "Looks like a general has accomplished what a colonel could not!" The Bear smiled, "When in Rome!" I have been working with the general's staff to improve their reconnaissance techniques and it was felt a less *razvedchiki* look might help." "A toast gentlemen, to the hero of

Yartsevo and may he kill more fascists!" The toast was downed and soon some soldier's bread was consumed to help empty the bottle and preserve the toast.

Rokossovskii smiled again. "Comrade Colonel, it seems you are going to Moscow to be head of senior GRU staff at the 'Little Corner' (Stalin's office in the Kremlin). They must be in the pay of the Germans to give them a break like that! These orders come from the new Chief of Staff comrade Marshal Shaposhnikov!" Now it was Dmitry's turn to be surprised. "Is comrade Marshal Zhukov promoted? Where is he?" "No, Dima. He has been demoted for arguing with the *Vozdh* about Kiev. The situation is hopeless there but the *Stavka* has given another stand and die order. Zhukov protested and now he is in Yelnya, near here, with orders to recapture the town. We need to wish him victory if he is to survive, Dima." "God and St. George, what are they thinking?" The general broke in, "My NKVD Commissar will be here in a minute so get it off your chest and do not say a word when he arrives. Just act the Soviet hero when he starts gushing! We will talk more about the comrade General soon."

Rokossovskii continued, "We are still in a desperate situation, although a bit improved thanks to you and others. We have blunted the German assault and if we have some luck at Yelnya, we might just push them back. Kiev is going to fall no matter what the Politburo thinks and because of their stupidity compounded by Budyenny and Khrushchev, as his commissar, we will lose many men. We held the pincers back and allowed tens of thousands to escape. We are rearming and reforming them now. Additionally, our spies in

Tokyo let us know that the Japanese have no stomach for war with us. They are in their own desperate situation in China and if they attack the US, which is rumored, they will have their own hands full.

Therefore, we have moved ten Eastern divisions including four tank divisions to the West and these troops are fresh and just beginning to arrive. Hopefully, they will be used well and not sacrificed needlessly. OK, here is Novorev, we are simple Red soldiers. Bear, at attention for him and no familiarity."

The Commissar entered the room and made quite a show lauding Dmitry. Who knew what he really thought. For once Bear was the Sergeant-Major and obedient to the officers and all came across as a perfect Pravda photo.

The one key piece of intelligence that the Soviets did not have was that Hitler and his generals were in the midst of a tremendous argument. Guderian wanted to drive for Moscow after being resupplied. Hitler had decided that the south, beginning with Kiev, was more critical in order to control the region's food and petroleum production. After a week of bitter wrangling including a Fuhrer visit to Guderian to promote him and award him another Knight's Cross, it was decided to encircle Kiev and leave Moscow for September.

Rokossovskii's observations proved correct and in a few weeks the city fell with over 600,000 Soviet casualties. The Red Army was on track to incur 4 million casualties in the first six months of the war, more than all the other Allied forces combined! This would be the trend for the rest of the war. Civilian casualties were just as high, and mainly uncounted. However, the German victory at Kiev gave the Soviet forces in the North time to regroup and Zhukov proved what Red Army fighting could achieve at Yelnya.

Later that evening after a quick meal and before Rokossovskii went to meet with his staff, Dmitry and the general talked. "Dima, as I mentioned you are being sent to the Kremlin. As I know comrade General Zhukov discussed with you, there are enemies there, be very wary. However, their acceptance of you as Chief of Staff for Intelligence was a very strong result of your action at Yartsevo. We in the field desperately need a strong, correct voice in the 'Little Corner'. As you know many of them are idiots in that closed circle and will lose this war before they know it. The army has gained them valuable breathing space and it must not be wasted. You are the very person to lead that effort, the savior of Lenin and now a proven field commander while still representing the staff. The last almost beggars the imagination!

Stay true to Zhukov and all will be well but keep a wary eye! Stop and see your uncle on the journey to Moscow and, by the way, you are ordered to report to the medical center at Vyazma for a complete check-up after your recent efforts." Dmitry began to protest but the general held up his hand to signal there was no possibility of argument. "Just do it, Dima. Gods, I will miss your help. Know that you have been invaluable to our efforts and that your stand at the river will be a part of the Red Army forever. Go with my blessing and preserve yourself in these dark days. Thank you again." With this Rokossovskii saluted and then hugged Dmitry. Dmitry returned the hug and saluted as he said. "I will do my very best in Moscow, comrade General. I understand what is needed and will fight for you cucumbers." He spun on his heel and the general again wondered, will I see him alive again?

Dmitry collected Bear and asked about the Georgians and the *razvedchiki,* Felix and Lev. "Comrade Colonel, they will be with us in Moscow. Taka will be your driver and will be taking *razvedchik* training with Sachino. Lev and Felix have been assigned GRU functions at Moscow HQ. Even our handsome knight of the air, Shanislav, will be with us! He has been assigned permanent liaison for the Western *front* air forces and GRU. This is due to his success with aerial reconnaissance. He will be training pilots at Monino air base to better fly reconnaissance for the GRU. All together, the Bear and his cubs, that's very nice, eh! We will make the most of our stay in Moscow, comrade Colonel!"

Dmitry was both pleased and surprised by the assignments. Clearly Zhukov and Rokossovskii were behind these new assignments. They made sense and every man would be a better soldier after their stay in the Red capital. "Well, then Sergeant-Major, what is the delay? Why are you standing there without moving! We must leave immediately for comrade Marshall Zhukov's HQ outside Yelnya." The Bear only smiled, "Comrade Colonel, we are loaded and ready to go. We were only waiting for you. We travel at night to avoid the fascist air pirates." With that Bear led Dmitry to the truck and the reunion with his team. Their eyes gleamed as they welcomed him a bit raucously and again Dmitry's heart lifted with the sight of these men and their spirit. Gods, we will eliminate the fascist horde with true Communist hearts like these! He climbed into the truck smiling and paying back the comments in kind.

The trip to Zhukov's field HQ was uneventful and they arrived just before daylight. God, what day is this? Dmitry wondered. I have lost the date! "Taka, what is the day and date?" The Georgian thought this might be a test so he launched into an update on his and his brother's new reading skills. While pleased Dmitry cut him short. "But what date, comrade Sergeant?" Taka replied, "The 28th of August, Thursday, comrade Colonel." "*Spasibo*" (thank you), Dmitry replied. "Comrades, get some food and rest. We only stop for an hour or two so I can meet with the comrade General. Do not stray far as we will leave as soon as our meeting is complete." They dutifully saluted and began the search for some breakfast. Dmitry strode forward to find Zhukov and learn what the hell was going on.

He found the General at work with his staff and senior commanders in the pre-dawn. The minute he walked into the crowded room, formerly party HQ, the dour strained General broke into a huge grin and virtually flew to him. "Nephew, I have heard of your actions and the praise they have received. May your parents know this and smile on you. Have you met my comrade generals?" Zhukov led him around the room as he made the introductions.

Dmitry was pleased to see some of the stalwarts from Mongolia with Zhukov. He was particularly glad to see Konev and Vasilesky present. Tried, tough, and true was all you had to know about them. He also noted that Major-General Rakutin of the NKVD Border Troops was now a Red Army general. Well, the Hitlerites are going to get a hard time from this outfit, he thought while greeting each general. Zhukov announced, "I need to talk with Colonel Zhankovskii, let us break for an hour and reconvene then. We will call Moscow at 0700. Thank you, comrades."

Zhukov hugged Dmitry after the generals had filtered out. "A good bunch, huh! We will bloody the fascists with this team," Zhukov stated. "I know, I know," he continued. "What am I doing here? Well, it was a week or more ago when the *Vozdh* and I had a major clash over Kiev. There is no hope of saving it and I disagreed with the stand and fought the plan which would only lose us more men. I wanted us to withdraw and save the troops. The Party boot lickers all backed the *Vozdh* and I was gutted like a sturgeon for caviar. That yes man, Shaposhnikov, is the new Chief of Staff. I have been given command of the Reserve Army with orders to recapture Yelnya and hold the road to Moscow. With these men and fresh troops from the east, we may just have a chance."

"Damn, the politics in Moscow. It is getting worse rather than better and we play into the German hands every time we disagree and don't consider our strategy carefully. That is my speech. I am alive and in a fighting command and that's all I ask!" Dmitry had been silent for the whole speech and understood perfectly what he was being told. He could only respond with a soft, "The fools!" to the news. "As you know, comrade General, I am heading for staff work in Moscow. What can I do to help from there? Do have any advice for me? Can I get word to your wife and the girls?" Zhukov smiled, "Yes, to all of those."

"First, we need the *Stavka* to stop sending out of date battle orders. They only make things worse. Do what you can but it will be tough. Without me or Timoshenko to control the *Vozdh,* things will be done in the most shamelessly political manner. Try to inject some reason into that situation. But to continue our interrupted talk, be aware that you are under Beria's eye. Even I don't know the real reason but again it goes back to Poland, Tukhachevskii, Stalin, and your parents. Be very careful. I know you will do your best. Just be alert. Beria is capable of anything in order to impress His Supremacy (Stalin), that's his new title, you know? Very Bolshevik, eh?"

"Finally to Galina and the girls give my love and these notes. Tell them I think of them daily. Finally, my gods, Dima! What a stand on the Vop! It is the talk of every fighting unit. You have given us all great heart in this dark hour. And where did that bridge trick come from? Even I would have been fooled. Keep up this work and there are generals' tabs coming for you. But now we need you in Moscow directing intelligence gathering. As you already have observed, it is woefully inadequate and our generals and field officers have no clue what to do."

"I know you hate being assigned to a behind the lines assignment during a fighting time but you must draft new field orders to direct improvements in these areas and also in aerial reconnaissance. This is critical." Dmitry gave a look waving this off but Zhukov said, "No, listen. You can do more for the Motherland now by directing this improvement than even by another brilliant battle. The army has lost itself and needs to learn technique in order to regain its confidence. This is all extremely vital. Do this well and we will reward you by allowing you to experience more life and death situations! Understood?" Dmitry saluted, "Understood, comrade General!"

"Good, now get some food and get moving, but before you leave I need our old Sergeant-Major for a moment for an errand in Moscow." "I'll send him in, comrade General and please stay safe." Dmitry embraced the fireplug-like old soldier and bending over gave his bald head a kiss. "Take care of yourself, Uncle. You are indispensable!" Zhukov blushed and they separated. "Gods, your parents would be proud!" he said with tears as they parted.

Bear reported to the General as ordered. "Sergeant-Major Rasilev, as always you are a disgrace to the uniform but a sight for sore eyes!" "Comrade General," Bear responded, "Fighting the Hitlerites is demanding work when the *Stavka* is so helpful. This leaves little time for neatness of dress." "I know, I know" Zhukov interjected. "Damn good work out there, Rasilev. But now you go to Moscow with our comrade Colonel." The Bear was expectant at this opening. "Yes, comrade General, staff duty and a training mission. I will attempt to honor you by my appearance." "Do, do," Zhukov said and relented a bit.

"Comrade, we know the world. We are not bright eyed idealists like Dima. This war will be the most terrible in history and death will be everywhere. I do not want it perched at Dima's or his pretty surgeon's door." At this Bear was fully attentive and any sense of casualness vanished. The General continued, "As a precaution I have put the word out to the Commissars and NKVD officers that if anything happens to comrade Irina, the officers involved will be immediately assigned to the front lines, blindfolded. They seemed to act surprised but vowed to protect her after they had heard of the previous "German" attack."

"This smells all the way to Mongolia, my friend. I need your help. Here is what I think but I need your ideas also. This is not just about Major Petrova but somewhere this touches Dima. Please listen and comment." The two were in conference only fifteen minutes but when done Bear seemed even taller and his dark, black eyes frighteningly bright. "Yes, my General. You can count on me!" With a brusque nod and a '*Dasvidonya*', the General signaled his staff to enter and Bear exited.

"Bear are you and the comrade General all set?" "Yes, comrade Colonel, some things to forward from Moscow. You would think I was his personal attendant!" Dmitry smiled and said, "Bear, he respects you as a real fighting Red. Never doubt it." An enigmatic, "I never have," was the Bear's response.

The team reassembled shortly after dawn and established that a lone truck could take a chance moving during daylight. Dmitry ordered them to start on the Moscow road but after a half hour they turned off at Mozajsk. Studying maps and photos he looked up and shouted, "Where the hell are we going? Why have we left the Moscow road?" Bear casually answered. "I am sure that the comrade Colonel recalls comrade General Rokossovskii's orders for a medical checkup." "Forget them," Dmitry ordered. Again, casually, the Bear responded as the Georgian brothers took in this very mild but deepening confrontation.

"The comrade Colonel will forgive me but I have direct orders from both Generals to have you examined at our field hospital. Comrade Sergeant Sharadze, please continue as I have directed." Dmitry swore but would not violate the orders even though he considered it a waste of time. "Damn it, Bear, someday you will go too far. What kind of Red Army is this with Sergeants ordering Colonels? Lenin is turning is his grave." Bear nodded his agreement and kept his own counsel. A short while later they pulled into the field hospital.

"Comrade Colonel, please let me find the doctor to whom we have been assigned. The rest of you men, a few hours break. No vodka, but hunt up some tea and food and I'll join you." Bear set off to find Dmitry's examiner and soon returned. "The house over there is where you will find the Doctor. They are waiting for you in the rear of the house."

Dmitry entered the former farm house. From its odor it was clear the animals had also lived inside during the long winters. The interior had been established as an area for recovering patients. He nodded and said a few words as he went by the reclining soldiers. The wounds were all consistent with major air and armor attacks. Large caliber munitions produced terrible slicing and puncturing wounds where they did not require amputation. Crushed limbs certified the bravery of those taking direct wounds from tank treads.

My god, Dmitry thought, these men are the bravest we have. As he penetrated the unlit house he heard a woman's voice softly singing. It was the song 'Katyusha' which had swept the country since the beginning of the war. The caressing voice and gentle words seemed to come from another world. The words were evocative, 'While she walked she sang a song about a grey eagle of the steppe, about him whom she loved, about him whose letters she held in her hand. Oh, you song, you little song of a girl, follow the bright sun and fly to the warrior in the foreign country and bring him greetings from Katyusha.' The voice was sweet and the scene melancholy.

The men drank in the sounds and words like nectar. Dmitry didn't move for fear of breaking the moment as he saw the beautiful nurse singing and changing dressings. She ended the sweet song and was joined by another voice. The two women's voice rose in the 'Internationale'. "Arise ye workers from your slumbers, arise ye prisoners of want..." The men took in the changing mood and began to join in; soon the ward was filled with the hope of a nation near death, from soldiers who had defeated death.

Dmitry was moved and sent his voice to join the chorus and as he did so, what he thought was a nurse was a petite, dark haired surgeon who finished what she was doing and ran to him. In front of the ward she drew him down and kissed him hard. The men cheered and a renewed rollicking version of 'Katyusha' was soon echoing around this home of grief and sadness. When the kiss concluded there were yells for more. "So that is how officers are cured," was shouted. There was much kidding but soon the word spread, "That is Zhankovskii, HOSU, hero of the Vop. My god, boys, that is him. I was there! He was a true Red hurricane! We banged the fascists good, let me tell you." The excitement spread through the makeshift ward.

At that the cheering became louder and other staff rushed in to see what the matter was. Soon word spread and the chant, 'Kiss him again," forced Irina to plant a somewhat more subdued kiss on Dmitry.

Neither had yet spoken. In a hushed voice Dmitry asked if they could get away for a moment, just a moment. He now realized that he was the victim of a set-up from Zhukov, Rokossovskii, and Rasilev! But it was a sweet set-up and it did his heart wonders to see her well. "Irina Marieovitch, are you well? How are the wounds?" "Nothing to mention," she said. "But look, my great Soviet hero, I am now wearing a wound stripe which I notice you never do," and grabbing her *gymnastiorka*, she also flashed her Order of the Red Star.

"Direct from comrade General Rokossovskii himself," she smiled and it was with pride. "Careful, Colonel, in war we women will best you men." At the next sentence she collapsed into his arms. "Oh Dima, I heard about the Vop. What were you doing standing up to the *SS* with a scratch force. They would have slaughtered you all." "Well" he responded, "They didn't because we got them first. I knew the risk but the General needed the time and I knew we could do it."

She stared at him and softly reminded him of her love with another kiss. "Dima, I am glad they are sending you to Moscow. It will be safer for you." He was not so sure but said nothing and squeezed her hard. "How are you? Are you sleeping and eating? How is your work?" he asked. She shook herself and the sharp eyes blazed. "Don't worry about me! But the work is going well. The wounds are like nothing I have ever seen. The tanks are the worst. But we are using new techniques which greatly increase the survival rate and save limbs. Therefore, I serve the Motherland and am proud to be part of the Red Army."

What a woman, Dima thought. She is the greatest of us all. So amazingly unaware of all she does, what a woman! He knew it all sounded naïve but when in her presence you felt it and could not deny it. He crushed her again and said, "We have to be off but come see the men and give Bear a hug. I swear he lives only for you." She smiled in return and walked with him to the truck.

Bear, the Georgian brothers, Lev, and Felix were all there. At the sight of her they all came to attention. She smilingly gave each a kiss and remarked on Taka's new sergeant squares. Then she hugged the Bear and he blushed wildly as the men hooted. He did not move for fear of hurting her. "Are your wounds healed, comrade Major?" "Yes, but only thanks to my heroes," and now Felix and Lev also blushed. "I hear you are all off to Moscow for a party! I envy the Moscow Katyusha's. They will get more than they bargained for! You are all my heroes, and I want to see you all again soon. Blessings on you, and thank you for your bravery."

"*Spasibo*, comrade Major. Call us any time for a rescue!" The Bear responded for all of them with a great tear running down his cheek. The men drifted into the truck giving Dmitry and Irina a final moment. "Dima, stay well. Stay safe in the 'Little Corner'." Dmitry smiled but had no words. He pulled her close and with a final kiss bounded into the truck and they were off. She gazed at the disappearing truck and wondered as always about their future. She hoped to see him again, soon and in one piece.

Chapter 11

Dmitry and the team scattered to establish quarters and get set up for their new assignments. Dmitry reported to Marshal Golikov, the GRU chief, for his new assignment and was told that his new duties had him reporting directly to the Red Army Chief of Staff, Marshal Shaposhnikov, who had replaced Zhukov. "Comrade Colonel, we have been following your actions with interest," the politically oriented Golikov commented. "Very impressive, very impressive. However, we are constantly criticized by Comrade Stalin for not being precise enough with our intelligence. You will remedy this situation and quickly. Daily briefings are held every day in Stalin's office, the 'Little Corner' in the Kremlin. You will conduct the assessment portion of the briefing. It is not necessary to review your materials prior to the meeting with me."

At this Dmitry's mental antennae went on alert. He was clearly being given enough rope to hang himself. Well, we'll see how that goes, he thought. Golikov continued, "We also have a call with the major *fronts* after the planning session. Please stay and assist with direction for reconnaissance with these units. Finally, you are to draft new directives for the *Stavka's* signature regarding *razvedka* at all levels. We are being constantly surprised by the Fritz's and need to direct front-line commanders in proper technique. Do you have all that?" Dmitry replied, "Yes, comrade Marshal. It will all be done. Do you have a roster of my staff for this assignment?" Golikov produced the list and directed Dmitry to a Major who would convene his staff. "Your first briefing is tomorrow, so get moving!" was all the direction he got from Golikov, and Dmitry exited the office.

As expected, Bear and Captain Shanislav were on the list. There were also other familiar names that Dmitry recognized. Amazingly, they had assigned this group of some 20 officers and men a Commissar, and Dmitry's eyebrows went up at this. The name was even worse; they had chosen his onetime torturer, Yedved. Gods, this vermin sticks to me like shit, he thought. He could only imagine how this was going to work out. The Party works in strange ways, came unbidden to his mind as he traversed the halls and met or renewed his acquaintance with his staff. "Comrade Major Yedved is with General Mekhlis and will join you later," was all the mention that was made of the Commissar.

Someone with a brain had chosen his staff, thought Dmitry as they got to work. He could only wonder who that was. They were young, energetic, and many had already seen combat. Shanislav had good liaison skills and both the army and air force found his instructions simple, direct, and helpful. Sergeant-Major Rasilev was responsible for the drafting of the new directive and he and Dmitry would work very closely on it. His new Major, Galanin, had worked with him before in Berlin and he put him in charge of the daily briefing preparation. He and Galanin would meet daily, outline the briefing and Rasilev would assemble the materials and information. He, Galanin, and Shanislav would brief Stalin and the *Stavka* each day. There was much to do in a short time so they quickly got to work.

The next morning they had assembled the maps for the day and had chosen to focus on Kiev. Marshal Budyenny and Commissar Lt General Khrushchev would be on the phone from the embattled city but before they called in, Stalin wanted to understand their situation. "Comrade Colonel, good to see you in Moscow." Stalin intoned. "We saw your holding action on the Vop as very effective and recognize the value reconnaissance brought to that action. We will review your directives on these matters. Now, present the situation in Kiev."

With this Stalin lit his pipe and began to pace in the small room. Dmitry had made the maps oversized from their previous renderings and the various positions were marked with gross, heavy lines. He felt that detail could be added but Stalin and the *Stavka* needed the big picture in its clearest form. The room was packed with the *Vozdh*, Golikov, Beria, Mekhlis, Molotov, Malenkov, Chief of Staff Shaposhnikov, and a host of others.

"Comrades" Dmitry began, "As you know the situation in Kiev is becoming critical. Hitler has redirected Guderian and other forces to the region to ensure its capture. Their pincers are already searching behind the city for contact. We must prevent that at all costs." A soft grunt from Stalin was taken by Dmitry as assent. Being aware of the heavily laden political nature of this debate, he did not recommend but painted the scenario in its starkest terms. "Comrades, note the positions of the First and Second Panzer Groups. They are positioned to separate our Kiev forces from

our other southern forces. This will allow an encirclement operation."

Beria looked at Shaposhnikov, "What does the
army intend to do, comrade Marshal?" Shaposhnikov
replied, "Fight, comrade, fight!" Beria huffed and gave
Stalin a look which publicly registered his disdain for
the military. "Not enough, comrade Marshal! We cannot lose this key city and its food and industry. We
must win, not just fight." Shaposhnikov hastily added,
"We understand, comrade Beria, and are sending more
forces to the region. We will have almost 850,000
forces there but they are woefully short of tanks and
aircraft, especially the newer models. Our factories
must increase production!"

Stalin stopped pacing and said very quietly,
"Comrades, do not accuse each other but fight together. The situation is grave but with Marshal Budyenny
on site I am confident. Draft orders for him to
strengthen his defenses and probe the enemy with attacks." Dmitry knew, from Zhukov, that this was a
remedy for disaster but also knew that his opinion
would only worsen the army's position. He held his
voice even though Beria and Mekhlis were staring at
him almost forcing him to comment. Stalin noticed
their glares but ignored them as he turned to Dmitry.

"Comrade Colonel, I note we are to award two
Orders of Glory to soldiers of your command on the
Vop." "Yes, comrade Stalin, that is true. We have arranged the ceremony for after this meeting." "Good,
let us call Budyenny and Khrushchev and discuss our
plans and then to the awards." The call was made and
the always malleable Budyenny thought the *Stavka*

suggestions "brilliant'. Khrushchev backed the Polit-buro's "no surrender" stance which Dmitry knew would seal the fate of the Red Army in Kiev. Dmitry made a mental gagging sound and stood at close attention without commenting. The call was soon over and the meeting broke up.

"Comrade Colonel Zhankovskii, accompany me," said the *Vozdh* and they moved down the hall to a larger state room. There, present and looking like newly shorn lambs, were Taka and Sachino Sharadze. Bear was also present as their enlisted commander. Stalin took the awards and noted the names. "Georgians! Where in Georgia?" Taka replied, "My Supremo, we are from the Caucasus and are proud to serve the Motherland!" Stalin looked slyly at the men. "Bandits, hey? You were probably stealing our stores before you enlisted. Right? Well, no matter, Georgians always find their way. Comrade Colonel, what have these men done to deserve the Order of Glory?"

Dmitry explained their now numerous actions directing attacks against German armor and their great personal success with over ten personal Panzer kills. Stalin puffed quietly and listened. When Dmitry finished, Stalin pinned the Order on both of them, and as they threw their smartest salutes he simply said, "Georgians!" He turned, shaking his head back and forth as he repeated "Georgians!"

He left and everyone took a breath. The brothers were congratulated by Dmitry and Bear and hugged each other. "We will now live as Georgian heroes when we return from beating the Hitlerites," Taka stated. Dmitry only smiled and wondered if any of them would see that day. Bear let them know that they were to return to barracks where special refreshment had been arranged for them and their squad mates. With a final bug eyed look around the Kremlin they were escorted out.

Chapter 12

Bear glided down the blacked-out street clinging to cover and shadow when he could. In his long
black leather overcoat, slicked back hair and clean
shaven face he hoped he looked like an NKVD agent
to both the populace and the NKVD. His mission from
Zhukov would begin with this first step, a meeting
with an old GRU comrade who had made the unusual
switch to the NKVD and had lived to tell about it. The
agencies were supposed to partner in all aspects of
overseas intelligence gathering but over the years each
had their political ups and downs and in truth there
was little cooperation, and much competition. The violent purge of the Army had made this worse and right
now Beria and his NKVD were clearly ascendant.
However, Bear needed information and he knew that
the NKVD's predecessor, the Cheka, might have been
involved with the death of Dmitry's parents in 1920 so
he had to have a link into the current organization.

His enormous pockets held two bottles of vodka which he hoped would be sufficient to get the project launched. "My gods, Vladimir Levonovich, it's
been too many summers since we met. You have not
shrunk, that is for sure. Come in, come in, I thought
you were probably permanently attached to a fascist
tank tread by now. What brings you to Moscow?"
Stefan Nikoman was pulling the Bear into his small
flat and commenting at light speed all at the same
time. "Stefan, I am fine and have racked up some Hitlerite kills as well. But now you are looking at a Sergeant-Major assigned to the staff of a GRU colonel in

the 'Little Corner'." "My gods, you fly high, Vladimir!" Nikoman responded. "What brings you to an old comrade's door? Looking for women, no, you never needed help with that. In NKVD. trouble is more likely, eh? Come on Bear, spit it out."

Bear silently pulled the two bottles out of his pocket and Stefan smiled. "Ah, something serious! Good. Spying on artists and musicians has me bored to tears. What is the plot, comrade?" "Stefan, Stefan, something to drink first please, and then I will tell all. "First," as the glasses arrived, "How goes the Lubyanka, have you stayed out of the cellar?" "Oh yes, comrade, except when I am questioning a stupid intellectual who knows better than the *Vozdh*. My gods, they are like children. We stuff the east bound trains with them every day or just shoot them at the "horse farm" outside town. No, I am in good standing as long as I bring fresh fish to comrade Beria. Why do you ask?"

Before responding, Bear thought that all of this was occurring during a war for survival; yet the restless, irresistible state continued to hunt and capture those it didn't trust. By heavens, we need these people to fight Germans, not Russians, he mused, but when he spoke it was of other things. Taking several pulls on his glass, Bear began. "This colonel I work for, Zhankovskii, is very interesting. Hero of the Soviet Union, for saving Lenin's life. Good GRU career with posts in the US and Berlin. Good fighter, you might have heard of his operation on the River Vop."

Stefan responded, "So that's him. Yes, he appears to be quite the comrade colonel. Why do you bring him up?" "Well, comrade, there is some mystery here and I am worried about my skin being close to him. It appears that your boss has something against him and I would like to find out what." At this Stefan stiffened and his eyes clouded. "My gods, Vladimir Levonovich, I owe you much including most of my career but anything near Beria is desperate indeed. Just get transferred and forget the whole thing."

Bear sat silent and drank. The first bottle was gone and he knew now things would get serious. "Oh, I would love to Stefan, but I can't. Zhukov himself has given me this job. God knows why but there it is. I am stuck, but we bears are cunning. This will be no trap for the Bear." Stefan broached a small smile, "We all know your talents, Bear, but Beria! My gods, I don't even like to think his name. I say forget it and get transferred. Appeal to the Commissars for help. Tell them you want a Party job." "That's it exactly, Stefan, this is a great billet and with thousands being killed daily I'd be a fool to give it up. This works great for me. Maybe I can even help you with the *Vozdh*. I see him almost daily."

Stefan's eyes lost some of the clouds as he parsed this possibility. "That's very interesting, comrade, perhaps a commission in the Blocking troops or some such. That's both safe and profitable." The Bear rolled his frame, "I don't see why not. That is not a big deal. Say, a captain of blocking troops, very nice, very nice." They both drank in silence.

"OK, my friend let me make some very, very discrete inquiries and see what comes up. Maybe you could start work on my commission as I begin."

Bear looked at his friend very carefully. "Yes, Stefan, but only if things can be found out. I am going to trust you as an old comrade. I need real information. This is my hide on the line. I can't live with half answers, right?" This was delivered with the full glare of the Bear's black eyes on Stefan. Stefan shrank a bit but greed overcame all. "All right, Bear. Don't get worked up. I'll get the story and we'll both be better for it." "Very good, comrade," Bear responded. The rest of the bottle was consumed with tales past and present where the truth remained a far obscured horizon.

A week later Dmitry called Shanislav and Bear to his Kremlin office, "Captain Pilot Shanislav, I require you to fly the Sergeant-Major to comrade General Zhukov's headquarters at Gzhatsk. Sergeant-Major, you are to review the draft Directive regarding the fronts and *razvedka* with the comrade General. Please get his comments and let him know that within the week we will present the draft to the *Stavka*." Bear saluted and acknowledged the order.

Dmitry continued, "Comrades, this is a critical mission as this Directive will reorganize the army for intelligence and reconnaissance improvements. This is not, I repeat not, simple paperwork and that is why the flight and interview with the General is authorized." "Comrade Colonel, with no disrespect but isn't there going to be a major attack from Zhukov's command?" Dmitry looked sharply at Captain Shanislav, "Piotr, where did you hear that?" Captain Shanislav stumbled a bit on the response, "Oh you know pilots, Dmitry. They are abuzz at Zhukov's reconnaissance orders with both ground and air working every day and night. It can only be preparation for an attack." "Well, I hope the fascists are not as observant. It is true. But both of you never heard it."

"Actually, the attack has been delayed to assign some more troops and armor to the effort so there should be only minor action when you are there. However, you both know to not bother the General! He will be absorbed in planning. Get in, have him review the Directive, and get out. Additionally, here are some letters from his family. Bear, please hand them directly to the General."

The Bear smiled and accepted the packet. "Letters from home, that should take the crust off of the old man. I just think I will present these first!" "Good idea, Bear" replied Dmitry. "But also be sure you look sharp. The whole *Stavka* is on watch for a return of your lax uniform and appearance. Remember you are a Sergeant-Major of the Red Army, for heaven's sake!" The Bear rustled but withheld any comment.

Dmitry stated. "I've arranged an Il-2 for the flight." Bear and Piotr eyes gleamed. "I want a report on its capabilities from both of you. Bear, think about its firepower and how it could better support ground troops. Piotr, no stunting but I also require a combat pilot's opinion of its capabilities. I reviewed the new instructions for ground support pilots and in my opinion they are much too cautious. Let me know what you think and don't break anything except a fascist tank or two! Off with you both!"

Piotr and Bear both saluted and left Dmitry's office talking and gesticulating like school boys. Dmitry grinned at their enthusiasm and mentally noted their friendship and cooperation. That is good for the State and our war efforts, he thought. If these two, a committed flyboy and overgrown cucumber, can get along, anyone can. With the thought of his next meeting in his mind his smile turned to a frown and deeper thoughts distracted him.

"Comrade Sergeant Tsetkova, who is the next appointment/" Dmitry asked although he knew the answer. The youngish, perhaps a bit mannish and certainly not starving, new female Sergeant saluted and said, "Comrade Commissar Major Yedved, comrade Colonel." Dmitry was pleased with her efficiency. She had worked as a junior factory manager before the war and was clearly very competent. The only question was, who were her political "friends"? Oh well, Dmitry mentally sighed, no answer for that, just be thankful for the good help. Before he could answer she said, "I will bring in fresh tea when he arrives, yes, comrade Colonel?" "That would be excellent," Dmitry responded and returned to his less than spacious office.

He was glad to be in the Kremlin, as it saved a major amount of time moving around the city. Every once in a while he could get down to the Embankment apartment to catch some privacy and much needed sleep. Now with a permanent driver he could be home in five minutes and back at the most urgent summons in minutes. With surprising quickness, country boy Taka had gotten a handle on Moscow and now was rarely lost and always on time. A good soldier, Dmitry thought. Soon we will all return to combat and I hope that the two crazy brothers survive. They provide the breath of life to this country. At that thought, Yedved entered.

"Comrade Commissar Major Yedved, how good to see you again." Dmitry intoned. Yedved saluted and giving Dmitry a close look to ascertain his attitude, replied. "It will be a pleasure to work with the comrade Colonel." Dmitry said "Oh yes, with me, not on me, eh? An interesting development, comrade Yedved?" Yedved started, but replied calmly, "We all have our State duties, comrade Colonel."

Dmitry only raised an eyebrow. "So comrade Major, what do you intend for our small command?" he asked. "Oh I'm sure nothing out of the routine, comrade Colonel, investigations of the men, listening for traitorous talk and ideas, interrogation when required. Of course, advising you is my main duty." This was all by the book and Dmitry knew none of it was true but went along with it. Yedved was here to spy on him and his closest associates and report to Beria. They would all have to be on their toes to avoid trouble. "Right, comrade Commissar. We meet several times daily to prepare the briefing and accomplish other duties, the comrade Sergeant-Major will provide you with the schedule. Regarding the men, nothing goes beyond you without first being discussed with me. Agreed?" "Oh yes, comrade Colonel, nothing."

Dmitry could only mentally roll his eyes but the physical result was a good head brushing to remove the thoughts before they were vocalized. "All right, comrade Major, see you in two hours." Yedved rose and casually slouched from the room without a salute and no sense of an officer's bearing. My god, Dmitry thought, how can we win a war shackled to these fools? I don't even know how to describe them. Perhaps after the war we can clean up this mess, was his final thought punctuated by, if we win, if we live.

Out at Monino airfield, Piotr and Bear eyed the gleaming new Il-2. Piotr took Bear through the aircraft's weaponry and power capabilities. "Comrade Sergeant-Major, note the armor placed around the two crew compartments. Thick enough to stop a 20mm cannon shell! Also, note the bulletproof canopy and self-sealing fuel tanks. All of this so we can get in close to the ground action when you cucumbers get into trouble, which seems to be all the time!"

Bear only sniffed, "No offense, comrade, but the air army seems to be in trouble too! I understand that they have lost thousands of planes with only several dozen fascist bastards shot down." Piotr looked very melancholy at this statement. "Please don't repeat that comrade Bear, but it is mostly true. We have not done good service for the Motherland, We of the air are starting to carry our share of the battle and by god we will help win this war. You have my promise!" Bear smiled, "I never doubted you, my young knight of the air! Tell me more about your pride and joy."

"Well, as you see, there are two forward firing 20mm cannons, perfect for taking out panzers and two forward heavy machine guns for cleaning up on troops or unarmored vehicles. Finally, while in our dive, we are protected by the rear gunner with a machine gun. How is that for a 'flying tank'?" "Very good, very good," Bear responded and somewhat gingerly poured himself into the rear seat and prepared for takeoff. The flight to the Yelyna sector was uneventful and the Bear headed for Zhukov's HQ while Piotr went to see the reconnaissance pilots and evaluate how their efforts were progressing.

Bear had to wait for almost an hour to see the General although their office had been notified by Dmitry of the visit. During this time Bear lounged with the office Sergeants, who he knew, and engaged in the usual bullshit. He was pleased to find them an efficient group but to a man they were unhappy about the level of the forces being provided by Moscow. Manpower was getting better but tanks and aircraft were desperately low. There was no fighter cover at all so the reconnaissance pilots were taking enormous casualties and their assigned aircraft were noticeably dwindling daily. The tanks were mainly obsolete types and the anti-tank forces were primitive. Still they felt they had good leadership and Zhukov's careful marshalling of available forces gave them hope. As he waited, Bear was treated to the General's booming voice informing a pair of generals of their shortcomings and needs for development. In the course of this exposition, Bear learned some new phrases with questionable military application or derivation.

Zhukov's Chief of Staff signaled for Bear to enter. He presented himself and saluted. "Comrade General, I bring communications from Moscow." Zhukov looked up from the map and signaled for the room to empty. "Well, comrade Sergeant-Major Rasilev, you are looking like a soldier instead of your nickname. What do you have for me?" Bear stepped forward and said, "Two things, sir. First, letters from home. Second, the draft *razvedka* Directive. Which do you prefer?" "You sly old bear, trying to ease my view, huh! Give me the family letters please; I'll be just a moment, sit, my old friend."

The tough, bullet headed General opened his wife's letter first and quickly scanned for bad news. When he saw that all was more or less normal at home he folded it up for later. He opened his daughters notes with one written in crayon and the tears formed as they wished "Papa every good thing and to win the war soon and come home." The General turned and stood staring at the wall for a moment, shook himself and said to Bear, "We have to win, comrade Sergeant-Major, our families, our dear families count on us. God, we have to win." With that he put out his hand for the Directive. They sat and both were silent as he scanned the document.

"Most of this is very good, Bear. The detail on required organization and performance of *razvedka* is good. There needs to be more direction to the army commanders. The *fronts* don't have the experience yet to know what they need. You heard my educational development lecture on deception for some of my commanders. They have no idea. Others like Vasilesky and Rokossovskii are good. More specifics will help. Finally, punishment must be noted for failure to comply. We'll shoot them if they don't figure this out." At that statement Bear blanched but said nothing. The General had clearly been hardened by both his Moscow experience and his time at the front. Bear replied, "Yes, sir."

Zhukov scribbled some notes and handed them

to the Bear. "Here are some thoughts. You and the comrade Colonel are on the right track but realize these Directives are for idiots or worse. More direction is required. Leave little room for initiative for now. Later it will change but for now this is kindergarten.' "As you say, comrade General."

Zhukov turned his always opaque eyes on Bear. "Well, what's new in Moscow and with your assignment?" Bear went through some of the continual staff and organizational changes that revealed the chaos of Soviet war planning and fighting. Zhukov waved his hand. "I know most of that. I'm still a *Stavka* member but who knows for how long! What else?" Bear described Yedved's appointment and Zhukov nearly destroyed his chair. "They stop at nothing. Well, we'll leave it for now but I will have that dual command order repealed! I swear it! But we'll need victories to make that so. Fighting and winning is everything, right, my friend?"

Bear nodded. "Comrade General, I have begun the other operation we discussed, as yet there are no results but I will need a Captain's promotion for an NKVD agent to assist with the plan." At this Zhukov almost fell out of his chair. "Have you gone mad? The NKVD! That is the enemy we fear." "Precisely, my comrade General. It brings us in close." "Bear, you are sly indeed. The GRU is lucky to have you. Alright, give me the name and other information and I'll see what I can do. The promotion will appear to come from within the NKVD." Bear acknowledged and said, "Here is what you require, sir."

Zhukov took the paper and glanced at the name

and raised an eyebrow. "The woods are deep, my Bear." He dismissed Rasilev and signaled for his Chief of Staff. Bear saluted and exited the office. My, my, he thought, where are we headed with this? The State and its best general spying on each other. Where is Lenin when we need him?

"Well, groundhog, ready for some flying?" Piotr addressed Bear as he arrived at the airfield. Bear only grimaced but signaled, OK. Piotr indicated that on the trip back to Moscow they would explore the far flank of the German forces for a target or two if that was alright with him. The Sergeant-Major could only roll his eyes and imagine the worst. "Take some test shots with your gun, Sergeant-Major." Bear complied using the rear-seat machine gun and they were ready. Skirting massive German concentrations they looked for a weak sector and kept an eye out for Heinkels or ME-109s. The region was strangely quiet with both sides massing forces for the next contest.

Finally, a German reconnaissance car and armored vehicle were spotted. "Perfect!" yelled, Piotr. "Watch our ass!" He nosed over and brought the armored vehicle into his sights as the German machine gunner opened on him. Closing at over 150 klicks it was no contest. 20mm shells chewed up the armor and hit the fuel tank, lifting the vehicle into the air and exploding the gas tank so that not a sign remained of its occupants. The car had headed for the forest but Piotr came around and easily finished it off. "What a plane!" he screamed back to Bear. Bear was just glad for the level flight back to Moscow but only after Piotr executed several violent maneuvers to test the plane's

ability. Highly satisfied with both the Il-2 and the reduced condition of the Bear, Piotr headed for home.

Chapter 13

"Konstantin Piotrovitch, you ask so many questions!" Dmitry surveyed his fourteen year old nephew and thought, how in the late 1950's do they still hide the truth, even after Khrushchev attacked Stalin's memory in the Presidium! The boy was asking very astute questions regarding the time when Dmitry served in the Kremlin and had put his finger on a number of inaccuracies in the official accounts. Not surprising given his very intelligent parents! "OK, young historian, here is the story of late August and September in 1941, terrible days indeed but with hope beginning to show through the disasters."

"First, let's discuss your special Uncle, Zhukov, and his stand at Yelnya. The truth was hidden by the *Stavka* at the time but it was a signpost on the road to victory. The *Stavka* buried the news since they had no hand in the fighting, but we in intelligence knew what had happened. It told us that our road was long but if we were brave, persistent, and above all, smart, we could win. When I returned to Moscow in mid-August and took up my duties as Chief of Staff Liaison for the GRU, Uncle Zhukov had already developed a plan."

"However, he did not have enough men or weapons from Stalin to accomplish his mission to retake Yelnya. Why was this small city so important? First it was a salient, meaning a bulge in the German lines, so we could attack on three sides, not just frontally, giving us a good chance for victory. Second, it would slow the German advance on Moscow which along with Hitlerite air attacks on the capitol was becoming a source of panic. These air attacks, we now know, were more severe than the famous 'London Blitz.' We stepped up evacuations and housing consolidations to help with the fire-fighting."

"The fascist Germans came every evening and our air forces rallied valiantly. It became a real battle instead of a one sided victory for the Germans. We had some pilots who rammed German bombers and lived to tell about it! Can you imagine their courage! It was inspirational to a desperately demoralized air force and soon they became our heroes. New fighters arrived and really helped, the famous YAK-1 you have seen at the airfield was our greatest fighter." "Oh yes" Konstantin jumped in, "Papa flew one and was very brave." "The bravest!"

Dmitry remembered those days and a tear rose in his eye. "By the way, where is your papa?" Konstantin answered, "Now that he is Major-General of Missile Forces he is gone much of the time. Of course, we don't know where. But we are so very proud of him!" Dmitry smiled, "That is right. Honor your parents. I still miss mine terribly. But back to our story, now the *Stavka,* including Stalin, slept in the Kirov Metro Station every night and the rest of us dispersed around the city. I didn't like being surrounded by the NKVD guarding the *Vozdh* so I always went home and I figured the fascists probably couldn't hit anything anyway."

"Soon we built an immense bomb shelter under the Kremlin and that became the Supreme HQ for the rest of the war. Any way, it was all very chaotic and seemed to be teetering on the edge of outright panic."

"As I said, Uncle Zhukov was permitted time to prepare for battle. He received more men, mainly from reorganized Divisions that had been mauled in combat. Also at this time our agents told us Japan would not declare war on the Soviet Union because they were preparing to attack the US and British in the Pacific. So we were free to move fully equipped Divisions from the Far East to the front. This saved the capitol and the country as we will see later in the winter. Anyway, at the beginning of September, Zhukov attacked."

"He threw everything at the Hitlerites. He still had almost no air support so all his moves were desperate indeed. However, his timing was good. We did not know until after the war when we captured Berlin and German Army records, but Hitler had ordered much of his Army Group Centre south at this time to encircle Kiev. This included much of Guderian and his ferocious Second Panzer Group. What a welcome factor! But at the time we had no idea. Zhukov was still facing *SS* Divisions and regular grenadiers so it was bad enough and they were superior in tanks. The fighting was terrible and hand to hand. No surrender was allowed on either side; it was kill or be killed!"

"Uncle comrade General, where were our tanks? The T-34 could best any Panzer." "Yes, young Marshal, that is true but we did not have enough of them yet. During June, July, and August we rightly dispatched many of them to the front but due to faulty intelligence on the location of the fascists, whole trainloads fell into Hitlerite hands, right from the factory! It was a terrible loss. Also, our tankers were not yet familiar with the power of the T-34 and often did not fight it as it was intended to be fought. It was our fault entirely and only made worse by brilliant work by the Germans. I hang my head now when I think of it. OK, what did our Uncle do to beat the supposedly unbeatable *Blitzkrieg* and force the Germans back, buying valuable time?"

Konstantin jumped in, "Why he tried many tricks on them. He even had bombs attached to dogs to attack tanks. He was so clever the fascists turned and ran!" "Well that is partly true, Konstantin Piotrovitch," Dmitry stated. "However, there was much more to the plan then dogs, although those dogs did pretty good work! They were trained to run up to and underneath the tank and explode their mine. It worked fairly well but did not stop an army! It really upset the fascists because we used German shepherds!"

"Anyway, there were more than just the famous Red Dogs! Fighting had been going on for weeks when Timoshenko had been in charge but there had been very little heavy fighting. Zhukov massed his artillery and used it very effectively after conducting in depth *razvedka* and getting fascist positions from partisans and captured German prisoners. He took his time to map out their positions and then slammed them with artillery and *Katyushas*. It was all extremely effective. He also used night paratroop drops to get in their rear and organized partisan attacks, so that the Fritz's felt like they were being surrounded. This was all delivered around the clock and mainly targeted at their rear and very front positions. It caused great confusion and chaos in the fascist ranks."

"After a huge artillery barrage on September 2nd our men broke through and the Germans gave up the whole salient. Our first victory! In fact it was the first German retreat of the whole of the Great Patriotic War. Our troops poured through the gap and some of Konev's men even made it to my old position on the Vop. The brave former NKVD general, Rakutin, was killed during the battle but the victory was immense. It really hurt the Germans because the salient had been a great place to jump off from for an attack on Moscow. Of course, we knew that too and felt really elated by our victory."

"However, all this good work would be for nothing due to Stalin and the *Stavka's* handling of other *fronts* at Kiev and around Vyazma and Bryansk. These defeats would take us back to the gates of Moscow itself and the city experienced a major panic. It was a great tragedy and almost broke our hearts."

Dmitry looked at Konstantin, "Are you interested, should I continue?" "Oh yes, yes, Uncle. I want to know everything. It is important. I need to be a great soldier like you and father, and I need to learn. Also, I want to be able to tell the truth to my children in the future." Dmitry just smiled, so much like his parents. Maybe there is hope for this country after all, he thought. "OK, well at the time I was conducting briefings for Stalin and we really focused on Kiev. I will just mention that commanders were being appointed and fired daily. No one was in their job more than a few weeks. It was extremely disruptive and hindered the best commanders."

"For example, General Zhukov more or less wiped up the Yelnya Salient by the 8th of September and on the 9th he was ordered to take over in Leningrad! Can you imagine the disruption this caused? The city was in a desperate situation but then we all were. Zhukov obeyed but knew not much good would come of this. These changes were happening everywhere, all the time. Even the toady Budyenny was eventually fired and poor Timoshenko given the Kiev command just as the pincers closed. But we are getting ahead of ourselves. Kiev, Kiev, what a disaster. Guderian thought it was his greatest victory! Maybe it was, at the time it hurt us very badly and set up the collapse of the whole Moscow region."

"So what happened? Well, basically there had been terrible fighting for months around Kiev. Then Hitler decided that this great store house of food and the door to the Caucasus oil was the next target for the *Wehrmacht*. He sent major portions of Army Group Centre south to assist von Rundstedt and his Army Group South forces. This helped save Moscow in the long run because it gave us time to prepare but at what a price! You cannot dream of how many soldiers and civilians were killed or captured. Now the *SS* was in the country in force with what they called the *Einsatzzgruppen*, the death squads, and to be captured was actually a death sentence."

"The suffering was immense and the food and property that was destroyed ensured starvation and a frozen death for the survivors." Now Konstantin was crying and Dmitry moved closer to put an arm around him. "I am sorry, Konstantin Piotrovitch; I should not upset you so." "Oh Uncle, you do not upset me. It is the thought of the people suffering so much. Hitler and his armies were monsters!"

"On that we can agree, my young friend. This was a very sad time. For those of us of the old Red Army, every day you heard of a friend or acquaintance killed or severely wounded. But we knew if we didn't fight, if we didn't win, we would all be dead or slaves. This was powerful motivation. However, the mistakes at the top were devastating morale and there were many desertions and surrenders as the men didn't yet know what was in store for those who surrendered to the Germans. Even our Uncle ordered many executions to stop the tide but with little effect."

"Only victory could restore a soldier's confidence. But this was not a time or place which granted us victory. With fascist armies in front of them and now Guderian and others over 100 miles to their rear the forces around Kiev were trapped and desperate to escape. But the *Stavka*, especially Chief of Staff Shaposhnikov, would not let them. Daily the orders were, stand and fight, even when the fascists were closing off their escape routes."

"Finally by mid-September it was obvious there was no hope. Stalin and the *Stavka* authorized retreat but it was much too late. Brave General Kirponos, the last of the long list of South-Western *front* commanders, organized a break out with 1000 of his remaining men and they almost made it but he died fighting as the fascists completely surrounded them with tanks and blew them to heaven. Budyenny, Khrushchev, and Timoshenko were all flown out by special missions.

They left behind over 500,000 men killed or captured and we never saw many of them again."

"Did Stalin shoot the three of them when they got to Moscow?" "Oh no, they were his cronies so they lived. Timoshenko and Khrushchev eventually redeemed themselves but I spit on Budyenny right up until today. I tell you nephew, things were starting to look very bad. Panic was slowly capturing the hearts and minds of regular citizens and the highest leaders of the Party."

"However, there were a number of factors beginning to help us. At the time we did not know of these things and we made some bad assumptions about German intentions.

"First, after Kiev there was a lull in the fighting. Yes, there was fighting and some of it very desperate especially around Leningrad where Uncle Zhukov now commanded. But from north to south clearly something was happening with the Germans. Troops were being realigned and moved about. Stalin thought it was a massive refit for possibly a spring offensive! Little did we know! He and others believed that the Hitlerites had exhausted themselves. Well, to some degree they had but there was more to come in that worst of all years, 1941."

"As we now know, Hitler and his generals were planning Operation *Typhoon,* intended to capture Moscow in one massive blow. We knew they would attack but we argued and argued over where and when. Time was on our side but at this early stage we squandered some of its gifts with unneeded offensives and the frontal attacks! We were still killing more of our own men with our tactics than the fascists were."

"Slowly, slowly, we began to learn and good commanders started to get the key assignments, like Zhukov and Rokossovskii. They soon removed Vasilesky from his staff position and gave him a fighting unit. They were all good leaders but there was great shortage of line officers and sergeants. They are the ones who fight the war! We had slaughtered them like sturgeon in the first four months of war and we missed them severely." "Uncle, it was a dark time for the Motherland, what were you doing and where were you?" "Yes, those were bad days. I was still GRU liaison to the *Stavka* and briefing Stalin every day. We were making progress about intelligence and knew more about the Hitlerites' positions, but their exact plans were still hidden in a fog from us. So we soldiered on as best we could and waited, waited for the massive blow to fall."

Chapter 14

It was midnight on September 16, 1941 and the Kirov Subway Station in Moscow was ringed with NKVD troops as the *Stavka* met for its evening brief- ing. During the day most meetings were still held in the Kremlin due to the Germans' propensity to bomb at night. The night was too dangerous to risk Stalin and the *Stavka* being killed by one bomb so here, deep underground, they met. Dmitry had arranged enlarged aerial photos and the new "strategic" map as best he could in the unorthodox setting.

Beria, Molotov, and Shaposhnikov sat while Timoshenko, summoned from the front for the meet- ing, and Dmitry's new boss, Panfilov, and other mili- tary paced with Stalin. "Comrades," Dmitry began. "We have many challenges at the moment, Leningrad is coming under siege, the center is somewhat quiet for the moment but we can expect more there, and in the south we have lost the Ukraine and we will soon be under siege in the Crimea. The strategic picture is not a positive one but we have some hope. If our northern and southern flanks can hold we can bolster the center and save Moscow."

Dmitry took a breath and Beria jumped in. "The comrade Colonel is as always too defeatist, comrade Stalin, we should launch offensives to drive the fas- cists back from our borders. They are certainly weak- ened and ripe for the taking." Some others nodded agreement but the new head of the GRU, General Pan- filov, did not follow that lead. "Careful, careful," was all he said and Stalin nodded to his old Bolshevik friend.

Dmitry knew this was an uphill argument. It had been so for days now. The army had to be ordered onto the defensive if it was to survive the next blow. More frontal offensives would sap its strength and make the defense of Moscow problematic at best. Dmitry began again. "Comrades, may I present our latest photographic research of the fascist positions?" Stalin looked at Dmitry closely. "Comrade Colonel, I know you are not defeatist. Your fighting proves that, but it does seem you want us to hide in holes when we need to slaughter the enemy. Why are you persisting with this line?" Dmitry nodded and blessed his saints that Stalin was at least reasonable on this very early morning. "Comrade Stalin, Supremo, the problem is one of numbers. The Hitlerites are tired but if they can achieve local superiority anywhere, they beat us." At this the room shuffled and Dmitry's chief gave him a warning glance.

Dmitry corrected by saying, "It is not inevitable, comrade Stalin, but it has proven the case in the last months. Indeed, as comrade General Zhukov demonstrated at Yelyna, the same rule applies for us. Local concentration and a combination of defense, offense, and preparation does yield results. However, the number of troops is not the only important variable in this calculation. Until we can get more of our new T-34's and more aircraft into the fight our troops are mauled by the German mechanized war."

"Our men are brave, but Man of Steel; we cannot stand flesh against iron as you can." Dmitry hated himself for this suck up to Stalin but the discussion was too important to sacrifice. Shaposhnikov must be having heart problems because he was very silent and Beria, my god; he is letting me set the rope! I must push on, was all Dmitry could think. He moved closer to the aerials, "Comrades, please note the fascist tank and supply columns in these photos. They are moving armor, supplies, and troops forward. This clearly presages a major offensive. We should consider what those moves might be. Also, this shows that the Hitlerites are not exhausted. They have fresh troops and materiel moving forward. This column alone includes almost 500 vehicles. These photos were obtained at great risk by Pilot-Captain Shanislav and forwarded to the new Briansk *front* as this activity is in their region."

Beria lumbered into the conversation, "Josef Vasilievich, maybe this represents signs of old units moving around. How do we know these are fresh units? Maybe the Germans are staging a show for us! This is just a photograph, it does not tell us all." Stalin switched his glance to Dmitry. Dmitry knew this was the moment. "Comrades, I have dispatched several GRU *razvedchiki* to this area to grab some fascists to answer this question. They will return in a day or two. Can we bring this question up again at that time?" Stalin removed his pipe and stared at his shoes and finally nodded.

Shaposhnikov stood up and asked for the group's attention. "Comrades, this may be difficult and challenging work but our men are facing even worse challenges." He glanced at Stalin's hooded eyes and continued. "In discussion with the Supremo, we have decided to reinstate the title of 'Guards' for those units performing heroic actions in the defense of the Motherland. These units will have special insignia, flags, and wear a special chest badge. They will be considered the best of the best and receive both rank and financial special privileges. We have selected three units from the defense of Smolensk to be the first to receive this honor. Their commanders will be at the Kremlin state office at 1400 to accept this great honor. We will all be present."

The room was hushed and slowly, applause led by Beria began to build. Even Dmitry applauded. This was a powerful idea on many levels, he understood. The men would feel special and be rewarded. This would slow unnecessary retreats and desertions because of the peer pressure to perform in these units. Dmitry allowed a glance of admiration towards Stalin who was enjoying the response. This was the first positive moment since June. The *Stavka* and staff broke up to get some sleep. Noticeably no one came near Dmitry and he just shrugged to himself. I am doing my duty, I am doing my duty, he repeated to himself as he gathered the maps and left the room with his guards.

As he left the station a nervous Piotr Shanislav was pacing in the entrance way to disguise the light from his cigarette. "Comrade Colonel, how did it go? Did we convince them?" "Not yet, comrade Captain, but at least I am still alive and kicking, as the Americans say. We will have another chance when the boys return from Briansk with some interrogation intelligence." Shanislav sighed and stomped on the cigarette butt. "I hope they don't wait too long," he said. "Every day the traffic and air cover is heavier. However, my brand new Yak-1 is a match for anything. Thank you, comrade Colonel!" "No thank you, Piotr Ivanovich, you are making it possible for our new science of war to advance. This will be critical in the long run. Please walk with me; I have a special favor to ask."

They turned to head for the Kremlin and the guards asked, "The car, comrade Colonel?" "Not tonight boys, get some sleep. The heroic Red air force here will keep me safe. We will walk; the fascists are clearly deceived tonight as they are bombing some fields west of town." The guards saluted and departed for their own subterranean quarters. "Piotr Ivanovich, this is purely personal but I need a day of your time." "Anything Dima, please just name it." "I have been unable to find my sister Natasha since I returned to Moscow. I visited her flat. She lived in a Party building which is now deserted due to the evacuations. An old building keeper told me that she left with the other scientists. She is a physicist, you know." Piotr just nodded. "Anyway, being GRU has its uses. I found out which city the Moscow physicists were taken to and I would like you to fly there and find her. They are in Murom temporarily but will probably move further east. If you do find her just confirm that she is safe and give her my love. Can I ask this favor of you?"

"Oh Dima, this is nothing, in the Yak-1 I can be to Murom and back in no time. I am sure I can find them, Murom is not so big. I am off at first light, comrade." "Thank you and stay safe," Dmitry responded as they parted at the Kremlin's Watchtower gate.

With the Sharadze brothers and Lev, led by Felix, off to ruin some young German lives, Bear was free of his team for a few days. He knew that a meeting with Stefan Nikoman to discuss his research was required. The continual night bombing and the deserted buildings resulting from the evacuations provided well hidden locations, far from prying ears. With the two operatives being sure they were not followed, they both arrived at about the meeting time designated. Bear arrived first and set a small shielded candle for light and produced three bottles of vodka and glasses to be sure every bit of information was extracted. When Stefan entered Bear greeted him with, "Comrade Captain, is that not so?" Stefan looked at him closely, grabbed a bottle and drank right from it, sans glass. "Now, how are you so well informed, my brother? How high are you placed with this?"

Bear just rolled his shoulders and said, "The GRU is all knowing, my neighborly brother!" Stefan grimaced at the vodka and took another pull. "I am appointed Captain and sweet it will be. No blocking troops for me but a Division Commissar! How do you like that? I think I'll have you shot some day!" "Congratulations, comrade, you always land outside of the manure pile. Where are you headed?" "Oh a little town called Leningrad. Heard of it?" At this the Bear could only smile, oh what a player the comrade Zhukov was. Little did the rabbit know that the hunter had him in his sights? "Perfect, comrade. I congratulate you!"

With this as a toast Bear also drank straight from the bottle. "Now Stefan, what have you found out?" "Oh much, much as you well know. This assignment is like stealing the Tsar's underwear! What have you gotten me into? OK, here are the details but the rest is up to you. I am gone to a vacation on the Baltic to shame you useless Red Army types into action." Stefan had almost finished his first bottle and the Bear knew that soon after the next bottle was finished, unconsciousness would follow, so he had to get the information from him quickly! "OK, OK, comrade and old friend, what do you have that is so important?"

Stefan took another pull and Bear thought, this is some serious drinking. Gods, he might pass out in moments. But Bear was wrong and a confirmed NKVD drinker like Stefan had a huge capacity for vodka, sometimes aided by drugs. Stefan stared at Bear, "It all began long ago right here in Moscow at the Lubyanka." The Bear moved gently forward to hear Stefan's wheezy slightly slurred words better. "Yes, right near here. Lenin assigned Felix Dzerzhinsky, Head of the Cheka, who was Polish, as the political leader of the invasion of Poland in 1920. The whole idea was to get through Poland and start a worker's revolt in Germany with its weak post-war government. Well, it didn't work but this war sowed the seeds of vendetta across the Red leadership."

"Lenin also assigned his favorite, the dashing Red Lieutenant and future Marshal and future bullet in the back of the head recipient, Mikhail Tukhachevskii, as the military commander. Tukhachevskii was all of 27 at the time. Well, the famed Red cavalry would also be at the party commanded by Budyenny with Stalin as his Commissar. In practice they were under Tukhachevskii's command but these two wrought havoc with the campaign by ignoring his orders and acting independently. They devised their own plans and barely acknowledged Tukhachevskii's direction. Well, this was alright for a while. The cavalry mopped up the Poles while Tukhachevskii was also successful against the main Polish forces.

However, with all the important commands coming from Lenin in Moscow things got a bit confused. Finally, the Polish general Pilsudski figured out the disorganization of the Bolshevik armies and devised a plan. He baited Tukhachevskii forward even as he inserted forces between different Bolshevik armies. Tukhachevskii did not really understand this, but did understand that his forces were scattered and not focused on the capture of Warsaw. He ordered all armies to converge and support the Warsaw efforts. Budyenny disobeyed and encouraged other commanders to disobedience. Stalin jumped in and telegraphed Lenin that he would lead the army to Warsaw through the Polish city of Lvov.

This would give him and not Tukhachevskii the credit for the capture of Poland. Well this was all rosy until Pilsudski unleashed his forces in stunning counterattacks that separately defeated the disorganized Bolsheviks. We fled like cattle from their forces and got back to the border as fast as we could. The Poles call it the "Miracle on the Vistula." It was an awful defeat and nothing good came from it. The Red Army left many behind and was a broken shadow of itself when it stopped running. The Poles recovered large tracts of land from us which we only regained after the invasion of 1939. As you can guess the finger pointing really started in earnest and Lenin was mad beyond belief. He even said of Stalin, 'What idiot would go to

Warsaw through Lvov!'"

"Hey, Stefan, where are we going with this? How does this affect my boss?" "Easy, easy, Bear. As with all stories of our people, it is deep and complicated. Why else are there so many like us? Here's the thing. You know that your colonel's father, Alexander Zhankovskii, was Polish and married a Russian girl. Well, I guess they were red of the deepest color. *Bolshoi Krasnya*! Lenin assigned them to go with Dzerzhinsky to organize Polish Bolsheviks and begin to construct the nucleus of a government that would take over when we were victorious. They were very close to Lenin before the Revolution and only more so after your colonel, as a boy, saved his life. They had impeccable connections!"

"They traveled with Stalin and Budyenny and yes, that is where they met one of Budyenny's regimental cavalry commanders, the young Georgi Zhukov. Are any lights going on in that bit of mush up there, Bear?" Bear knew most of this already but something grim and dark was beginning to form in his mind. Emptying his bottle he nodded but said, "What Stefan? I must be too dense for this political work. What are you saying? Spit it out for a poor soldier." "Just as I thought, Bear. As a commissar I'll be the brains to the Red Army muscle. I will finish this war a General or even a Marshal!" Bear could only salute with his glass. Now the almost comatose Stefan came and directed his comments right to Bear's ear as if someone was listening. "So where were the Zhankovskiis when all this arguing and disobedience of Tukhachevskii's orders was going on? What did they see and hear between Stalin and Budyenny? What did two pure idealistic intellectuals think of this infighting?"

"You know the answer to that. Well, when all went to shit, Budyenny and the others tried to stick the mess on Tukhachevskii but guess what? It didn't stick. Trotsky and Lenin knew enough about intrigue and began to talk to expedition members about what happened. Now if I was Lenin I would try and get in touch with my dear close comrades, the Zhankovskiis, loyal and smart to a fault. I'd want to talk with them and get their opinion of what happened. Wouldn't you do that Bear? Yes, I know you would."

"Well, the call came during the retreat for them to head back to Moscow as there would be no Polish communist government required. They packed up and were ready to move out when their tent was destroyed by a stray Polish shell. In fact this shell was so lost, that it was the only Polish shell that fell on the camp that day. They were both killed and as they say, that was that. The infighting continued but the true story never really surfaced. Isn't it interesting that some of those who knew the real story were soon dead, exiled, or later executed. Lenin and Dzerzhinsky were both dead within several years. Trotsky was driven out of the Army and eventually the country, Tukhachevskii and others on the expedition were purged in '38. Deep and dark, deep and dark," Stefan muttered as he lost consciousness.

Bear withdrew his shoulder and hid his eyes. Oh my god, this is bad, this is fucking bad. He now knew why Zhukov was so worried; he also had pieces of the story but not the whole picture. A stray shell, sounds like a stray German grenade, eh? What are we into? He wondered. Well, now I know and the General will know and we, the morons of the Red Army, will design a plan to protect our knight and his lady, but can we? Can we?

Chapter 15

Near Briansk, Felix inspected the *razvedchiki* for the 'snatch' mission. Besides the Georgian brothers and Lev, he had selected eight other *razvedchiki* from the Briansk *front* to fill out the mission billets. He had learned the technique from Bear who had learned it to perfection fighting the Japanese in Mongolia. Two teams would be formed from the twelve men. The first team was comprised of four men, Felix and his companions, and they were the snatch team. They were supported by the other eight men who would observe and preserve the track back to the Soviet lines. The final member of this team was stationed with the regular troop's forward line to prevent any 'friendly fire' incidents.

Felix carefully reviewed Taka, Sachino, and Lev who were dressed in German uniforms. The other men wore typical *razvedchiki* camouflage uniforms. As he closely looked over each of his companions, he tried to use the eyes of a German officer. "Lev, you are some Hitlerite! You look exactly like a good Bolshevik trying to be a Hitlerite. You are too immaculate. They are living in mud and lice just like us. You have been kicking the shit out of us sub-humans for four months without a fray on your uniform. Come on! Get into this role."

Of course these comments were for everyone but Felix knew Lev could take it and even understand his strategy. Felix did not want to spook Taka and Sachino on their first true mission. "OK, another uniform inspection at dusk. We move out at midnight. I want these uniforms to look right, not perfect. The rest of you will be examined by your sergeant for correct field gear. Once we move, hand signals only and no light! No smoking! I'll shoot you myself for breaking field discipline. We are all armed with German weapons so I intend to visit each one of you so you can demonstrate its use for me. Questions?"

Everyone shuffled in place and finally Taka spoke up. "Comrade Senior Sergeant, we have been talking. We know our mission is to retrieve a fascist officer and private but we want to slit some throats while we are in their lines. They have been murdering our people for months. We need to kill some of them for revenge. This is an ancient Georgian virtue but applies to all of us in this case. What do you say, comrade Senior Sergeant?"

Felix stood very still. What he said next was all important for the growth of these men into expert, fearsome *razvedchiki*. "I know, comrade junior sergeant, the feelings you speak of are in my heart also. If we were common soldiers I would agree with you but we are not common soldiers. We are the head of the great Red Army. We kill not just with our hands but with our information. We are *razvedchiki*! We know where the enemy is. Where to make the Katyushas sing, where to send the 'flying infantry' in their Il-2's, where to let loose the artillery, tanks, and cucumbers! We kill not one or two but by the thousands."

"Without us this army is blind and a blinded bear is useless in a fight. No, comrade junior sergeant, no killing unless, unless, it is required for the mission.

The mission is everything. We must help the comrade Colonel convince the Supremo and the *Stavka* that he knows the fascist plans. This is critical to everything! He would be here and wants to be here, but his mission is larger than allowing himself the glory of combat. He trusts us to do the job. We will do this job and we will do it perfectly. If some fascist bastard bares his neck to you and there is no mission reason to kill him, you let him live. Is this clear? This is very important."

The men nodded very soberly. The eight regulars had been stunned to hear of the reason for this snatch. They thought, my gods, this is for the Supremo. Felix had let this slip intentionally to put more urgency into the mission. What they didn't realize was that because they knew this he would never let them be taken alive. Their senior sergeant understood and gave Felix a nod of support. "OK, let's break and get geared up. No fucking drinking! The man who has even one sip of vodka gets left behind and can explain this to the comrade Colonel. Get tea and food, I've brought special rations which comrade Sachino will distribute. We might be gone for days so prepare well."

Again the men nodded and broke up. As they were leaving Felix had one more comment. "No talking to anyone outside the team, nothing, or some throat slitting will be done right here. Go comrades and prepare!"

Their target was a staff group far behind the German lines, almost fifteen klicks in back of the front lines. On their passage through the German lines they

would encounter forward listening posts, troop concentrations, and anti-infiltration squads, some with
specially trained dogs. He was hoping that since the
fascists had seen so little reconnaissance action from
the Red Army that they might be a notch below real
combat readiness.

They would know soon enough, Felix mused.
Once past the main line, discipline would be less and
Felix was expecting downright laxity in the staff areas.
The trick was getting there in the dark, observing for a
day, making the snatch the second night, and getting
back. He knew these missions, but this one was critical, and he asked his famous namesake to give him
and his team great buckets of luck.

At midnight, the team silently moved out
through the outer Soviet lines and began to break step
and crouch and move forward. Captain Shanislav's
pilots had located a cabin in the German rear near a
tank park that seemed like a very likely staff site. It
was miles away and they had to get there by dawn.
Depending on their progress it might take two nights.
Progress was good and as this part of the line had been
fairly quiet very little was seen of the fascist inhabit-
ants of this portion of Soviet territory.

Felix strung out the support team and ordered
them to dig in and wait. As they passed through what
they suspected was the main German line they went on
high alert for anything indicating movement. They
noted that the Germans were not dug in terribly deep
and this also presaged an offensive move by them.
Gods, I wish we had the strength to attack, Felix
thought.

He stopped himself because he had to focus on the job at hand and he knew the Red Army was not yet ready to attack even this casually defended location. Felix placed his last *razvedchik* right behind the main German defenses. The sergeant understood well both the danger and the responsibility. If they were to get out with their captives it all depended on him.

Now the four member snatch team moved as a unit, trusting their uniforms for protection and making good time. Without too much counter marching for misdirection they fell into a position near the hut which had been identified as a likely target by aerial *razvedka*. It was just before dawn and they waited silently. At dawn, several officers came out from the hut to relieve themselves and all of a sudden curses and shouting broke out. Felix and Lev looked at each other as a partially clad Russian woman raced out of the hut and tripped on a rock outside the door. She went down, sprawled on her back with her sex exposed, seeping blood. A German officer stepped out of the hut and shot her in the face and groin with his pistol. For good measure, he emptied his Luger into her twitching body, kicked her, and then pissed on her.

Felix and his men hardened at the sight and Sachino almost bolted forward, only a look of steel from Felix prevented it. Lev looked long and hard at the sight and then at Felix. Felix slowly moved his head back and forth, no. They dug in to wait.

The day brought forth activity from the hut and it was clear that the officers there were command and staff. Soon after dawn, breakfast was brought for them by privates and they left in great haste, likely heading for a command session. The privates cleaned up, including the dead woman, and all was quiet. Felix decided it was safe enough to look around for better targets. With his German language skills, which Lev also possessed, and Sergeants' insignia, he should be able to talk his way out of anything.

"OK, I'm going to look around. You three stay hidden. If challenged, don't say a word. Lev will talk you out of it, comrade Georgians, for the moment you are Romanians serving under Lev and are being trained in sentry duty, OK?" They nodded and as casually as possible Felix drifted into the clearing and headed in the direction the officers had gone.
In the trees and out of sight he knew there were Panzers and their crews.

Having studied the aerial photographs, and from previous recons, he knew the units and his insignia were proper for one of their neighboring grenadier troops. He acted like a man on a mission and strode with great purpose towards the headquarters tent. He got close and almost froze. Heaven and St. George, it is "Hurrying Heinz" himself, he thought as he spotted Guderian leaning over a platform outside one of the tents. This guy and I must be destined to go through this war together, was all that Felix could think, remembering the time he saw him during the first days of the war. Someday, if I'm lucky, I'll kill the bastard!

Felix moved on toward an outer tent to scout security. There was some but it was not too tight and they all seemed very casual. Perfect, he thought. Perhaps we can pick up a nice German map or two for the Supremo!

Slipping back to the others he described what he had seen and how it would fit into the night's plans. The officers returned late in the day and as the fall's shorter days worked toward darkness, the team prepared for the next events. Felix and Taka would head for the staff tent and try to retrieve maps or papers. Lev and Sachino would wait for an officer to leave the hut and as he was relieving himself, blackjack him from behind and pull him into the forest. Having observed the morning routine, there was no doubt that this would happen at some point.

When full darkness had fallen, Felix and Taka moved out. They approached the tent gingerly and noted two staff officers working on maps and two sentries standing guard outside of the tent. Felix boldly walked up to the sentries and asked for a certain major. The sentries didn't know him, of course, but told him to ask in the tent. Taka stayed outside to distract the guards with his 'Romanian' poor German. The tank park obliged by providing the roar of Panzer engines being put through their daily maintenance paces which drowned out casual sounds. Felix entered the tent and came to attention. He asked again for the ersatz officer and the staff lieutenants shook their heads no and went back to work.

This was the moment. Felix turned to leave and as he did knocked over a small table holding water and alcohol. The officers immediately yelled at him calling him clumsy, stupid, and worse. They came over to retrieve the alcohol and as they bent over Felix blackjacked them both. He quickly stepped to the table, grabbed maps and papers which he shoved into his ready haversack, and exited. Collecting Taka outside the tent, they wished the sentries a *Guten Abend* and quickly melted away. They reached the relative safety of the hut.

Felix was surprised and pleased to see their 'package' ready for travel. "Quick work," was all he said and they started to move. Felix turned to Lev, "Start out and pick up a German sentry as you go. I am going to try for more information in the hut with the other three officers." Lev studied Felix's eyes. "Do you think that is a good idea, cat? This could turn bad in a second."

Felix nodded, ending the conversation, and passed the haversack to Lev. The others moved out and Felix ghosted towards the hut. At the door he sang out that he was here at their comrade's request and had brought food and alcohol. They opened the door and as he entered Felix calmly shot all three using three bullets from his silenced Luger. He took a minute to piss on them before he left.

Rejoining the team he said, "Nothing of value so I bolted. Let's go. By the way who is our package?" Sachino spoke up proudly but quietly exclaiming, "I read his papers, comrade Senior Sergeant!" Felix's eyebrows went up. "You read German?" "Yes, I can now read Russian and a small bit of German that comrade sergeant-major Rasilev has been teaching me." Will wonders never cease, was Felix's thought. "So who is he?" "He is Lieutenant Colonel Strauss of the Second Panzer Army and he is assigned as terrain officer." Good snatch, Felix thought as they moved on.

Several days later, Dmitry sat cross legged at

the table in the very damp basement of a GRU facility in Moscow. He slowly smoked and stared at the German lieutenant colonel standing in front of him. Bear sat in a corner with all insignia removed and heavy black leather gloves on. Light came only from a small wall slit to the outside covered in bullet proof glass. What a hell hole, Dmitry thought. He wore the insignia of a captain of artillery to confuse his prisoner. "Well, Lieutenant Colonel Friedrich Strauss of 2212 Moltke Street in Berlin, married to Ingrid with three delightful daughters; Mara, Elsa, and Anna. How are you today?" The German could only stare at Dmitry's recitation of this information. Dmitry had used Soviet sources in the Berlin government to get personal details on the Lt. Colonel and he had a whole pocketful if he needed them.

"Welcome to the Lubyanka? You know, the Lubyanka?" The German blanched and nodded. Good god, he has heard of our little world of horrors. Of course, he was not in the Lubyanka but just the mention of it was enough to cause sweat to break out on his forehead. "Well, my friend, as you can guess we would like some information. The sergeant here is ready to use our tried and true methods of persuasion followed by a nice bullet to the back of the head." The German looked defiant and said nothing. "Oh, I can see very well that you are a brave man. You are in an elite unit, the Second Panzer, commanded by my good friend, Heinz Guderian."

At the amazed look Dmitry only smiled, "Oh yes, he taught me much about tanks. How were the Polish girls? Did they treat you well? But I bet the

French were better. Survival is always first in their minds, no nasty patriotism to get in the way. Eh? You have seen much of the world from an armored car and now you visit Mother Russia. Well as you can guess, we need some information to make your stay more pleasant. Let's talk a bit. Sergeant, please leave us for fifteen minutes and have a smoke." Bear nodded and got up and left the room.

"Colonel, there is something here that we can work through, I think. You see, you have been snatched to confirm our predictions on German strength, especially armor, and your plans to attack us for the final time very soon. Based on this information, a number of us in the Army and other organizations are trying to convince the Politburo to surrender now, so that we can have some negotiating position. This would also rid us of the hated commissars and the monster, Stalin. To make an effective argument and overthrow Stalin, who will never surrender, we need to prove the picture of overwhelming strength on your part. Can you see where I'm going with this?"

The German nodded ever so slightly. "I mean what a shame. We put a bullet in your head tomorrow and within two weeks the war is over and Hitler rules Russia! What a waste, only 14 days. We have peace envoys working through the Italians as we speak." This was partially true and had been rumored about the army, who rejected any peace feelers. As Zhukov said, "I'll give them a peace feeler in the ass and when they notice that, I'll plant my boot so far up that my toes will be in Berlin!"

Dmitry sighed, "What a waste! Those little girls

will miss their father forever. The beautiful Ingrid will have to marry again to support the family. Maybe there's someone already that she relies on, a close friend, a staffer in Berlin? Life is suffering, we Russians say. This picture is too tragic but will become real very soon. The really tragic part is that if you resist we'll get the information from you anyway. The sergeant is very persuasive and in an extremely bad mood as his home village was trampled in the first weeks of the war. Normally he beats up Russians but I think he will have a few extra surprises for a Hitlerite. It's all too sad, really."

Dmitry put out the cigarette and stood. "Why don't you think this over for a while, Colonel? If you choose to give us information, which will convince us to surrender, we will send you to a camp here in Moscow to wait for your comrades. They will likely be here in two weeks anyway. Why be a missing person? Really, most sad." With that Dmitry stood, grabbed his cap, and left the room.

Bear was down the hall and had been listening to everything. "Well, comrade Sergeant-Major, what do you think?" "I'm not sure, comrade Colonel, he is a smart, tough one. To be in his position with Guderian he must have a good record and performance. You almost convinced me but I think we need to turn up the heat a bit. I suggest the recording."

"You know Bear, you amaze me. When you suggested we make a torture session recording in German, a year ago, I thought it a waste of time. Well, here we are and it sounds like a good thing to try. Give him an hour and then play it and then we'll let it sink in for a couple hours and try him again." Bear saluted and went to retrieve the record and get the equipment set up.

Dmitry had gotten a report from Felix of the young sentry they had also snatched on the return to Soviet lines. After interrogation, very little new information was gained. There was a sense that morale was a bit fragile and that supply was a continual problem. At least it didn't paint a picture of an overwhelmingly confident troop base, but an average attitude for the foot soldier as opposed to the tankers and air forces which were very positive based on interviews with troops snatched from those units. The only other bright spot was that in all units there had been severe losses in officers and NCO's. That would help the Soviets in the future battles.

The gruesome recording of a German officer being beaten to death and shot finally ended. After some more time elapsed, Dmitry headed for the cell. Bear joined him but standing and with a length of heavy wood this time. "Well, comrade, what do you think? Can you help me understand something about your force?" Dmitry nodded back at Bear to indicate they could not speak freely as before. The German colonel stood and straightened his somewhat filthy uniform. "If you promise to put me in a camp here in Moscow until I can be returned, I will give you some information," he stated. Dmitry nodded, "Good, very good comrade, a wise choice. We will put you in the camp."

"Let's get down to business. How many tanks, how many planes will you hit us with and where?" The questions went on for hours and when finished, Dmitry could not only support the aerial *razvedka* but do so in great detail. The officer had given him the name of the German operation, *Typhoon*, and confirmed Moscow as the target. He did not know, and Dmitry believed him, the start date or specific routes other than those suggested by the captured maps as they were still in planning. However, this was incredibly valuable information and gave a good picture of German intentions, if not specific plans. In keeping with the deception, Dmitry acted pleased with what he got from the German and reported to the *Stavka*.

Based on this information, on September 27, 1941 Stalin ordered the three *fronts* defending Moscow, *Western*, *Briansk*, and *Reserve* to go on the defensive and prepare for a massive German attack. A few days before, the *Stavka* released Dmitry and Bear's new directive concerning the responsibility of *front* commanders to conduct *razvedka* before all operations. As suggested by Zhukov, the severest penalties were applied to those who ignored these orders. The revolution in Red Army intelligence began to show immediate results in the next weeks.

Dmitry had Bear use Taka and the team to transport the prisoner to the holding camp outside Moscow. When they returned Bear sadly reported that the German had tried to escape and after a chase Taka had been forced to slit his throat. Dmitry raised an eyebrow and Bear just saluted, leaving the story between them.

The Soviets waited for the German attack on a line almost 400 miles long. Tanks began to appear but air support was still almost non-existent. With 1,250,000 men and 1000 tanks, mainly the older models, and a motley collection of 700 out of date aircraft, the line was not in depth. There were no reserves. On 29 September 1941 Hitler unleashed *Typhoon*, the crescendo of *Barbarossa,* against the Red Army. The German commander, Field Marshal von Bock, mustered forces including the Second, Third, and Fourth Panzer groups supported by the Second, Fourth, and Ninth armies and supporting air forces. Guderian, of course, was used as the spearhead of over two million men, 1000 tanks, and 1400 aircraft smelling the blood of the wounded bear. One week after the attack began, the first snow fell.

Chapter 16

One week after the beginning of *Typhoon*, the *Stavka* was very worried. Various *Front* headquarters were getting routinely cut off from communications and the picture of the German advance was piecemeal at best. Dmitry had watched this developing and had gotten permission for the newly appointed Major Shanislav to lead his Yak squadron as fighter cover for reconnaissance flights. They were huddled over the newest photos in Dmitry's office with his Chief of Staff Galanin reviewing friendly and enemy positions in the *fronts*. As predicted the major German advances were just south of Moscow and moving quickly.

Dmitry pointed at a tank column on the photo, "Comrades, look here. These are elements of the Fourth Panzer; you can see the letters on the tanks and see where they are. They are already in the rear of Konev's Western *front*! His battle is already over and he doesn't know it."

Major Galanin, who was running the ground teams, concurred. "Comrade Colonel, these photos are backing up Senior Sergeant Felix Vasilev's and the team's findings but with a better overall picture. I have asked General Vorolov to study these positions and determine what fire we can bring to bear on them. He said that Marshals Budyenny, Eremenko, and Konev had no idea where he and his artillery should target the Hitlerites! What is going on out there?"

"Murder, dear comrade, murder, that is what is going on. The *Stavka* is always a day or so behind the fascist thrusts and then we lose communications with the front lines so things get even more confused. It is simply murder for our men. Ok. Here is how we will brief the *Stavka*. Comrade Major, prepare maps showing the situation in each *front* from the photos. We will not use photos for the briefing but have them outside the room. Comrade Pilot-Major Shanislav, continue your missions but close up on the leading Panzers. We need to start predicting where they will hit next. Got it everyone?" "Yes sir," echoed in the map room.

As Shanislav and Galanin turned to leave, Dmitry grabbed Shanislav's arm and held him back. "Piotr Ivanovich, thank you so much for the news of my sister. The note from Natash was very calming. The scientists seem in good spirits and are moving to the Urals, she tells me. Did she mention anything else?" At this there was a moment of silence and shoe-staring. Finally, Shanislav spoke up, "Dmitry Alexanderovich, she just sent her love and told me how proud she was to be your sister. She said that they all have great faith in the Red Army to save the country."

Waving at the map table he continued, "Of course, they don't know what we do. My god, this is getting bad. Anyway, she sends her love and, and…" "What is it, Piotr? Spit it out." Shanislav drew himself up and faced Dmitry directly, "Comrade Colonel, I am in love with your beautiful, smart, wonderful sister." "Oh come on Piotr, you were only together for minutes. What is this?" "No Dima, this is real. As a pilot and I would add, a good looking one, women have never been a problem for me except as a nuisance when I need to fly, but the minute I saw Natasha Alexandrina that was it. Gods, what a beauty, and she's smart, she's a physicist, smarter than this engineer any day. No, I am serious and I had to let you know."

"Well, well, what does the lady think?" "That's just it Dima, I don't know and it's killing me. I don't know when I'll see her next and that makes it worse. God, Dima, this is the wrong time and place but I'm in heaven." Dmitry smiled and shook the young major's shoulder. "It's never a bad thing to be in love, Piotr Ivanovich, I'll see that she hears a hint of this and let you know what she says. I already had a letter in the works to her and who knows, if we survive the next couple of weeks maybe airmail might be the way to deliver it. Eh?" At this Shanislav looked like a condemned man with a new lease on life.

Dmitry continued, "Now Pilot-Major, I want photos and piles of them. We need to brief the *Stavka* with the news and soon. Move out and think only of killing fascists. No soft thoughts that might get you killed. Dismissed!" Shanislav came to attention and saluted, left the office and seeing his second in command waiting outside, gave him a massive hug and said, "Let's fly, Vasily, let's fly." Lieutenant Vasily Tovarich only shrugged at his always crazy commander and muttered, "That's our job isn't it?" to himself and left the building with Piotr.

That evening the briefing of the *Stavka* was again at the Kirov Station. The ground shaking and the sound of the bombs seemed to punctuate every statement. Dmitry was ready for a battle with Beria and Shaposhnikov who had been relentless in not letting outflanked troops retreat to escape encirclement. This meant they were hemorrhaging forces as in the past and would open the roads to Moscow for the Hitlerites. Dmitry once again addressed the complete *Stavka* except Zhukov, who was in Leningrad.

"Comrades and Supremo, the picture I paint today is very black." Now the room bristled but Stalin held up his hand to check the group from drowning Dmitry out. Dmitry gave a small nod to the *Vozdh* and continued. "The strategic map shows our situation from Leningrad to the Crimea. The war front is our whole west facing landscape. Today however, we focus on Moscow."

The room tensed and Dmitry strode with great purpose to the map table and invited everyone to join him. Major Galinin had out-done himself; the map was like looking at a bird's eye view of the approaches to Moscow. Only the most critical roads and towns were shown to enhance the simplicity of the presentation. Dmitry slammed his pointer on Konev's Western *front* HQ site. "Comrades, this is Konev's HQ. Comrades, fifty miles closer to Moscow in his rear is the 4th Panzer! He is cut off and in the process of being completely encircled. Eremenko and the Briansk *front* are in even worse trouble. They are already encircled in two small groups."

Now there was stunned silence in the room. Finally, Dmitry continued. "We cannot even find Budyenny's HQ but his men are fighting to get out of the pincers approaching them near Vyazma." Now the room collapsed into accusations and shouting. Beria rounded on Timoshenko, Voroshilov, and Shaposhnikov, the senior Red Army men in the room. "You have sold out, you bastards! You are in Hitler's pay! How else can you explain this disaster? This is worse than June 22. Where is the army? The NKVD should be put in charge and the firing squads kept busy. Maybe that will put some meat into the defense."

Stalin himself had turned a shade of pale associated with the dead and could not speak. Timoshenko tried to reason with Beria but Mekhlis, the head Commissar, jumped in and said, "We political officers should be put in charge. We'll show these tin soldiers how to fight!" Everything was chaos and Dmitry was appalled at what he had unleashed. This was the government of his beloved Motherland, these screaming fools who were only thinking of their own advancement at a time like this.

Finally, Stalin gestured for silence. "I will shoot the bastards who have caused this. We are being led to the slaughter by fools. Timoshenko and Bulganin, get your asses to the front and find our dear comrades Konev and Budyenny and see what the fuck they are doing. Shaposhnikov, I want Zhukov back from Leningrad tomorrow to take over the defense of Moscow. Now comrade Colonel, tell us in your words what we should do."

Dmitry stood to attention and directed his words only to Stalin. "Supremo, we must allow the men to retreat to the Mozhiask line near Borodino. I know it is under construction but at least there is some protection. Even a half-finished trench and pill box is better than nothing. We must allow troops to retreat when they are out-flanked. The GRU indicates that we are outnumbered two to one and every man we lose makes this worse. We must establish areas for forces to regroup."

"We need to save troops for the final fascist assault on Moscow. We still do not have enough force on the line, and we especially need tanks and aircraft. The only good news is that as we fall back, our overall front becomes shorter and our forces can provide more defense in depth. Also, the fascist supply lines are being stretched and stretched. We must get organized to provide fast, responsive support between the *fronts*. Now we are always a day late without enough punch. This must improve. We must listen to the GRU."

"Secondly, we must work even harder on Moscow's defenses. We will need them. It is unlikely that we will be completely successful at Mozhiask so we must prepare for the worst. These must be proper, deep, anti-tank defenses with supporting fire zones. They must be in at least three layers and ten miles deep. Also, we must flood areas to slow the fascist even further. But overall we need troops, planes, and T-34 tanks."

Dmitry stopped and saluted, "That is my report as ordered, Supremo." Stalin paused, slumped and spoke, "Comrade Marshal Shaposhnikov, make these thoughts into orders. I want half a million laboring on Moscow's defenses by tomorrow. Beria, we evacuate the Party and government to Kuibyshev. You are in charge, get it organized. That is all for now. We meet again at noon tomorrow to see how this develops." The shocked room could only stare at the *Vozdh* and nod with a few, "Yes, *Vozdh*," thrown in as they left.

Stalin turned to Dmitry. "Comrade Colonel, we

have known each other since I pinned the Hero of the Soviet Union on your chest for saving Lenin. Today's work may have been more important than what you did that day in 1918. Thank you, comrade." With that Stalin left the room and Dmitry allowed himself to slump into a chair.

The word of the evacuation order raced through the city like wildfire. The feeling of disaster was enhanced by the extremely heavy German night bombing. The city was burning, being looted, and being deserted, all at the same time. Hundreds of thousands of men and women were sent to work on the anti-tank and other defenses of Moscow, further depleting the city's population and infrastructure. Additionally, tens of thousands of men were organized into volunteer battalions to bolster the Red Army. Poorly equipped and with no training they became lunch for the *Wehrmacht*. But they went and went proudly. The thought that the Germans might land at Moscow's door was frightening to even the staunchest heart. This was also inflamed by the stories of the now real and proven Hitlerite atrocities at the front and behind the German lines. The city panicked.

The panic started at the factories when many arrived to work and found the factories closed. Rioting broke out at the various sites and the special targets were Party officials or NKVD troops. Many were beaten with tools and shovels since these were the populace's only weapons. The city was littered with looted debris but other types of debris began to appear. Communist tracts, Party membership cards, trade union identifications were all being burned by the populace. Anything that could tie them to the regime was taken out and burned. The NKVD was summarily executing any Party member who could not produce their card on their person.

The scene at the railway stations was worse. People fought for places on the trains leaving Moscow and threw off the old or children who could not fight back. The roads leaving town were clogged with *apparatchiki* in their cars, taking their family and possessions east as the workers trudged by trying to escape what all knew was death or slavery. The city was going mad and no one knew what would stop it.

Dmitry walked down the hill from the Kremlin to his flat. He passed a baker's shop where the bakers were giving out three days' worth of bread for one days ration card. This further inflamed the crowd who believed this meant that this was the end. They started fighting each other to get even more rations and hoard all they could. Dmitry sized up the group and fired his TT-33 into the air.

"People of Moscow, you are an insult to the Motherland. Get in line for your bread and leave those others alone. The Red Army is dying for you as we speak." "Yes, they die well but they don't stop the fascists," someone cried out and the crowd muttered. Dmitry began to wonder what he had gotten himself into. "Hey, why aren't you at the front? Are you a coward like our leaders?" The small crowd sensed some purpose for itself and Dmitry fired another shot into the air. "Muscovites, I have lived here my whole life and I am just back from the front. We will save Moscow but it will take all of us. If we act only for ourselves the Hitlerite beasts will kill us all. I have seen it, I know."

Someone in the crowd, maybe an ex-soldier who had noted Dmitry's gold Hero of the Soviet Union shouted, "Listen to the hero Colonel, and look at his chest. He is a Hero of the Soviet Union. A brave and true fighter, I think he's right. We must band together like Lenin taught us and show no hole in our solidarity. Listen to him."

This speech was not met with wild cheers or an outbreak of singing of the Internationale but it did seem to quiet the crowd. Dmitry went to the front and said, "Give my ration to a mother with children." The baker nodded and shouted to the crowd, "We were giving out three days rations to help you out, so you don't have to queue so often. There is plenty of bread, please go home. The man out there is right, we must stick together, not fight each other."

With this the crowd began to drift apart and Dmitry quickly departed the scene and vowed to avoid police work in the future. By the way, he wondered where the police were. He had not seen any. He later found out that they had deserted and that Komosol members, young communists, had donned arm bands and side arms to try and keep order. Order only came with the arrival of train loads of NKVD troops who were dispersed throughout the city and slowly calm returned. However, the most important moment for the restoration of order was when Stalin announced he would never leave Moscow, now the people felt that if they fought next to Stalin perhaps there was some hope for survival.

The bombing was beginning to have an effect. Great swaths of the city were on fire. Lenin's tomb had been buried in tons of dirt and structurally protected against any direct bomb hits. The NKVD was tasked with camouflaging Moscow's city center and Red Square to disorient German fliers. They were partially successful but the Moscow River's course directly in front of the Kremlin could not be disguised. Smoke machines were brought in to reduce visibility and the stifling stench of the kerosene generators combined with the cold to produce a depressing fog over the usually bright city. The air force went on a desperate round-the-clock schedule. When Major Shanislav was not flying daylight recon air support, he and his band of YAK's were assaulting fascist bombers either in advance of Moscow or directly over the city. The YAK-1 was proving to be a great fighter but there were never enough machines or pilots. Slowly the Red Air Force began to regain control over Moscow's night skies. Piotr himself landed twice in Red Square, out of fuel from the desperate air combat overhead that he had been reluctant to leave. Even though the city was under light discipline and curfew, whenever he did so there were girls present to shower him with kisses and flowers. God, it's good to be a pilot, he thought.

As ordered, hundreds of thousands labored on the Moscow defenses under Beria's direction. The work was exhausting and driven at break neck speed with no regard for safety. It was all too desperate for that. The anti-tank ditches and various infantry redoubts and bomb shelters began to take shape. As the city was restored to some balance the defense became first in everyone's mind. A system was devised for the orderly evacuation of people rather than the 'every man for himself' approach seen earlier.

Finally, things began to quiet down and when they did Beria launched the largest purge since 1938 ostensibly to root out traitors but really to settle old scores and clean up embarrassing NKVD failures. Marshal Tukhachevskii's wife, Nina, who had been held captive for years, was shot, just as the Marshal had been in 1938. His daughters were raised by a foster family until they were eighteen and then taken out and shot. Scores of former Generals were shot including Dmitry's former boss, Proskurov and his wife. He was possibly the most progressive figure in the Red Army and had fought bravely in Spain and other theaters.

Smushkevich, twice Hero of the Soviet Union, and triumphant Red aviator in both Spain and Mongolia, was shot after years of torture under which he never confessed to his 'treason'. As the fascist beast mauled the front line of the Motherland, the Communist monster proceeded to devour its own possible saviors. Dmitry took the word of these shootings hard. Purges in peace time were bad enough but when your very life is threatened? He did not understand and thrust these thoughts from his mind.

At the very center of this destroying whirlwind, Yedved stood in front of Beria's desk in the Lubyanka's upper story and noticed the fresh blood on the floor. It must have been one of his own officers for the beating to take place in Beria's office, Yedved thought. Beria sat back from the pile of papers and

removed his small round spectacles. This always high-
lighted the weak chin and small eyes. He looked up.
"Well, Yedved, I go blind in the service of the Party.
These lists go on forever and if I miss a name or don't
make note of one of Josef Vasilevitch's comments, he
is all over me. The nice thing is that once in a while I
see a name of an old acquaintance and think, what an
ass! It will be nice to be rid of him! That's a good
day."

Beria slouched in his chair and studied Yedved.
"You wear the uniform well, comrade Commissar."
"Thank you, comrade Commissar," was all Yedved
said. He knew from the past that it was important to
say nothing or not appear nervous otherwise Beria
would pounce like a wolf. "Well comrade, I am reas-
signing you." Yedved allowed his eyes to look quizzical. "Tell me, how goes the Zhankovskii project?"
"Not well, comrade Commissar. They are playing with
me. Rasilev never lets me near the Colonel except on
official business and every time I'm around, the Georgian brothers follow me about singing Stalin's praise
which are echoed by the whole staff. They are playing
me like a trout."

Beria nodded. "Yes, they are too clever by half
but pride comes before the fall, eh? We'll let them
have a small victory but we will win this war. The
Vozdh told me how impressed he was with Zhankovskii's work at the *Stavka*. That confused the hell out of
me. I think we just let these fish swim for a while and
watch. You know in war many are killed with no ex-
planation. We will get our moment."

"For now, tell comrade Chief Commissar

Mekhlis that you are to be a roving political officer with a pass to go anywhere to assess the work of the commissars. That ought to scare the hell out of him. Then visit the fronts and keep an eye out for traitors and slouches, especially amongst the generals and marshals. They have won one or two fights and are getting quite big for their trousers. I need a few examples to keep the rest in line, maybe Rokossovskii, what do you think?" "I think that this is a good plan, comrade Commissar, and I will do as instructed." "Good, good, and don't be afraid to summarily execute some soldiers or an officer or two."

"The commissars are becoming too chummy with the Red Army and I won't have that. We are their masters, not their fucking pals. In fact, blow a Commissar's head off to get the attention of the others. OK, that's it, off you go, my friend." Yedved stood, nodded his understanding, and exited the office. Beria went back to the GULAG deportation list and groaned. The print was so small and there were thousands and thousands of names. Pissed off, he wrote, 'Death', in the margin of the next fifty names just to improve his spirits. War is hell, he thought.

Finally, several days later at the Kremlin, Dmitry and Zhukov were able to meet. Zhukov had been sent to the front to assess the commanders and had reported to Stalin that a combination of their inexperience and the *Stavka's* rigid stand and fight orders were virtually opening the road to Moscow. Now back in Moscow at his new office in the Kremlin he wanted to review the strategic situation with Dmitry before making any further changes.

"Dima, what a fucking mess! The worst fucking mess I have ever seen. Fucking Voroshilov doesn't know how to fight in the twentieth century and the *Vozdh* follows his every fucked up suggestion. I am ready to turn the guns on the *Stavka*!" Dmitry just smiled and hoped that his daily screen for listening devices was completely successful. At some point they would have to submit to the 'bugs' as the Americans called them but for now there was still some freedom for the General's colorful expressions.

"Yes, comrade uncle, this is mostly a mess but some units are beginning to fight well. Comrade General Rokossovskii found his feet only two weeks after the Hitlerite invasion and has been fighting well since. As we speak, Generals Lukin and Boldin are attempting their second or third breakout since Minsk to save some of the troops enveloped at Vyazma and Briansk. This is also affecting fascist progress as they have been unable to close the pockets or *Kessels* as they call them. So it is not such a mess as Minsk or Kiev."

Zhukov gave a curt nod but was silent. Dmitry continued, "Observe here on what we now call a *front* strategic map, this small village, Mtsensk. A great story has been reported and confirmed from there. Colonel Katukov and his Tank Brigade got in front of the German advance and went into complete hiding in a heavily forested area on the Hitlerites' flank. This was possible because of *razvedchiki* reporting the developing situation and pointing out an opportunity. This was then all confirmed by aerial *razvedka* and the comrade Colonel developed his plan."

Zhukov was now interested and paying attention. Dmitry elaborated, "The fascists were using the main road in the area and without any trouble from our air force felt free to barrel down the road at 40 klicks per hour. Well, just like an old bandit, Colonel Katukov waited in the woods until he could spilt the Panzer column in two, then moved into them, surrounded each section of about twenty tanks and blasted the bastards to hell. The new T-34's with the improved armor took direct hits from the Panzers with no problems! They killed them all!"

"That's what we need, that's what we need," Zhukov repeated, "People who have good intelligence and know their business. Your *razvedchiki* are coming into their own, Dima, and your Directive is having an effect already. I knew it would. Get the comrade Colonel here when he can and we'll make him a General and his Tank Brigade a 'Guards' unit and then give him a Division! God and St. George, that is how to fight! Make sure you brief this to the *Stavka*! I want that old wives group to understand what it is going to take to beat the fascist!" "Yes, comrade General, I will do as ordered," Dmitry replied.

Zhukov turned and made sure the door was shut. "Dima, Dima, you are doing very well. I'm like an old cow with only one sound but I must say it again, your parents are smiling with pride in heaven. Even though they were Bolshevik to the core I'm sure they are with St. George directing his aid to you. You have been brave and brilliant. Even look at this map, simple and accurate! A small thing but since you introduced the strategic maps to the *Stavka*, they can't argue make believe any more and with each engagement their faith in the truth of the maps grows. This has changed the whole discussion at the meetings from just currying favor with the *Vozdh*, to one of real battle planning and by God, we need that now. Very well done, nephew, very well done!"

Dmitry was always uncomfortable with Zhukov's praise but realized how heartfelt it was. He always made sure to respond very correctly with a curt "Thank you, comrade General," or other military form as he knew that Zhukov would be embarrassed otherwise.

"Well, comrade Colonel, I have praised your staff work. Do you wish to remain with the *Stavka* or go to the field?" "Wherever I can serve best," was Dmitry's immediate reply. "Oh, I know, my dear nephew. If you ask me, you have proved an invaluable staff officer but I have a field job in mind. I don't know who to trust with this mission other than you and your band of cutthroats. So I am ordering you and your merry men to the field." "Very well, comrade Marshal. What is the assignment?"

Zhukov led Dmitry over to the Western *front* strategic map. "As you have so accurately depicted, Dima, we are not yet concentrated enough to resist the fascists in front of Moscow. We are falling back as you recommended to the *Stavka* to the Mozhiask Line and will try to hold. As you well know, that is on the old Borodino battlefield. Think of it! We are fighting the invader where our forefathers fought the invader! That must be an omen! But we will need some help. With the fall of rain and snow we are in the *rasputina* (time without roads) season. That will slow the fascists down for a while but will also slow our forces. While that is happening and before the hard freeze in November we must fortify the line. We are doing that and the orders have gone out as you have seen. However, we need to apply more friction to the Hitlerites and I have become aware of where it can come from."

Dmitry raised an eyebrow and the stout Marshal rose to his diminutive full height and looked Dmitry in the eye, "From the rear." Zhukov stopped for effect as if briefing Stalin as he shortly would. "We have tens of thousands of troops trapped behind the fascist lines and even more Party cadres who have escaped to the forest in order not to be shot by these so-called death squads. Gods, before I'm done with them they'll have earned that name! But these forces, partisans, are disorganized. During the Civil War against the Whites we used them very effectively but since they are not regulars they need training and leadership. I am going to ask the *Stavka* to para-drop *razvedchiki* to locate and organize these units to harass fascist supply and communications in their rear area. This will accomplish a number of things. First, we will hurt their supply as winter comes. Second, we will disrupt their communications which up until now have been better than ours. Finally, we will draw troops and equipment from the front line in order to hunt these subversive elements down. It will be nasty, dirty war with no holds barred. Does this interest you, my Hero of the Soviet Union.?"

"Of course, sir. I have also been thinking along these lines and have some ideas." "Excellent! I knew it," said Zhukov. "OK, get with the merry men and develop a specific plan and brief me tomorrow. If it looks good, we brief the *Stavka* the next day and you can launch whenever possible after that. All set? Dismissed."

Dmitry strode out of the office with his mind racing; there was much to do and not much time. First thing he needed was the team to research likely drop areas and how many men they should take. He called Major Galanin of his staff and outlined what he needed and headed for their office to get things underway. He did not see Bear enter Zhukov's office moments after he left it.

"Well comrade Sergeant-Major Rasilev, what an honor it is to receive a visit from you? How goes your personal annihilation of the fascists?" Bear smiled at the General and while towering over him threw a massive salute that shook the office. He held the salute until Zhukov returned it and then still stood at attention. "Ah" said Zhukov. "I see, I see. Look at this immaculate new Guards uniform with even more tinsel on your chest. A haircut and shave also. I am simply amazed, comrade, your turnout is impeccable. Maybe you can become a trained bear after all." In response, Rasilev boomed out, "Anything for the cause, comrade Marshal. War is hell," which seemed to be a favorite expression from everyone those days.

Bear continued, "Allow me to congratulate the General on his new command. You will see great success." "Well, Bear, it is out of that finery and into the field with you. I have just given Dima his orders and they will be eventful for all of you pirates. Deep behind fascist lines you go to organize partisans. Huh, what do you think of that?" "Comrade General, I think that will be just fine. Bears are happiest when in the woods and free to hunt."

Zhukov smiled. Whenever he was around his nephew and his GRU crew he just felt better and hope was alive. With men like these they would not only beat the fascists but annihilate them. "Now, Bear, down to business. What have you found out?" Bear brought Zhukov up to speed with what he had learned from his NKVD source. The General listened quietly, leaning forward with his arms resting on his thighs, deep in thought. Finally Bear wrapped up the report with, "But you must have had some sense of this, comrade General. Not so?"

Zhukov looked directly at Bear, "Oh yes, my friend, for 21 years I have thought of this event and had many sleepless nights with it. The other part of the mystery which your friend didn't mention is that it was Stalin who went to Lenin with the request that I raise Dmitry. Stalin! What does that mean? This whole thing stinks and gives me a massive headache. Just yesterday I returned from the front and briefed Stalin. By the way, I begged him not to shoot any of the *front* commanders."

"While they acted stupidly, the breakthrough was mainly the *Stavka's* fault. It took a lot of convincing but they live. We might even restore Konev to be commander of a *front* again, if we form a new *front* to the north of Moscow. But enough of that! Anyway, the *Vozdh* looked hard at me with that almost Asian face and said, 'Your nephew is doing good work. He is rising quickly. We should think of a promotion and award for him.' I can tell you, Bear, I almost threw up my tea. Whenever the *Vozdh* notices someone it can go either way. That confused the hell out of me. If the *Vozdh* killed Dima's parents why would he intercede for him with Lenin? Why would he now praise him? Why not just have him shot? What the hell is going in?"

Bear nodded and said, "I agree, comrade General. This is very deep and very bad. I think organizing partisans behind enemy lines sounds very safe right now." "Yes," Zhukov agreed. "That is probably best for now but you and I must continue our search. Who is after Dima and why? Where does this all lead? By St. George, this is scaring the hell out of me. My friend, I thank you and want you to stay close to him with your eyes peeled." "Of course, sir. I am sorry that I don't know more but this is like rot in your house. The more you find the deeper it goes and the worse it gets. I will stay alert and thank god we are only fighting the fascists right now and not these invisible monsters. The one thing we know is that no matter where the *Vozdh* is on this, Beria has it in for Dmitry."

Zhukov laughed, "Dmitry can join a select society including me and comrade General Rokossovskii and others then. That is okay, Bear; we are all at risk from the monster of the Lubyanka. Again, thank you my friend, I'll see you tomorrow when you all brief me on the mission. Go find Dmitry, he needs your help." Bear turned to leave but before he did he threw another room shaking salute and then advanced and grabbed the General and kissed him the traditional three times. Zhukov was a bit taken aback but returned the kiss and reached high to give Bear's shoulders a squeeze. No words needed to be exchanged.

Chapter 17

Dmitry's team met the next day with Zhukov in a spare room at Western *Front* HQ in Alabino, about 100 klicks from Moscow. Zhukov had not wanted to discuss the mission at either Kirov Station or the Kremlin. Gathered in the room were Zhukov and his Chief of Staff, General Vasily Sokolovskii, Dmitry, Bear, Felix, Taka, Major Galanin, and Major-Pilot Shanislav. "Well," Zhukov announced, "It is my favorite group of bandits. I need to get you into the field to spare the Moscow ladies any further overwhelming passions! Comrade Colonel Zhankovskii, please introduce your team." Dmitry started with Bear and Zhukov waved him off and said, "I need one of your famous hugs like we used to have in Mongolia. Eh, Sergeant-Major, those were the days! Come to your father."

Bear obliged and the newer team members were quite astounded by this familiarity between a General of the Soviet Union and a sergeant. Next Dmitry introduced Galanin and Shanislav. Zhukov was expansive regarding Galanin's development of the strategic map system and its proven accuracy. "How can you kill fascists when you don't know where they are?" he stated. He also praised Shanislav's refinement of air *razvedka* until the pilot blushed. Finally, Felix and Taka were introduced along with some highlights of their exploits.

Zhukov's eyebrows went up and he whistled, "I heard the tales but I didn't think they were really true. That was your snatch of the fascist bastard Lieutenant Colonel, eh, comrade Senior-Sergeant?" Felix looked the General in the eye and replied, "Yes, my General, and I saw Guderian up close for the second time, some day he will be in my sights." "Well, may God have mercy on him then," Zhukov replied. "OK, comrade Colonel, what is the plan for these land pirates?"

Dmitry smiled and unrolled a map showing the strategic situation in front of Moscow. He knew how much the General loved maps and also knew that it was the easiest way to communicate with him. The story was that at Advanced Training School after the Civil War, Rokossovskii used to have to climb over Zhukov in their dorm room as Zhukov crawled around the floor-sized map of whatever campaign they were studying! At any rate, the minute Dmitry unfolded the map, Zhukov was all over it. "Is this correct, where is this unit? Why are they placed here? Is Kaluga really there, I thought it was closer to Moscow?"

A whole raft of detailed questions followed and when they began to abate Dmitry spoke up. "Comrade General, our mission is to organize irregular forces behind the fascist lines but I believe this map also shows another opportunity." Zhukov stopped his study and with his balding head still pointed down he said, "I see it." The whole team was silent; it had taken them hours of study and argument to understand this point raised by Major Galanin.

Zhukov continued, "I should have seen this earlier, what a fool! My gods, I think I know everything and the fucking Hitlerites are laughing at me all day long. The problem is that there is very little fascist artillery spotted on this map and our artillery is too far away to do any good even if we knew where they were. Right?" Dmitry nodded, "Yes, comrade General, I believe this issue can be addressed along with partisan organization when we are behind the lines. I propose a night para drop here, at Kirov. It is well behind the lines and between the encirclements at Vyazma and Briansk. There will be few Germans there. However, many of our people trying to escape the encirclements and Party cadres having deserted their towns are hiding in the forest. We will seek out and organize the partisans there. However, on the way back through our lines, I propose we break into two teams and follow the seams between the Hitlerite units back to our lines."

"Along the way we can map artillery and supply depots. With comrade Major-Pilot Shanislav's help we can pinpoint these locations for comrade General Vorolov and his artillery. I estimate the total trip should last two weeks. One team will head for our center at Borodino. The other team will head north and find comrade General Rokossovskii and the 16th Army. Your thoughts please, comrade General?" "I agree, I see it," Zhukov concurred.

Dmitry nodded to Felix, who spoke up. "Comrade General, my comrade, Lev, and I were members of the 4th Airborne before being attached to the GRU and the comrade Colonel. I believe that Kirov is a logical location for remnants of that unit to be found. As you know they are fierce fighters and their training is almost as good as that of a *razvedchik*. They would be valuable troops to find and organize. Zhukov continued to nod. "How many men do you intend to take with you, comrade Colonel?" "I think about a dozen, comrade General. Also, we will need radios and several crate loads of the new PPsh's, their ammunition, hand grenades, fighting knives, etc."

Zhukov was deep in thought. "I have briefed Shaposhnikov and the *Vozdh* on this operation. I am declaring it a *front* initiative so that the whole *Stavka* does not have to know. Secrecy is everything here. The NKVD firmly believes we have been infiltrated so this remains just between us. When can you go?"

Dmitry looked at the men, "The last remaining task is to identify the landing site, and comrade Pilot-Major Shanislav leaves in one hour to select it. With that done, the only hold up is getting the equipment. I say we leave tomorrow night. Also, comrade General, can the newly established Central Partisan HQ here in Moscow help with contacts?" Zhukov gave a firm nod. "The timing is good. I will call the Partisan HQ myself to see what they know."

Zhukov paused and surveyed the men and turned to his Chief of Staff, "You see, comrade General, what men we have! The fascists have nothing like these. They talk about two weeks behind enemy lines as we would of a fishing trip." Sokolovskii smiled, he knew how his chief loved the *razvedchiki* but he too saw their value. "Men, comrades, I give my blessing and love to you. Good hunting and return heroes!" They all saluted and turned to leave and as they did so, Zhukov grabbed Dmitry's sleeve. "Go with St. George and come back to me, nephew but come back with that artillery information, it will make a huge difference in the coming weeks. Also, when you make contact with Rokossovskii use your own judgment to decide if you stay to be his Intelligence chief or return to Moscow. If you don't return, send Bear with the information. Take care, Dmitry Alexanderovich and success!" Dmitry left as the General called for his staff to plan the next day's fight.

The rest of the day was frantic with activity as the request for arms was processed and equipment organized. Bear surprised everyone with a new camouflage outfit that was dyed black for the night drop but with a white interior for snow. He had ordered the first ones a month ago. Since Dmitry had selected the other *razvedchiki* to fill out their dozen, the loose fitting outfits could be adapted for them. Noticeably, Taka and Sachino spent the day sharpening everyone's fighting knife until it wasn't safe for anyone including its owner to be near them.

After the scene with the woman during the snatch there would be no live fascists in their zone. The Georgians had been very much affected by the incident and were literally out for murder. Dmitry watched them and decided that their discipline had been exemplary so he just let them go for now. Later that afternoon, Shanislav, or the 'Russian Fritz' as he was now nicknamed because of his impressive flying hours over German held territory, had returned and the time was set for the final briefing.

Dmitry uncovered the large map and gave everyone a smaller copy. Soviet units had been removed and only crude fascist locations were indicated but the map was true in terrain and road detail. "Comrades," Dmitry began. "Tonight we jump into the lair of the fascist beast. Our mission is twofold. First, contact, train, and organize Red Army and civilian cadres into effective partisan units. Each of you will be assigned students and subjects. Comrade Sergeant-Major Rasilev and I will handle target selection, Felix, Lev, and Taka will teach correct concealment and assault tactics. Sachino, communications and explosives are your areas. The rest of you men will cover arms training and basic hand to hand fighting. Questions?"

Everyone nodded so he continued. "We will spend about a week accomplishing this effort. We cannot do everything but we will begin their education. From then on they will have good contact with Partisan HQ and the various *fronts* to get better at their new job. The second objective is to make our way approximately 100 klicks back to our lines and map enemy artillery and supply positions as we go. This will give the flyboys and big bangers something to do while the cucumbers are winning the war."

Much good natured slapping and wrestling followed this comment. "I will announce teams just before our departure from the partisans. Any questions?" Again only studied looks met his inquiry. "All right, we will operate in two squads under my command and second in command, the comrade Sergeant-Major. Sergeants Felix and Taka, cooperate and pick your men for the two squads. Taka and Sachino almost fell over as they realized that Taka would lead one unit. Taka sought Dmitry's eyes and gave him a firm assertive look. Dmitry allowed the shadow of a smile to cross his eyes and said, "We have the best *razvedchiki* in the whole of the Soviet Union here. You are all leaders and when we are with the partisans you must act it. Their discipline and Party spirit will be weak but by your example they will learn how to have confidence and lead. Clear?"

Now everyone nodded and Dmitry took them through a detailed briefing of the drop zone and approximate location of several bands of irregulars. He had two final comments. "Major Galanin cannot accompany us because he will conduct the *Stavka* briefings in my absence. I think his job is more dangerous than mine, eh? Good luck, comrade Major!" They all smiled at Galanin's obvious pride in this assignment. Taka nudged Felix, "He will be a light Colonel when we return, don't you think?" Felix nodded.

Dmitry continued, "Also, Major Galanin will be our contact with the General and the *front*. We will radio information as required but this will be very difficult. The fascists have excellent teams for finding radio operators. He and I have devised a simple but easy to remember system to keep our times and frequencies varied. Finally, and I want no groaning or swearing here, we will be assigned a political commissar. Our friend and comrade Yedved has been reassigned and will miss our little outing."

Now things went really wild as the men congratulated each other for Yedved's reassignment. "The General himself is selecting a political officer from his staff in Mongolia who he feels can keep up with us." The looks on the men's faces told it all but they needed to understand so Dmitry continued. "Comrades, this is critical for the success of our mission. These partisans are not only fighters but will be the Soviet government in these occupied areas. They need instruction in the latest Party views of the situation and how to enforce regulations and more important, which ones to enforce." The men didn't look convinced but nodded their assent.

"OK, comrade Sergeant-Major, outfit our man when he arrives. Comrade Major Galanin, please brief him on the mission and then bring him to me soonest. One final time, any questions at all?" The men were ready and Dmitry felt it. No pep talk was required for these true fighters. He saluted them and as they returned the salute, he thanked them and left them to their preparations.

In the afternoon, Major Galanin brought in Captain Commissar Nikolev to introduce him to Dmitry. Dmitry was wary of the NKVD member but this one seemed a real Bolshevik and had jump experience. He recited his combat background in Mongolia and the Winter War with Finland. Dmitry was satisfied for the moment especially since he was General Zhukov's choice. We'll see, he thought, at Nikolev's retreating back.

Later in the evening, Dmitry met with Piotr, his wing man, and the transport crew. They would fly at the transport's maximum ceiling to reduce friendly fire. The two Yak-1's would provide cover against either air force. Piotr was aghast at the risk but felt that it was manageable if they could get out of Moscow without being hit. He had personally visited the commanders of the two antiaircraft batteries he intended to over-fly and given them a bullshit story about a secret mission but hopefully they would hold their fire.

The reason for his nerves sat on the tarmac, a

German JU-52 transport, a real three engine monster. The plane had been captured near Yelnya when Zhukov had retaken the city. It would do great service tonight carrying Dmitry's team. Once over the lines the YAK's would peel off and the team would be on its own. German recognition signals were currently widely confused due to their rapid progress forward and overlapping areas of responsibility. It should be enough to keep them safe for the very short flight behind enemy lines. Or at least that's what Piotr prayed.

GRU guards were all over the air field keeping everyone back from the scene. As his men jogged out, the pilots and Dmitry headed for their planes. The men were loaded and Dmitry took a moment for drop assignments. "Listen up, comrades. We have over a ton of equipment to get into the drop zone. We go first. When on the ground Felix and Lev are the form up leaders, they will signal the aircraft for the equipment drop. Does everyone have that?" The experienced airborne trained *razvedchiki* had no problem with any of this and nodded. Dmitry saw the question in Taka's eyes and said to him and Sachino, "Georgians, I know how brave you are but night drops are special and this is your first. So that we can apply maximum force to the fascists, Sachino you jump with Bear. He will hook you up. Taka, you are with me. That is why you cannot lead the form up. We will be busy getting unhooked. Ok, comrades, this means no disrespect but it is very important for the correct beginning of the mission."

Taka and Sachino glanced at each other and nodded. As the Junkers started taxiing Sachino spoke up. "The comrade Colonel must recall that there are many instances in Georgian history when famous warriors were seen flying to the aid of their comrades. You do not trust us to fly?" Sachino finished with a very innocent expression. Dmitry loved it, "Yes comrade I trust you but today you fly with a bear." This seemed an acceptable answer and as the plane gathered speed, Dmitry sat and rechecked his gear.

The three planes escaped the Moscow zone without incident and Piotr knew some vodka would go to the AA crews on his return. The flight would be short as the distance was only 220 air klicks. Ahead they could see fires burning in dozens of locations. It was impossible to tell if they were towns, equipment, or supply depots burning but the fire and smoke from them were everywhere. This is not how our blessed Motherland is supposed to look, thought Piotr. In the transport the pilots were very active getting the navigation timing exactly right. Dmitry went up to check with them and got the thumbs up. At the same time he watched Piotr and his wing man roll over and head back to Moscow with their wings waving for luck. He went back to the men and they all prepared to jump. No static line today, free fall for 8 seconds on the count and then release. The snow should help with the landings.

The co-pilot waved and hand signaled 30 seconds. Dmitry thumbed up and got the men near the door. He and Bear were now tightly strapped to Taka and Sachino. At the count of twenty Bear roared and the men began diving out in the Russian head-first jump. It was a black night and even with the fires there was not much visibility. Finally Bear went and then

Dmitry and Taka of course followed. It was a clean jump. The air was brisk and cold with smoky aftertastes in it. Dmitry scanned the ground, nice work fly boys, there was the field bordered by woods and the river.

The town of Kirov was blacked out to the east. Nice, nice job he thought and at that second pulled the ripcord of his oversized chute. They shot upward with a rush and even now as they dropped, Dmitry spotted the lights from Lev and Felix. OK, he thought, let's get down before we get hit by a cache of grenades. "Hey, comrade Sergeant, what do you think?" Taka thumbed up and spread a huge grin. "*Bolshoi Khorosho!*" he whispered to preserve silence discipline. They hit the snow and rolled. As instructed Taka knifed off the harness and pulled Dmitry up, all in silence. They had arrived.

The next couple of hours was spent getting the equipment hidden and to some degree trying to disguise their tracks as that of deer or other animals. New snow would solve that problem. Early November was always a transition time between fall and winter with as much rain as snow. It was always just enough to make the roads extremely difficult to use, as both armies were experiencing. However, Dmitry sensed that winter was just around the corner due to the distinct chill in the air as they moved into the forest. After getting things organized in the night's semi-blackness, Taka and his team took the watch and the others grabbed a few hours sleep.

As Dmitry expected, the next morning was gray and heavy. Snow is coming, was on everyone's lips.

The smallest of fires provided some warmth. Dmitry had been up at dawn to see if the Hitlerites would do an air patrol behind their lines but he had heard nothing. Good, they are too preoccupied to worry about this sector. "Listen up comrades, our search begins. We will break up into four three man teams and search for any sign of semi-organized units. If contact is made bring their leader back here. In any case we rendezvous back here at 1600. Questions?" Sachino spoke. "Comrade Colonel what if they won't come?" In response Bear smiled and said, "You have to be persuasive, comrade," as he drew his knife.

"All right, Sergeant-Major, we want them alive. Sachino has asked an important question. We are now the Soviet government in this region. These groups of citizens or soldiers have been on their own for months with no authority. Make it clear that we are now the authority and they will come. Anything else?" No one spoke up so Dmitry continued. "OK, let's get ready and we'll use the skis. We move out in 30 minutes. Sergeant-Major and Sergeants, please stay and we will discuss assignments. Good hunting, comrades!"

An hour later they were all gliding through the Russian forest as silent as the snow which was falling. Dmitry loved the conditions. With their white camouflage they must be nearly invisible. He expected the bands of partisans to have lax discipline with quite a bit of noise and smoke so the patrol's silence was not only protective but attentive.

Dmitry had been briefed by an officer from the Partisan HQ in Moscow. He had said that there were at least four semi-organized groups in this area of about

100 men each. He had also said that the whole rear of the German lines past Smolensk was lawless in the extreme, with groups masquerading as partisans but stealing the villagers' food, murdering and raping at their whim. Dmitry had orders to apply summary justice in those cases. The damage being done to the population was awful enough without Russians adding to the misery. There was going to be mass starvation this winter and that thought was colder than the Russian frost, thought Dmitry, as he skied at the rear of his team.

As they went deeper into the forest they moved their senses up a notch. Here was where the bands would be, far from roads or open ground. The fascists would not attempt to assimilate this territory until the spring at best and that was only if they were still here, Dmitry allowed himself to think. In the lead, Sachino's hand went up and signaled them to halt and silence. Dmitry slithered to the front of the line where Sachino pointed out very fresh tracks. They agreed to follow them and spread their ranks wider and were even more silent if that was possible. They were soon rewarded with the sight of makeshift shelters covered by boughs and men huddled near fires. This was the most critical moment.

All the *razvedchiki* readied their weapons as they had no idea who these men were, bandits, deserters, or men trying to fight? They could be any or all of the above. Dmitry moved quickly into their midst on the skis and spoke. "*Razvedchiki* of the Western *front*, identify yourselves; you are surrounded by my comrades. Who are you?"

At first the men appeared too shocked to speak; as time elapsed Dmitry saw the shreds of uniforms on most of them. These were troops and that is probably best he thought. One man stood and asked, "How do we know who you are? Maybe this is a clever fascist trick?" Dmitry threw back his hood and his expression tightened. "If I were the fascists I would just have shot you all. Now quickly speak up!"

The man who had spoken nodded. "Well, comrade *razvedchik*, I am Lieutenant Andreev and you are looking at the remnants of General Boldin's assault in early July." It took a conscious effort for Dmitry to not look stunned. My God, these men had marched and hidden for almost six months and come over 500 klicks! As sternly as possible to keep the momentum of the questioning Dmitry asked, "What units?" "The Sixth Armored," was the response and Dmitry began to relax just a bit. That had been one of Boldin's temporary commands.

Dmitry motioned his men forward. "Are you the highest ranking officer?" he asked the Lieutenant and received an affirmative response. He told his men to distribute the rations they had brought to the other men who appeared to number between sixty and seventy, while he talked with the Lieutenant.

"Comrade Lieutenant, I am Colonel Zhankovskii of the GRU. I have been sent into the rear to find groups like this and organize them for partisan warfare." The Lieutenant covered his eyes and quietly shook. When he gathered himself he looked Dmitry in the eye, "I thought you were sent to execute us for desertion. If you are asking, the answer is yes, we will fight. They are not a bad bunch. We have a mix of shirkers and fighters but they have basically thrown together on this journey and I could make a fighting unit out of them."

Dmitry looked at the officer trying to size him up but he was so disheveled and clearly hadn't bathed for months that it was impossible to tell his quality. "OK, comrade, get a bite of food and we'll talk. We also have tea. Can we boil some snow?" "Yes, comrade Colonel, at once." As the word spread that the *razvedchiki* were not here to execute them the atmosphere in the camp noticeably warmed.

Dmitry explained to the Lieutenant that they were in an excellent position to harass the fascist supply lines about fifteen miles away. As they talked Dmitry began to get a favorable impression of the young officer. He was probably 22 years old and had gotten his training at the Frunze Academy in Moscow. He had led a rifle platoon in the Armored Corps; they were tank riders, tough shock troops who rode the tanks into battle. They had been encircled but had broken out with a few additional men. They had 'adopted' these others as they moved east.

The Lieutenant had been worried sick over what they would do when they got to the fascist rear echelon. How could they get this many men through the lines? Dmitry's proposal had answered that problem. He agreed to return to camp with Dmitry and they broke out the spare set of skis they had brought for that purpose. Dmitry observed how he detailed another member of the band to be in command while he was gone. With that taken care of they set out for their base and to see if other parties had been successful.

On their return they arrived first and Dmitry got some socks and underwear out for the officer. The expression on his face as Dmitry offered these small things of everyday life almost broke Dmitry's heart. Clearly, Dmitry thought, all of the tough assignments he had ever been involved with paled before this man's journey. Right at dusk the other parties came in. Felix had struck out but Taka and Bear were successful in different ways. Taka had fallen on Red Army deserters acting as bandits. He had quietly sized up the situation and broken contact with them without being discovered.

He advised a punitive expedition when possible as it was clear that these bandits were preying on the villagers and had even kidnapped some women as hostages and worse. Dmitry sickened at the thought but nodded curtly. '"Excellent work, comrade Junior Sergeant, we will attend to the bandits in due time." Bear had been more successful and brought in an unshaven but otherwise somewhat clean and well winterized man who identified himself as Captain Fedorov of the NKVD Border Guards who had assembled about forty irregulars and had already been in contact with Moscow. This was clearly one of the units Dmitry had been briefed on. He introduced him to the Lieutenant and they all huddled under white camouflage covers and warmed some tea and soup and talked.

After an evening of talking Dmitry summoned Commissar Nikolev to join them. "Comrades, the comrade Commissar will brief you on what is required from you to be recognized as an arm of the Soviet government in your area. You will protect our people from rogue elements and where possible the fascists. Your primary assignments will be disruption of enemy supply lines and intelligence; is that clear? But at the same time it is important to give the people confidence that the Soviet government is fighting for them. This you will accomplish by your behavior and example."

"You and your forces must be viewed as protectors of the people. They will in turn protect and help feed you. Moscow will provide clothing, arms, and assistance, if needed, for special missions. They will also provide funds for your use. There is much to discuss, and the comrade Commissar will take you through the details. Then tonight we will return you to your units and begin training. You will each command your own force but Captain Fedorov will be in overall command. Lieutenant, you will act as if he is your commanding officer and brief him on actions and results. I want both of you to compare rosters and be sure that each team is balanced. The Captain's team needs more men. Comrade Lieutenant, you will provide them and don't just give him the shirkers! Let's begin, there is much to do."

Dmitry left the three to work their way through Nikolev's brief. Dmitry sought out his sergeants and detailed training assignments. Then he drew them closer and had Taka review what he had seen. The effect was like lightening landing in their midst. Bear started a rumble as if a volcano was about to erupt and Felix just took out his knife and repeatedly stabbed the ground. "Comrades, we must move quickly against these bandits before they hear of us and either come for us or take more hostages. We attack tonight. Our plan will be designed by you three."

With that the NCO's glanced at each other and nodded. "It needs to be efficient and 100 per cent deadly. There are no prisons or camps to send these barbarians to. We hit them with surprise and wipe them out. Our new friends will get the credit for the job and it will help their standing locally. OK?" As one they nodded and Dmitry left them to their planning.

The sergeants briefed the men on the night's mission and waited for the Commissar to finish with the new partisan commanders. When he did Dmitry called everyone together. "Comrades, tonight we eliminate parasites feeding on the citizens of the Soviet Union. Comrade Junior-Sergeant Sharadze discovered a camp of bandits today. They have been obviously preying on the villagers.'

At these words Captain Fedorov's head snapped up. "Virlov's bunch, they were too well armed and too strong for us to take them on. They are a plague. Can you really eliminate them?" "Oh yes comrade Captain we can and will. You and the Lieutenant will accompany us as observers. After the action we will return you to your units. We move out in two hours. Here is the plan." With this Dmitry briefed them all on the plan produced by the Sergeants. Their satisfied looks convinced him that all would play their part.

They moved out in the early dark of a Russian winter evening. Taka took the lead and guided them on the two hour trip to the camp. As Dmitry had hoped there was much drinking taking place. The women were being roughly handled. The team dispersed per the plan. The partisan leaders stayed with Dmitry. All of the *razvedchiki* were equipped with PPsh's except Felix and Sachino who had their Moisin-Nagant sniper rifles handy. Bear and Lev changed into tattered Red Army uniforms the team had brought along and left their skis in the woods in order to tumble into the camp as refugees. They were only armed with their fighting knives which were concealed.

They broke into the fire light of the camp and began begging for food. Several drunken men came up and started handling their uniforms and kicking and generally harassing them. As hoped the leader, Virlov, approached them with some of his lieutenants. Sachino and Felix chose their targets and took a bead. At that moment Bear flung himself on the ground groveling and begging for mercy in the most spineless way possible. Lev got his fighting knife ready and Taka gave the 'Ready" signal to the rest of the *razvedchiki*. Every man removed their skis and coordinated targets.

The fight began when Felix and Sachino dropped Virlov and his lieutenants in several seconds with just a few shots. As the bandits' heads disappeared in a red mist, there was stunned silence and then Bear and Lev waded into their captors with their razor sharp fighting knives slashing. All hell broke loose and the bandits started to shoot and run but none of them got more than a few meters as deadly accurate PPsh fire took them down. The makeshift shelter where the women were being held was the last target and Taka emerged from it shooing the women forward with his knife dripping blood from a couple of bandits.

He kept the knife hidden behind his back so as not to frighten the women. It was all over in minutes. Not a bandit survived. The partisan leaders were stunned. They had never seen fighting like this, which was precisely the effect Dmitry wanted. "Comrades, in one week your men will have begun to be like these *razvedchiki*. They are the wind from hell for the Motherland's enemies." Dmitry's men dispersed and looked for anything of value. There were weapons and ammo so these were loaded on a sled for distribution. The women and village elder hostages were given food and pointed towards their homes. Dmitry told them all that Stalin had sent his team to control the bandits and fight the fascists.

When they looked around the camp they could hardly believe their eyes and went down on their knees crying and thanking him. Dmitry just said "Return home children, and help these cadres who will live in the woods and fight for you." They promised they would do whatever was asked and left for the journey home.

"Good work, comrades. We split up. Taka, take your team back to camp and rest. Sergeant-Major and Senior-Sergeant, return the Captain and Lieutenant to their camps along with your men to begin training in the morning. I go with Taka and will then visit each of you tomorrow. A job very well done, comrades. Death to the enemies of the Motherland!"

Those who had never seen Dmitry in battle were transfixed by his transformation, from thoughtful, even intellectual officer into a fighting demon that was death on the wind to his enemies. At this moment his whole body was alive and his eyes on fire. Their respect for him deepened and their confidence grew. They headed out into the night as the wolves began to gather for the feast.

Chapter 18

The training that began the next morning demanded an intensity that none of the partisans had experienced since the war began. Whether it was map reading, hand to hand combat, weapons, or radio training, it was all done with an urgency borne of the clock. The *razvedchiki* knew their time was limited and felt the need to transmit all they could to those staying behind. The few men who did not respond well in some area because of a natural lassitude or attitude against authority were weeded out and given permanent camp jobs. Peer pressure might bring them around over time. The rest became more disciplined and proficient at a particular skill. After the third day they were allowed to specialize. Dmitry watched his team in action and added a few thoughts along the way but mostly he let them have their way. They were fighters and knew what was important.

Dmitry, Bear, and the Commissar took the commanders and their seconds aside to spend time on strategy and tactics. The first thing they had to learn was that blowing up one tank was not a victory. Blowing up a column of tanker trucks loaded with fuel would take a brigade of tanks out of the battle and was a major victory. Similarly, kidnapping a fascist and killing him was a risk to the squad. However, kidnapping a critical officer and obtaining intelligence and getting it to Moscow or the *fronts* was again a major victory. The importance of critical target selection began to seep into the two partisan leaders.

Dmitry thought they were a bit above average

as their survival in their different war situations had demonstrated. He also felt that with time and guidance they would both develop into good, effective leaders. The other major message delivered by the Captain-Commissar was the importance of supporting the villagers and helping them in any way. This way the loyalty of the villagers would be to them and they would have a cloak dropped over their presence. There would be reprisals from the fascists. There was no way around that, but with the villagers' support they would all weather these challenges as best they could.

The example set by Dmitry and his men would go a long way in establishing this relationship but it would be up to the two bands to maintain this critical asset. Dmitry felt that a select target should be attacked by his men and detachments from the two units to both 'blood' the new fighters and test their newly acquired skills. The M-1 Minsk-Moscow Highway was about fifteen miles away and he thought there might be good hunting there. He had Sachino radio Galanin with orders for Pilot-Major Shanislav to fly recon behind their location and locate a convoy which they could schedule for demolition. The opportunity came a few days later.

In terse radio contact with Moscow and Major Galanin, Shanislav reported that almost nightly there were major convoys on the Minsk-Moscow highway. This was one of the few paved roads that could support heavy truck and armor traffic. The current fascist plan was to use the railroad to Smolensk and convoy from there. Each convoy only carried enough fuel for the Panzers for a day and therefore the need was critical. Ammunition was also part of the truck convoy. Of course, these were heavily guarded affairs, usually with about one hundred Grenadiers and officers.

A light tank might lead the column with a command car three or four vehicles behind the lead vehicle and troops dispersed in trucks throughout the convoy, a formidable but rewarding target, Dmitry thought. From the receipt of the signal he decided they needed at least 24 hours to prepare. They would move up to the highway the next day and dig in for nightfall. Piotr had also warned about Hitlerite recon aircraft during the day but felt their attitude was perfunctory at best as they thought they had the Soviets on the 'run'. We'll see about that, Dmitry smiled to himself.

"Comrades, a night attack on a convoy presents two major problems. First, we must engage the enemy quickly and efficiently to minimize combat time. The more time we give them, the more aircraft or other support they can call on. Second, we must deploy on both sides of the road to deny the fascists the use of either side for their own defense. This means that friendly fire becomes a major danger to your comrades. Here is how we can accomplish these tasks with extreme deadliness for our enemies and minimal casualties to our forces." Dmitry took them through the plan. His men and the partisans would be intermixed to provide training and guidance on their first major mission. The two leaders would function as staff with Dmitry and have specific areas of responsibility.

Based on the lack of air traffic and the prevalence of white smocks among the partisans they moved out during the day. Dmitry did not like this but felt that in this case they could take the risk. Everyone was equipped with skis. He had also taken the time to basically train and equip some of the former soldiers in medical skills. The partisans would be self-reliant in this regard and the men needed to have some faith they would be cared for in case of injury.

As with all military operations, much of the guarantee of success came from preparation. Dmitry and his team kept going over the details to be sure that everything was covered. Dmitry had carefully taken the leaders through this process, step by step. His sergeants had done the same with the partisan non-coms. The attacking force totaled about forty men and was well armed for a variety of situations. They traversed the forest in about four hours and got lessons in how to dig in on the roadside when they got to the eerily silent highway.

Posting scouts in series up to a mile away so they could not be surprised in either direction, they got quickly to work. Fire parties were established at different intervals along the attack lane. Most critically, Sachino and his select students laid undetectable wooden cased explosive under the not yet hard frozen road surface. These would be exploded at intervals during the battle and to best effect. New Corporal Sachino was in charge and would not allow any mistakes in front of these amateurs.

Finally, Bear and a very small, very select team were dug right into the roadside. They would be connected to Dmitry by a string that would signal when a Panzer PzKpfw II or other lead vehicle was just ahead of them. They would then plaster its treads with explosive and lob some grenades into the very likely open, occupied turret, and then disappear. This would signal the beginning of the attack. Dmitry completely trusted Bear to pull this off. Wisely, Bear had selected two of the most capable and proven partisans to assist him. Everything depended on wiping out the tank. Finally, Taka and Felix would man the anti-tank rifles and as in earlier engagements use incendiaries to blow the tankers to hell. If there were ammo transports included, they would be looted and demoed.

"Again, comrades, everything depends on discipline and cooperation. No lone cowboys here! There might be a search light with the convoy. What happens when that switches on?" "Well, we shoot it out!" Someone shouted. "No, comrade, if we all begin shooting at the searchlight we will not be effective against the rest of the force. The man nearest shouts, "It's mine!" and takes it out. Then his comrades know what is happening. Someone is wounded, what happens?" This they knew from training. "We keep fighting and call for a medical officer." "Right," Dmitry replied. "We are all military men. Remember discipline is everything. These fascists will be on alert, well-armed, and tough. We must demonstrate our Bolshevik solidarity to best them. Understood?" "Yes, comrade Colonel," was the response.

Dmitry scanned for Bear and saw him in his usual slouched, seemingly sleepy posture but knew this signaled confidence. "OK, comrades, let's take our places for the play to begin. You all know the most important discipline is not to do anything, no matter how tempting until the lead vehicle, probably a

PzKpfw, is blown. Comrade Sergeants, fight your units and support your comrades. Good hunting! Death to the fascist beast!" They broke up and went to their various positions and began the wait.

After about six hours and close to midnight, the western scout line began to come in. Lev had been assigned the key position there and his report buoyed Dmitry's hopes. "Comrade Colonel, the column approaches at about 30 klicks per hour. We have over thirty gasoline tankers and as many transports of hard goods. Troops are dispersed as anticipated and a command car with a heavy machine gun is three back from the lead which is a PzKpfw light tank. I suggest we also target the command car specifically because of the HMG." Dmitry nodded, "Excellent work, soon to be sergeant! You and a partisan use grenades to take out that car. Otherwise we are ready. What is your estimate for their arrival here?" "Five minutes, comrade Colonel." "OK," Dmitry gave the preparatory hand signal and also gave Bear and his team the three pulls to get ready.

The distinct sound of heavy engines started to echo down the road and in the whine Dmitry caught the sound of some captured Soviet tanker trucks. Well, the Motherland will re-claim that property he thought. Dmitry was camouflaged black as night and buried in boughs but with a good sight lane down the road. The blacked-out convoy approached and he steeled himself for the wait. The ashes rubbed into his hair and face gave him a wild appearance but inside his mind was calm and ready. These bastards were systematically murdering, raping, and looting his homeland; it was going to feel very good to strike back with extreme violence.

The convoy was approaching his position which was in line with Bear and his men. Dmitry waited until the exhaust of the Panzer PzKpfw was just past Bear's head and yanked the cord with everything he had. In the black night Bear rose up as only a shadow and tossed three grenades perfectly into the open turret. The tank's officer caught one but dropped the others. At the same time the two partisans slapped the plastique set for thirty seconds on the treads. They all rolled into the woods. The truck following the Panzer saw motion and dropped a man into the road to alert the staff car but there was still just a moment of silence. Then the grenades blew and the lead German officer disintegrated into a shower of blood and body parts which washed over the next truck. The light tank lifted off the ground and settled into a flaming wreck as its treads also disappeared in a fiery blast. The road side became mayhem.

As the lead tank ground to a halt the whole convoy reacted as an accordion. Some of the drivers tried to go around others but that only added to the confusion. Dmitry started to breathe when he saw Lev and another partisan toss Molotov cocktails and grenades into the command car. The fascist leaders burned where they sat and the smell was choking. A pool of melted fat collected under the car as the fire consumed everything. All along the convoy tankers were blowing as the anti-tank rifles came into play.

Sachino was conducting a tour de force explosives class as seemingly random but very well thought out explosions drove the fascists into even greater confusion. The burning trucks provided much light and little cover so the enemy grenadiers headed for the roadside. As they did PPsh fire dropped them in their tracks. These were the men who conquered Poland and France and they were also, as they knew, fighting for their lives. They sold them highly. Hand to hand fighting broke out all along the convoy.

Dmitry almost passed out when he realized he had not briefed anyone regarding the destruction of the radio which would be identified by a whip antenna on one of the vehicles. As he searched for the vehicle displaying it, he shouted a variety of supportive orders and kept his PPsh active. Finally, he saw one of the troop trucks displaying the antenna and with his heart in his mouth he pulled back the canvas prepared to fire only to be met by Bear's amused grin. "I've been enjoying a conversation with our young fascist friend here, comrade Colonel." He waved towards the now dead grenadier. "He has told me much about signals and was even willing to give me his codebook. All because I mentioned how I had once watched groin surgery done without anesthetic and found it very interesting."

Dmitry slumped. "Comrade Sergeant-Major, you are too much. Did he get a signal off?" "Perhaps an identifier signal but nothing else, comrade Colonel. I noticed we had left this little detail out of the plan and decided to see to it myself." Dmitry said, "But Bear, why didn't you say something?" "Oh comrade Colonel, you must look perfect to the children even if it takes a secret bear to help you out." With that Dmitry saluted and moved on. Gods, he thought, where do men like him come from? Maybe he really is a bear turned human!

Back in the fight, combat was beginning to die out. Indeed Felix and Taka were directing cadre in the truck search but at the same time there was still some vicious hand to hand fighting going on. As Dmitry slouched and moved down the column he spotted a small group of fascists suddenly break cover and head for the woods. Sachino saw them also and started in pursuit. Felix pointed several men in that direction. At that moment a German came up out of the ground and grabbed Sachino from behind bringing him down with stunning force. The German slammed him into the ground and slashed at his throat with his knife. In a dazed condition Sachino was vulnerable but managed to roll as the knife came down.

It sliced open his camouflage smock completely and slashed down his arm and chest. Blood immediately erupted from the wound. Felix took aim to get the fascist before a killing blow could be landed but at that moment the German's head disappeared. Felix looked up the line to see Taka drop his anti-tank rifle after a perfect shot and rush to his brother's side. "Sachino, Sachino, are you all right? Where are you cut?" "Oh, everywhere brother, but I'm OK. I think he split my head. What a monster! Was that you who took him out?" "Yes, brother, but quiet, we will patch you up." Taka signaled one of the medical personnel to take care of his brother and went back to continue to ignite the tankers and assess supplies.

Besides the radio operator there were a few

other fascist survivors they interrogated, with no major results except that they had no winter uniforms and that the attrition on the tank corps was very severe, almost eighty per cent! That at least was good news. As the last Germans were mopped up Dmitry called the leadership together, "Comrades, excellent ambush. Good discipline. You and your men show great promise. The next one is yours and I want to hear about it from *front* Headquarters. We all have wounded so the first job is to prepare them for travel. Never leave wounded behind. We all know their fate but they may be saved by the fascists just to be tortured for information about you. Do not let that happen." Knowing looks were exchanged across the group.

Dmitry continued, "As you know we split up here. We head back to the lines and you must head eventually to your camps but not for 48 hours. Travel circuitous routes that lead nowhere until you are sure you are not being tracked. The skis should help but they will bring dogs so use your skills in evasion which have been perfected the last few months. Also, Commissar Nikolev has requested to stay as your political officer and I support this idea. What is your opinion?" The Captain and Lieutenant eyed each other and the Captain replied. "He is not bad for a Commissar. We welcome him to our band." Dmitry smiled and nodded, "Good. Also, several of my men would like to stay and be a resource for you. What do you think of that?" This took no discussion but was met with smiles and "Of course, of course! That is fantastic."

"Comrades, we must leave soon. You never know when the fascists might appear. But let me say that I will report back to the Border Guards and the Red Army that no one here is a deserter and that the units have twice engaged in fierce combat against the enemies of the Motherland. I have everyone's names and will see that the information is recorded. Also, you will be contacted by a drop agent regarding future plans. If you must change location drastically figure out a way to let Moscow know without alerting the fascists. Is this all clear?"

Captain Fedorov spoke up. "Yes, comrade Colonel, that is all clear. However, the men wanted me to say that it was a great honor to fight with you and that we would follow you anywhere. Just ask us and we will go. Even to Berlin and back. We also ask that you never have Bear discipline us, as that would be too much!" At this good-natured cheers broke out and Bear actually blushed as he said. "Fine men, fine men."

The Captain continued. "Comrade Colonel because of our respect for you we ask a favor. Could you please name our two bands? This would be a great honor and a treasure in battle to shout it aloud." Dmitry was quite moved by the request and realized its importance. "Yes comrades, I am honored to do that but only if you agree with the names. OK?" They nodded in return and crowded in to hear what he thought. Dmitry drew himself to attention. "Comrade Captain Fedorov, you are now the commander of 'Stalin's Wolves'! How is that?" The men cheered and wept and loved it. Now Lieutenant Andreev was standing with great anticipation, waiting for Dmitry's pronouncement. "Comrade Lieutenant, you are now

commander of 'Lenin's Defenders of the People'!"
"How is that?" The lieutenant looked at his men and
saluted. "We will make you proud of that name, comrade Colonel!"

Dmitry signaled Bear to prepare the men for
moving out. As he did so he looked at the assembled
partisans. He came to full attention and for the first
time through his camouflage smock they could see the
gold star of a Hero of the Soviet Union on his breast.
"Comrades, you have opened a new war against the
fascists today. My fascist 'friend,' "Hurrying Heinz"
Guderian, will not be hurrying very soon when no fuel
arrives for his precious Panzers. This will give our
forces time to prepare a very nice welcome for him
and his friends. I salute you and wish you all the success in the world. Death to the Fascist Invaders! All
Glory and Victory to Stalin and the Motherland!" He
threw his best salute and as the men stared and nodded
at his decoration, he embraced their leaders, wished
them *Dasvidonya,* and skied into the darkness.

Dmitry had deliberately not discussed his plans
with the partisans or his men. The fewer who knew the
better, but now was the time to identify destinations
and who would go with each team. He called everyone
together. "Comrades, a very excellent job, training the
partisans and even better results with the bandits and
supply column. All was handled like the experts you
are. You should be proud of your actions. I intend to
recommend Sachino for junior Sergeant and Taka for
full Sergeant. Also, there may be more tinsel for some
of those tunics with which to impress the ladies, but
first we need to get to the ladies!"

"Here is the plan. I will take Taka and Felix and head for Volokolamsk where we should find comrade General Rokossovskii and the 16th Army. It should be about 200 klicks. Comrade Sergeant-Major Rasilev will take Sachino, Lev, and our two new comrades, Sergei and Mikhail, and head for Tula where they should find our southern flank. They will pierce fascist lines north of the city for safety and then figure their best way in. Once safely in our lines you are to get to Moscow as soon as possible to brief Major Galanin on the dispositions that you have reconnoitered. Is that all clear?"

They nodded but everyone was glancing at Sachino on the sled. His clothes were soaked and frozen with blood. Dmitry looked at Bear, "I think I remember you have great sewing skills, comrade Sergeant-Major, because those sergeant tabs keep coming on and off so often. Am I right?" Rasilev simply nodded. "OK then. Let's get comrade Sachino sewn up and bandaged for the journey. You men will have about 160 klicks to go and it won't be easy but Sachino needs attention and I'm counting on you to get it for him."

With that Bear and Taka got out the field first aid kit with the needle and sutures. They packed snow onto Sachino's arm and chest. This was going to be a long and painful sew job, Bear thought. He signaled for Taka and Felix to prepare to immobilize Sachino while he sewed. They gave him some of the field vodka and after about 15 minutes of the snow numbing the flesh they began. Hundreds of stitches later and having replaced the flesh over exposed bone, Bear sat back.

Somehow Sachino had not passed out and he smiled at Bear. "There must be a Georgian story of a soldier being nursed to health by a bear. If there isn't, I'll invent one! Thank you, comrade Sergeant-Major." Bear had gotten quite close to Sachino during their stay in Moscow and admired his determination not only to fight, but to learn, including reading. He therefore bent over, and gently kissed Sachino's forehead, "Rest, dear comrade, rest. You will be fine now." With that they wrapped the arm and chest wounds in clean bandages after sponging off the blood with newly boiled water. Sachino fell asleep and they all relaxed.

Dmitry stood, "Comrades, our journey is longer so we must leave now. You have two missions. First, get comrade Sachino to an aid station so he can collect his promotion bonus. Second, map Hitlerite supply and artillery positions as you move forward. We part now and I wish you luck!" Everyone stood and embraced. The team was being separated again and who knows when they would again be together? However, the longest good-bye was between Taka and Sachino. Taka had taken the orders like a soldier but was terribly worried about his brother. Yet somehow, leaving him with Bear, Lev, and their new comrades felt very good. He glanced at Bear with brotherly concern in his eyes and Bear returned the glance with pure determination. Taka was satisfied and joined Dmitry and Felix as they began to disappear into the early dawn.

Using back roads at night and the forest by the day, Dmitry and his team made good speed at over 30 klicks a day. It was still a long way to Volokolamsk. They pushed on every day and by intention stayed in

the German rear echelon. They noted supply drops,
tank maintenance parks, and soon artillery positions.
While they had a good sense of their position they
tried to use physical terrain markers wherever possible
as they wanted the fly boys to verify these sites. They
pushed on and started to head north behind German
lines. They ascertained that the Mozhiask line and Borodino had fallen but that for the moment there was a
hiatus as both sides reinforced and resupplied. I hope
our new friends will disrupt that resupply, now would
be the perfect time, Dmitry pondered as they skied
north.

Finally after a week of travel they knew they
had to turn east and also knew this was the most critical moment of the journey. They must find a seam between German units or a flank and move through that
area. They turned east on a woods road outside Rzhev
and headed for Volokolamsk, 20 klicks distant, and as
they did so they could plainly see signs of fascist occupation and Red Army 'scorched earth' tactics. They
got off the road and using compass and map they
headed north of Volokolamsk. Outside of a major
German supply dump they halted for a break. Dmitry
had Felix and Taka dig in and told them he would look
around and map out the situation for later demolition.

As dusk settled in, Dmitry skied forward and
paused at a clearing where he observed a set of buildings being used by the fascists. He decided to stay and
see what they were and put them on the target list. He
had already passed a massive dump and was a bit be-
wildered at the function of this site. Darkness came
down suddenly as it does in Russian winters and he

slid forward on his stomach with skis off. He saw motion and men being carried in and soon a man in a bloodstained white gown came out for a smoke. Ah, a hospital, Dmitry thought. As he watched something small was tossed out a window and landed in the snow, soon followed by another.

He could not figure out what he was seeing. He wanted to come in closer but needed to switch position to get closer to the area where these things were thrown and keep the woods close. There were no apparent guards and the doctors and orderlies appeared to be extremely busy. That's good, came unbidden to his mind. He moved slowly around and inched forward to the area where the unknown packages had been thrown. As he got close he shook his head several times. I must be weak with hunger, he thought. It looks like the snow is moving.

As he watched the snow seemed to rise and fall in a random wave like motion. Perplexed he moved right to the edge of the area and swept back the snow. He almost fainted, screamed, and went berserk when the blue frozen face of a young girl of about seven stared back at him. Her Russian blue eyes reflected the light and gleamed with youth but they were dead. What was this nightmare? He probed some more and found more recently dead children. He very carefully examined them but could find no reason for their death. At that moment another body hit the snow and he looked hard. Now he actually slithered over the moving snow to this body. A young boy looked at him with barely conscious eyes and tried to speak but no words came.

Dmitry smoothed the boy's forehead and carefully examined him for wounds. There was bleeding from the arm. Oh no, oh my god, he almost fainted and the image was too much no matter how much war he had seen. The bleeding was from a crudely inserted needle to act as a drain. The fascist bastards were using these children for a live blood source probably because of supply problems and discarding them for dead when they were emptied! This was too much.

Dmitry's head hammered and he hyperventilated. He slowly returned to the edge of the wood and tried to reason out what to do. His brain would not function and for minutes he just sought to control himself. Finally, under control, he realized he must complete his mission. This pit of hell would be on the target list along with a message to the bastards attached to 500 kg bombs. He realized he could not save these children and every fiber of his body strained at the thought. This was his job! This was the mission of the Red Army! The protectors of the people and here these monsters were in the Motherland, killing their children, their future!

As control returned, his heart was where the blow fell and the wound, while not fatal, would never heal. This became not a war but a crusade for his people. He knew he couldn't tell Taka or Felix, they could not be controlled with this knowledge. He went back to camp and talked about the depot and pretended to sleep as visions of murdered innocents paraded through his restless mind.

That same night they moved out at midnight to make contact with the Soviet lines. They felt around the Soviet defenses looking for the northern flank after leaving the German lines. Dmitry was most concerned about mines but as long as they were on skis and did not hit any recent placements they should be OK. They finally came close to the Soviet flank. Dmitry studied the terrain hard and decided they had to crawl the remaining half klick on the open ground rather than try and penetrate through the woods. He had signaled Felix and Taka to drop everything not required and start a line crawl towards the defensive trenches.

When they were outside the wire but very near to the Soviet lines Dmitry called out. "Comrades, we are *razvedchiki* returning with information for comrade General Rokossovskii, please open the wire!" The response was immediate, "Yes, and your mother is Stalin's favorite, I bet!" This was, of course, accompanied by loud laughter. "What do you fascists take us for, idiots? You have 30 seconds to retreat or be blown to hell!" "Comrades we are what we say. Please telephone the General's HQ, and just say the name Dima. He will order you to let us pass. This is an order from Colonel Zhankovskii.'

The sentries began to be a little uncertain and sent for an officer. Soon a Lieutenant came up and Dmitry repeated the request. After some consultation they sent a runner to the field telephone with the information and got an immediate response. "Let them in!" The sentries said, "We don't know how you avoided the mines but do not move. We will open the wire and show you the safe path." This they did and soon the three *razvedchiki* were in the Red Army trenches.

The Lieutenant introduced himself and detailed a sergeant to take them to Rokossovskii. "By the way, comrade Colonel, why didn't you use the forest for cover and come right up to the line?" Dmitry just shrugged, "It didn't feel right." The officer smiled. "Well, I hope the Fritzs are not as sharp as you, we have laid an impassable minefield there and hope to get some good results during the next attack." Dmitry smiled, "Good thinking. I think that we had a Felix with us because I can't explain why we didn't come in that way. Good luck, comrades and thanks for not blowing us to hell." With that they headed for Rokossovskii's HQ.

It was still a couple of hours until dawn but the General and his staff were already at work. The sergeant escorted them in and the General grabbed Dmitry in a massive hug. "Well the prodigal nephew returns! And he has a part of his merry band with him. Where is my favorite bear?" At this Dmitry launched into an account of their mission and how they had contacted the partisans and wiped out the bandits and a supply column and returned with targeting information. This was all stated matter-of-factly and as the story went on Rokossovskii's staff members just stared at the man speaking. "Who is this?" they wondered. At that point the General spoke up.

"Comrades allow me to introduce my long, lost good comrade, Colonel Zhankovskii of the GRU, Hero of the Soviet Union, and the man who saved our asses by delaying the fascists four days at the Vop!" Now they knew who he was and stared hard at this young, lean officer, who some had thought was only a legend to help the morale of the Red Army. "Comrade Colonel, please name your sergeants to my staff." Dmitry identified Felix and Taka and all shook hands around the room. The General looked at Dmitry as a signal for him to determine the next move. "Comrade General, I would like to brief my comrades on their next mission, to take information to Moscow. Then I will return and if it is all right brief you comrades regarding what we have seen on our journey through the lines."

"Splendid!" the General responded. "While you finish up with your men we will scout up some food and tea for you. Welcome back, my young knight!" With that Dmitry and the sergeants stepped outside to discuss their next journey.

"Comrades, you have done an outstanding job! That ski journey was one of the fastest ever completed. However, our mission is not yet over. I remain here to assist the comrade General with Intelligence. I have the dispositions of supplies, tank parks, and artillery copied onto two maps. Attend please, comrades. I will keep one map for our use here. You will take a copy and deliver it to comrade Major Galanin at *Stavka*. Is that clear? Please ask him to confer with comrade Pilot-Major Shanislav and General Vorolov regarding targeting. We will inform *Stavka* of the targets we hit from here. The second item is absolutely top secret and to be handed only to comrade General Zhukov. Get comrade Major Galanin to assist you in getting access to the General. Tell the Major this is of utmost criticality. Are you OK with all of that?"

Both Taka and Felix saluted and said "Yes, comrade Colonel." Dmitry smiled. "I have never fought with better men. We will get a truck to drive you to Moscow. Comrade Major Galanin will get you reassigned and we will all meet again, soon I hope. You are outstanding Red soldiers." They certainly were, as the blushing was of almost mythic proportions. Felix spoke up, "The comrade Colonel knows the high respect we fighting men have for him. We will follow you anywhere, sir. We hope to Berlin!" Dmitry hugged each of them and went off to get them some food and transport.

Later, back at General Rokossovskii's HQ, the staff brought Dmitry up to speed. In his new capacity as Intelligence chief he detailed more reconnaissance and sent it to Moscow for aerial surveillance of their front. The General returned and explained the action of the recent weeks to Dmitry, how they had been slowly beaten back from their forward positions but were forcing the Hitlerites to pay a large price. Then the rains had slowed both armies and compounded the supply issues.

Rokossovskii told Dmitry the story of the battle on his southern flank at the Napoleonic battlefield of Borodino. General Polosukhin had not been given enough men or armor to defend the area but had heartened his troops by reciting Lermontov's poem of the battle from memory to his officers. Indeed the General had visited the battlefield museum as it was packed up and written under 'Reason for Visit' in the guestbook "I am here to defend the battlefield."

Fighting on the exact same ground as Kutuzov, Bagration, and Barclay 130 years earlier and almost on the same date, the Red Army had met the German attacks heroically. The General himself was wounded in hand to hand fighting with the attackers. Although wounded, he continued to hold off the Germans for five days, giving Zhukov time to reform troops in his rear. In an eerie parallel with the past, the Red Army retreated unbeaten but damaged and like the French, the fascists advanced but were deeply wounded as they continued their march on Moscow. This, of course, was the reason for Rokossovskii's continual adjustments and where he needed Dmitry to focus.

The last two weeks had seen only intermittent skirmishing but it was Rokossovskii's opinion that they would be attacked in force soon. That was why Dmitry's intell was so critical. Anything they could do to reduce German effectiveness would help them in the coming battle. Now the ground was frozen and snow covered and this benefited the German armor, but the snow camouflage benefited the Soviet defense and better winter fighting capability. Both sides knew that the next fights would be to the death with Moscow as the Queen on the chessboard and in dire danger.

"Comrades, the *Stavka* have received Dmitry's report and have also sensed the Hitlerites preparing to attack. However, instead of sending our requested reinforcements and aircraft we are ordered to attack from our lines against the Third Panzer Army." Rokossovskii paused and let the wave of dismay pass over the group. Their exclamations of, "stupid, foolish, we will be overwhelmed" were also his belief, but could not be expressed. Since mid-October these so-called spoiling attacks had done nothing but drain the Red Army in men and resources. No significant benefit had been accrued.

He was relieved to see his Commissar also pale at the news; at least they wouldn't be shot for these statements. "Well gentlemen, those are our orders and we will do our duty. We are ordered to attack on the 16th of November in three days' time. Begin the planning, and comrade Colonel Zhankovskii, I need more intelligence and fast!" Dmitry nodded and signaled for his adjutant to begin getting the teams out.

However, Rokossovskii never got to make his attack. The Germans hit with massed force, from Tula in the south to Klin in the north, along the whole Soviet front. The Germans knew this was the last push to Moscow and the fighting was desperate. In Tula, hastily gathered militia, military cadets, and armed workers fought next to Red Army troops and delayed Guderian. They eventually forced him to halt and withdraw to outside the city, stopping the advance in the south. However, in the north things did not go well. This was where the main German fist was hammering and all along the front the Soviets were forced back.

Several days after the attack began; Dmitry and Rokossovskii huddled over their maps trying to find a place to halt the Hitlerite advance. Every day they lost several kilometers but there was no widespread panic. Additionally, the artillery was really weighing in, devastating German artillery and supply depots thanks to the information that Dmitry had brought in. No longer was the German rear a place of relative safety, the Soviet artillery hammered it day and night using Dmitry's maps, aerial guidance, and new, sound range-finding technology. The Red artillery sent a fearsome hellfire to the Hitlerites which they had not seen from the beginning of the campaign.

To the north the troops of the 30th Army had been decimated and the Germans were seeking a passage through their front to get into Rokossovskii's rear. This would finish the Red Army and open the road to Moscow. Rokossovskii sent General Panfilov and his 316th Infantry Division to plug the gap. The fighting was desperate in the extreme and at different points the unit was overrun but succeeded in pushing the Germans back and extricating themselves from disaster several times. With their backs to the wall they fought some of the most courageous engagements in Red Army history.

Panfilov and his men had been fighting hard but on 18th of November they were put to the severest test. At Rokossovskii's direction they were holding off German attempts to flank the whole of their line. At a critical moment in the battle Panfilov was killed while leading his troops. Even then they did not break but slowly retreated, contesting every meter of ground. The Presidium of the Soviet Union had just broadcast that the unit was awarded the Order of the Red Banner and had been designated the First Guards Rifle Division when their commander was killed. It hurt Rokossovskii deeply to think of Panfilov's death as he and Panfilov shared the same command style and had gotten very close in their short time together. Rokossovskii recalled one of Panfilov's wry remarks. They were inspecting the line and in one area it was very thinly held and the engineer's stakes outnumbered the defenders. Panfilov had remarked, "Well, they have us staked out very well. Haven't they?" That was the man.

Every day was a crisis and every day they had to reestablish headquarters. Dmitry watched the strain almost crush Rokossovskii. At one point they both felt they could not hold off the flank attacks any longer and needed to reestablish their defense along the river Istra. Rokossovskii called Zhukov and requested permission. It was refused. "Stand where you are," were the orders. Rokossovskii knew this would imperil the whole line so he did the unprecedented. He called the *Stavka* and spoke to Shaposhnikov, who after likely consulting with Stalin, approved the plan. Rokossovskii then began the maneuver but soon received a screaming call from Zhukov that Dmitry could hear from meters away. "I am the *front* commander and you will stay and fight or I will have you shot!" Zhukov screamed at his friend.

Rokossovskii replied, "It is unlikely that you will have the chance, comrade General, because of the Hitlerites." At that exact moment a dud German shell crashed through the wall of his HQ and failed to explode. He hung up and turned to Dmitry and said, "Well Dima, it seems your uncle is in a bad mood today." While he made light of it, the relationship between the two men was never the same. Proceeding as ordered, their forces were routed and a now forced retreat was made to the Istra line.

Dmitry went out of the headquarters to assess the situation in the village and the threat to the staff. When outside he looked for the customary tank unit guarding the HQ and saw none. He signaled to the sentry to come over to him. "Where is the tank guard, comrade corporal?" "Comrade Colonel, they have left to refuel." Dmitry was incredulous. "You mean they are gone?" "Yes, comrade Colonel. A senior Commissar came up and ordered them to the rear to refuel." "What Commissar?" "I don't know comrade Colonel; I had never seen him before."

Dmitry was beyond being stunned and for a moment fought panic. German shells and now mortar rounds were smashing around them. The Hitlerites were clearly very close and Rokossovskii was likely minutes from capture. "Quick, get the staff car and meet me here. Tell everyone you meet to retreat. We regroup on the Istra. Move, move!" Dmitry sprinted back to the house serving as Army HQ. "Everyone out, now! Take the maps and correspondence, nothing else! Arm yourselves. The enemy is minutes away!"

The staff and Rokossovskii stared at him like he was mad but then their battle sense kicked in and they moved. Dmitry grabbed the General and pushed him into the staff car along with several other officers. The rest piled into a truck. A soldier started tossing grenades and weapons into the vehicle and they were off in a flash.

Dmitry happened to notice that the ever calm and always unflappable Rokossovskii was loading a beautiful presentation PPsh. "From the workers of the Tula Factory. I think it makes me look like an American gangster. Impresses the ladies, eh?" the General commented. They headed out of the village using back lanes and even still were just a jump ahead of a Panzer as it drove through a block of homes. Screaming tires hit the road to Moscow in a blistering turn as the Panzer opened fire on them. While the staff car with Rokossovskii and Dmitry aboard was missed, the truck with the other staffers suffered a direct hit. The General slumped in his seat and cried.

However, they could not hold on the Istra. The line was too improvised. They did hold long enough for a better prepared position to be readied, albeit closer to Moscow. They eventually retreated to these lines at the end of November.

With their line reestablished and with fresh reinforcements sent from the *Stavka,* they held and gained a moment for their collective breath. For some reason German pressure on the Soviet center had eased and Zhukov took this opportunity to shift forces to the flanks to prevent the pincers from closing behind Moscow. Stalin called Rokossovskii and asked them to hold a bit longer. He asked Rokossovskii what he needed. "Arms and troops," was the response, and Stalin sent both. Fresh troops were hurled into the battle just as they exited the trains bringing them from Siberia.

The new arrivals were fully equipped and battle tested troops, and they threw the Germans back in severe fighting. The Red Air Force also appeared in large numbers. Their battlefield prowess was improving with every engagement. Finally, the new *Katyusha* rockets made their weight felt and not only Panzers and soldiers fell to them but several German generals were killed and wounded. On Rokossovskii's new right flank at Krasnya Polyanya the Germans got the closest to Moscow of the campaign. Stalin called him to ask that they drive the Germans back. He informed Rokossovskii that the Germans had siege guns which could reach the Kremlin from there. A cobbled together force was constructed and hit the Germans hard. They were successful in driving them back a few klicks which put them out of artillery range of the Kremlin, only 20 klicks away. The two antagonists were ready for the culminating battle of the Moscow campaign.

In all of this Dmitry began to sense an opportunity. He discussed it with Rokossovskii and received permission to go to Moscow and brief Zhukov on the kernel of a plan.

Chapter 19

Back in Moscow at the Kremlin, Dmitry entered by the Watchtower Gate and turned and headed down the stairs to the new bombproof HQ. The corridor was narrow and long and lined with small rooms. He sought out the General who was expecting him, found his office, and entered. Zhukov was on the phone with Konev advising him on improvements to the anti-tank fortifications in his *front* when Dmitry entered. He waved him to a chair as he scanned a map of Konev's Western *front* location and added a few other comments for the General and hung up. Zhukov looked like hell. He had lost weight and his skin was almost transparent. Worry did not describe the expression in his eyes, but the bulldog chin was thrust forward and his bearing still rigid. He can take it, thought Dmitry.

"Bless you, nephew. It is water for the heart to see you again. Let's talk of your mission and Rokossovskii for a few minutes before you advise me on your latest plan. I have invited no one because I know your need for secrecy and also have cleared the bugs for the hour. How are you? Are you alright? What a stupid ass thing to say at a time like this, huh?" Dmitry smiled. "I am alive and well, comrade General, and count myself lucky to be so. My team performed extraordinarily well behind the fascist lines and we not only organized two partisan bands but brought back some good mapping of Hitlerite positions."

"I know," said Zhukov. "In many sectors we

are using them and they have proved very valuable. They really gave the artillery a shot in the butt and they have now joined the party producing great head-aches for our fascist friends. No, that was all very good and well done. By the way, we have heard from "Stalin's Wolves," where did they get that name, I wonder? They are keeping close tabs on the Moscow-Minsk Highway and their reports of enemy movements have been extremely helpful with the positioning of our forces. Well done all around."

"But that letter you sent me. My gods, I have never heard of anything like it, not even during the Civil War. I know it's true but I still can't believe it. Children, to treat children worse than animals." A deep sadness appeared in Dmitry's eyes, "Yes uncle, it's true and haunting. Even today I can't talk about it without anger overwhelming my mind." "I'm sure," the General responded. "When I briefed the *Stavka* on it there was total silence. Shaposhnikov had tears in his eyes and others the same. Stalin was cold as steel in winter. He just sat there and repeated, 'They will pay, they will pay. When we are in Berlin they will pay for 50 years and our boot will never leave their throat.' It was a stunning moment."

"I sent your comrade Shanislav to escort the bombers to take out the supply dump and the hospital. I didn't specify what the target was or why they were hitting it. The report was confirmed by aerial *razvedka* that the horror was totally destroyed. Wipe it from your mind, nephew, but not your heart; we must focus on driving the fascists from the Motherland and then punishing them so they never come again, just as comrade Stalin said."

Dmitry took this as a cue to bring his thoughts forward. "Comrade General, my trip through the lines and the attacks I witnessed at the front with comrade General Rokossovskii have led me to believe that the fascists are reaching their 'culminating point' per their own teacher, von Clausewitz. The attacks are very focused on narrow fronts because they are running short of men, ammunition, and armor. The GRU believes that some Panzer Corps are down to only one-quarter of their strength in June and the infantry is not far behind. However, to hold Moscow we must be both defensive and offensive."

"We defend now and when they are truly exhausted we counterattack to drive them back and set up the next series of campaigns." Zhukov nodded, "We are of the same mind, nephew, so what is your thought?" Dmitry pointed to Rokossovskii's sector on the strategic map. "Here is where they are the closest to Moscow. They can smell the cooking. They must feel that with one more all-out push, we will collapse and they will roll into Red Square. It must be driving them mad. What I propose is that we oblige them by providing a very tempting target. They will then focus their remaining forces on this sector and since we have invited them in we can spring a trap that annihilates this last effort and sets up our counterattacks."

Zhukov's eyes had new life and shone as lanterns on the map. "Where and how?" He demanded. Dmitry pointed at the flooded marshes more or less in the center of Rokossovskii's lines. "Sergeant-Major Rasilev and I will be 'captured' and provide the information on how the marshes are frozen and passable by tanks. We will tell them that this leads directly to the weakest point in our lines. They will test our theory so it must be set up as a massive *mastroika* (deception). We will weaken the line but bunch camouflaged divisions behind the gap. We will entice their armor to lead the spear point and blow the marshes as they cross. We will drown or massacre the whole fucking bunch of them. They will have concentrated most of their remaining armor and best troops for this final assault. Once we have defeated them, they will be exhausted and demoralized, and ready for your kind attention, comrade General."

Zhukov was electrified. For the next two hours they pored over the maps even as he missed a *Stavka* meeting and critical briefings. They identified units to be put in place, artillery to be pre-sighted, and aircraft to bring in for massed fire support. But it all depended on secrecy. Zhukov would brief Stalin and Shaposhnikov but no one else. He would have to let Rokossovskii in on the secret and a few others but he would keep the number to a minimum.

After they exhausted themselves working the details, Zhukov eyed Dmitry. "This is brilliant, nephew and it will work if they fall for it. But the danger to you and Bear will be immense. You might even be tortured to verify the information." "We are ready, comrade General. This is the moment. I can feel it in every bone of this soldier's body. If we can pull this off, Moscow and the Motherland will be saved and we can go on the offensive. Their supply lines are being constantly harassed. They are not ready for our winter. We saw desert camouflaged tanks brought from Africa to attack us in the last weeks, that all looks pretty desperate to me. Whatever it takes, the Sergeant-Major and I will make the deception happen. We are ready."

Zhukov reached up and put his hands on Dmitry's shoulders and gazed into the ocean blue eyes. "Nephew, we will not talk of rewards as this mission is too sacred to tarnish by that type of discussion. But rewards there will be. I tremble at what you will have to endure but I know that you and your trained Bear are the ones to do it. So with a broken heart I say yes. Let's take three days to prepare and I will brief the *Vozdh*. You and Bear get outfitted and we will take care of the rest."

"Thank you, comrade General. May I suggest that my team is the forward liaison for the operation and that they are responsible for mining the marsh?" "Granted, anything else?" "Only your blessing, uncle, and hold my memory if things don't go as planned." Zhukov looked away as a tear rose in his eyes. This toughest, most brutal of soldiers was in the presence of true bravery and knew it. It was blinding. He kissed Dmitry three times and they parted to accomplish their individual tasks.

Chapter 20

Lenin studied Dmitry carefully. He sat forward in his wheelchair as he framed his response to Dmitry's question. "The army, why the army, Dima? Soon there will be no need for armies. It will be a forgotten profession as socialism marches to victory around the globe. You are better to serve the state and people as an engineer or teacher like your parents." "Beloved uncle, your vision is as always correct but I seem to live more in the present than you. I look at the capitalist invasion, the assault on Poland where my parents died, and the just finished war against the Whites. The movement needed soldiers to fight these actions and that is where I see myself."

Lenin sat back and pulled his comforter more evenly over his body in spite of the summer heat. He appeared shrunken to Dmitry as if some magic had advanced his age 30 years. His translucent skin belied the old vigor and the defiant face and fist thrust into the view of the rest of the world. Periodically his face seemed to slip and almost melt. Dmitry had been crushed when he learned the carefully guarded truth of the Leader's real condition following a stroke. He had asked permission to speak about his decision with him and the doctors had refused. His wife, Krupskaya, had intervened as she knew they owed him a debt too large to repay. They also still mourned the death of his parents and perhaps felt some guilt at having placed both of them together for that mission.

Lenin looked away. "Are you not happy with the Zhukov family? Perhaps someone less military might be a good parent for a while?" "No, that is not it, beloved Uncle. Captain Zhukov is a model Bolshevik and soldier. He understands the military in a communist context. We have talked many hours about this but do not blame him. He did not convert me. My father had always told me when grown to defend the people. 'Dmitry Alexanderovich, always remember the people. Those who are naturally stronger must defend them against the capitalists who would exploit them. They must be protected so the communist state and the dictatorship of the proletariat can work its transformation on society. You must be a Bolshevik soldier, who serves the people, not harming them when he has the strength to do so. Is this clear?'"

"That is how he spoke to me, Uncle. So it has been in my mind for years." Lenin looked again at Dmitry. "Did we all fight so that the old ways would continue? No! The world will change. The time is near. I can feel it in this sorry old body as truth. Yet here we have a most promising young man joining the world's second oldest profession. Dima, I want you to speak with comrade soldier Tukhachevskii about this. He is of course, of your mind, but he is truthful. Share your thoughts with my dashing Red Lieutenant, so young for so much responsibility. He will guide you correctly for he too is a true Bolshevik. The future of our movement lies heavy on me. I wanted it all resolved before I pass but still the capitalists don't give in. They do not understand the inevitability of history and that will be their end."

Lenin paused and studied Dmitry. "Well, we are all young once. The one thing I ask is that you do as your father told you, defend the people! It is the task of the Bolsheviks to do this. Do not be a strong but stupid soldier. Be a smarter one. Know your enemy's move before he makes it. Understand why he does things and use this against him. That is how we bested the left wing reactionaries and the Tsarists. You must fight with your head, not just the arm. I ask this of you."

"Yes, beloved Uncle, I will do as you ask. I will remember my father's words and always protect the peasants and workers. I hope I can also be smart." "Well, we can help with that. Paper please, and a pen," Lenin asked. He could barely write but write he did and the note asked that Dmitry be admitted to the new state military academy in Moscow immediately. "Study hard, young Dima, and please come see me again as you become the soldier you want to be." "Of course, comrade Lenin, I am honored to be in your presence."

Lenin brushed this off but motioned Dmitry closer. He hugged him in a feeble grip and as his breath rattled against Dmitry's ear he whispered, "Beware comrade Stalin." Dmitry jumped back as if struck by an electrical charge and stared at the now enfeebled leader of the greatest revolution the world had ever seen. As he stared, Lenin just held his eye and nodded. They never saw each other again.

Chapter 21

Dmitry had recalled this conversation in the past, always with a certain pride that he had the blessing of the Leader himself for his career. Today he recalled the words on fighting smarter and took them into his mind and heart. That would be the only way that he and Bear could survive this mission, by being smarter. Yet, their survival was not as important as the success of this ploy. Dmitry understood that, but to be able to fight the fascists again in what he knew would be a long and bloody war was critical.

Two objectives were to be considered but one subordinate to the other. He sighed as he moved through Red Army HQ to the room assigned to him and Bear for their planning. Smarter, they must fight smarter! His brain was locked on this thought as he entered the steel-doored room in time to catch Bear napping. "Well, Sergeant-Major, this is what you do when your country and people are under attack by foreign monsters, sleep?" Bear grinned and eyed Dmitry, "No, my comrade Colonel, I was just musing on what bit of major trouble you had gotten us involved in this time. I feel it must be something truly awe inspiring and was just trying to figure how we are going to lure the fucking Hitlerites into the comrade General's trap."

As always Bear had worked out the plan, and Dmitry smiled at the one-upmanship. How the hell had he figured out the core of the plan with absolutely no information? "Have you been talking with comrade General Zhukov?" Dmitry asked and for once Bear could honestly reply, "No." Will wonders never cease, Dmitry thought and pulled up a seat next to Bear and unrolled the map of which only two copies existed, one was his and one was Zhukov's. "Come close my friend, and I think this might just excite your bearish instincts for hunting the hunter."

Huddled over the map, the two old comrades began by discussing the tactical situation on Rokossovskii's front. This consisted primarily of the failure of the recent fascist attacks and the limited but successful push back by the Soviets to get the Germans out of artillery range of the Kremlin. All of this implied not Soviet victory but Hitlerite exhaustion. The trap had to be designed to present a signal opportunity for a spectacular breakthrough and a 20 kilometer rush to capture the Kremlin.

This would be irresistible to the German command which was under intense pressure from Hitler and the General Staff to wind up this phase of the campaign. At the same time overwhelming force had to be in place to utterly destroy the attack and push the fascists even further back from Moscow's gates. Deception (*mastroika*) was the key to these seemingly conflicting goals and here were two of the best at the game preparing the welcome for their friends from the west.

Dmitry smiled as Bear succinctly framed the operational goals for the plan. He then moved on to discuss how the lure could be set. Bear walked around the room musing, "We can make a show of withdrawing troops and guns and sending them to help out at Tula where things are very tough still, although they have done wonders stopping "Hurrying Heinz." However, before we do that we have to move a heavy division in place to replace them without being seen. This implies night movement. We can't deploy as early as the comrade General wants, we need time to get the troops in place. I think two nights would do it."

Dmitry picked up the phone and asked to be put through to the General. Zhukov came on the line, heard him out and OK'd the delay. He also said that was the longest and only delay permitted. The operation had to move ahead no matter what. Secondly, the newly arrived 1st Siberian Shock Division was perfect for the task. They had been in some hard fighting but were nearly at full strength and even more critical, their armor and artillery were all in place. Dmitry and Bear moved on to other planning and decided it was time to get Dmitry's staff in on the plan to draft orders.

The call went out for now Lt. Colonel Galanin and Major Shanislav. The room was getting crowded but the two new invitees were buoyed up by the focused but positive looks on Dmitry and Bear's faces. "Comrades" Dmitry began, "We have a significant opportunity to hurt the enemy. But we have to be ready to execute in three days, no delays. Here is the situation." Drawing them to the map Dmitry outlined the plan and goals. As Galanin and Piotr absorbed the magnitude of the operation; they were by turns amazed, excited, and overwhelmed.

"Gods, comrade Colonel," Piotr stated, "This could save the city and throw the fascists on their heels. We could swing into offensive action." "That is so, comrade Major, but the blow administered must be of overwhelming strength and depth. It must cripple the Hitlerite forces north of the city completely and allow us to push them back at least 20 kilometers or more. To do that, we need absolute cooperation from cucumbers, air, artillery, and armor. Everything must be coordinated, and specific frontal and breakthrough tasks assigned. Is that clear?"

"We have at our disposal the 1st Siberian and we must handle them like a rapier to pierce and wound but not kill. The artillery, armor, and air will be the heavy saber crashing through the fascist front to their vulnerable rear, which we will annihilate. Clear?" Both officers nodded and Dmitry continued. "You three will form the plan today and begin issuing the orders. Only the commander of the 1st Siberian, Rokossovskii, Zhukov, and Shaposhnikov are to be in the loop. The air and artillery will be handled by comrade Major Shanislav. Comrade General Vorolov commanding the artillery has been informed of new requirements by Zhukov but has no further need to know. Surprise is everything. Questions?"

After intense detailed discussions on various issues a lull ensued. Lt. Colonel Galanin took the chance to speak up. "Comrade Colonel, I understand the depleting and replacing strategy but how do we get the fascists to know that the line is weak at that location? Their air forces are curtailed both by the weather and the heavy smoke cover being generated by us and their recon teams are not penetrating our lines. How will they become aware of the opportunity?"

"Oh that's simple" Dmitry replied. "Bear and I

are going to tell them." Spoken in a light tone, the room still went suddenly cold and silent. Shanislav and Galanin exchanged desperate looks. They both began speaking at once but Dmitry held up his hand for silence. "The comrade General has authorized our plan, so we go. This is actually the most critical part of the whole operation and must be handled seamlessly or Bear and I will be awaiting you in warrior's hell. Comrade Sergeant-Major, please give them the outline. This is to be shared with no one, no one but our immediate team and the General."

The looks of amazement grew into astonishment as Bear took them through the personal deception to be carried out by him and Dmitry. Bear wrapped up, "The fascists will clearly want to confirm our statements and proceed with a recon. They must be allowed to see what we want them to see but nothing else. They are too arrogant to really be on guard but we must assume the highest level of paranoia and work from there. Comrades, our *razvedchiki* are the only ones to be seen on the front line and they must play the role to perfection. Then you must be ready for the attack which could come at any time. However, the weather and Berlin will not let them wait too long."

"When the attack begins we must lure them onto the ice of the flooded marsh and from there spring the trap." Piotr and Galanin were now dumbfounded. The plan was brilliant but the risks immense, not just for Bear and Dmitry but indeed the army and the city. They slowly drew themselves to the task and the discussion became general. The orders began to flow and preparations at all levels got underway.

"Comrade Major Shanislav, a word please," Dmitry asked as the meeting broke up. Piotr held back and the others moved out of the small conference room in the underground bunker to attend to thousands of details. "Yes, comrade Colonel," Piotr responded. "Piotr, you know that air and artillery are the main focus of this operation. Please make this your total life for the next few days. Everything depends on their effectiveness. Also, strengthen air cover over the area to prevent German snooping but once we are ready, lighten up a bit to let them sneak a glance. OK?" Piotr nodded.

Dmitry continued, "By the way, how is my sister?" Piotr was astonished at this question. "How did you know?" he asked. "I am GRU, you know. We are supposed to know everything. It's OK; I'm not having you followed. I got a letter from Natash where she mentions one of your visits." Now Piotr blushed. "Oh, she says nothing too personal, just how dreamy this brave young pilot is and how she hopes he visits again and is he OK for her? Of course I answered he is just short of Ivan *Grozny* and she should take all precautions."

At Piotr's crestfallen look, Dmitry smiled and put an arm on his shoulder. "Not at all, brother, I told her you are trustworthy and whatever happens, I bless you both." Piotr now stood straight and with his lean pilot's frame hugged Dmitry. "Perhaps someday you can call me brother in truth," Piotr stated and continued, "She is wonderful, Dmitry. Just what I've dreamed of but I am unsure how to proceed. The war is terrible. I don't know what to do." "What is this here, a pilot actually thinking before acting? That is completely out of character. Follow your heart, dear friend, follow your heart. Whatever happens will be right."

"Now I have a request. During the next day or two I must write some letters. If for some reason I am delayed in my return, I ask you to deliver them. Can you do that for me?" "Of course, Dmitry but you must return, we need you desperately. Look at the brilliance of the plan. I know that the General and Bear were involved but it is yours. It is a work of military art. Please come back!" he concluded as a single tear curved a course down his face.

Dmitry looked away. "I will make every effort to return but I feel a hand on my shoulder with this operation. I cannot shake it so I am a bit apprehensive. Just jitters. Now friend, to work and bring the biggest bang you can and don't forget their rear areas!" After a strong salute Piotr hugged Dmitry and whispered, "May all of heaven and earth support you, brother, and please tell that awful Bear not to forget how to return home to his cave." Dmitry laughed as they parted.

Chapter 22

Even after many years together, albeit infrequent and random encounters after their initial affair, Dmitry was still astounded how this most rational of medical practitioners lost all abandon in lovemaking. It was as if a different being emerged from her body and took both of them into a whirlwind that was soft, immediate, and all encompassing. As he gazed up at the now softly breathing Irina he realized what sacrifice was. He could throw over everything for this woman and go live on the steppe tilling a field.

Now he smiled at that thought. He had learned on the Zhukov farm that he was the worst farmer imaginable. He was everything except stoic, patient, and unimaginative. He wanted those crops, now! She sensed his smile and shifted onto her side. "Ah, you are comparing me to those Berlin hussies you cavorted with in the interest of state security before the war. I think, perhaps that actress, Olga Tschechova? Am I correct?" "No, Irina as usual you have made a diagnosis without enough facts. Actually I was remembering what a terrible farm boy I was." Now her forehead wrinkled in puzzlement. "What does that have to with anything?" she asked tracing a line down his chin.

"Oh, I was just thinking of taking you away so I could have every moment with you. I know, I know," he said as she gazed in him in amazement. "This is in a world without wars and violent death," he added. She now gave him a falsely harsh stare, "Well comrade, a fine thing for a dedicated Bolshevik to say. What about the collective farms. They need more families. That is the state approved method of farming."

Dmitry smiled, "Somehow that doesn't fit my Tolstoyian vision but enough of farming. Irina, let us marry. We are in love and have been for years. We have and will continue to sacrifice for the state but think of our life together. It would inspire my every moment. Children, Irina! The little ones pulling at you and gravely listening to stories of their mother's fame as the Soviet Union's foremost doctor. What a life!"

He knew her answer but he had never directly asked before and somehow this felt right. He understood the terrible danger they were all in, but why wait? Piotr and Natash had stirred something in him. A longing for some stability in his life and he had to admit, the vision of a future where, even if he was not in it, at least his children would be. The foreboding he had experienced about the mission was a heavy drag on him and he knew this was very dangerous. Somehow this feeling had translated into the need for Irina. Not surprising he thought, as he let his hand slip down her hip to the satin of her legs. In her thirties, she was beautiful beyond words.

She had been very still and silent after his question and very slowly he became aware of tears rolling down her cheeks. "What have I done, *mon cher*, to cause this?" he asked. She let the tears fall as if in blessing on his shoulder and chest. "Oh, Dima, I too long for us to be together, with little ones that would drive us crazy. I sometimes, when grabbing a few minutes sleep on the hospital floor, use that thought to calm myself from the storm around me but dearest, it is not to be. Not that I don't love you more than anything in my existence but because I could not bear bringing children into this horror of a world that we are in right now. When the Motherland is safe for new life, I will be your wife and an eager mother but not before. Do you understand, Dima?"

He did, of course, and knew what the answer would be in advance but he was still disappointed. He was also determined not to hurt her. "Of course, I understand. But let us be together more frequently after this mission. I need you." She smiled ever so gently and brushing her hand over his short blond brush cut hair said, "Oh Dima, it means everything to me. We will find the moments and now that we are both stationed in Moscow with two apartments that should be no problem."

Now he smiled, "Yes, all of a sudden there are many vacancies which never existed before in the city. Think of that!" "Dima, how long will you be gone on the mission? I know that you cannot tell me any details but at least give me an idea of the time I'll have to worry myself sick." Dmitry frowned, "Please don't Irina, *dorogoj*. This is my life and I chose it so please don't worry every single day, it will hurt you, but to answer your question, no more than a week." She smiled and brought him closer. "Then we had better make up for that week right now," she said, drawing him over her.

They both enjoyed their first full night's safe sleep since the war began and woke with spirit. As they dressed he told her about Piotr and Natasha. Irina was very excited at this surprise love affair. She had watched Piotr grow as a man from a foolish young pilot to a self-controlled, crafty warrior but with a heart. His constant watching over Dmitry pleased her and allowed her to relax a bit. She knew that all of them, Bear and the men, were too grown for hero worship but the feelings they had for Dmitry were just a notch below that.

They would, and had, done anything for him. No fascist bullet would find him if any of them were around. The news about Piotr and Natasha helped her carry a false front about their parting which she knew she desperately had to maintain to support him. She did not know the exact content of the mission but she did know she had never seen Dmitry so distracted from her. They had to part in a way which supported him. No tears, Major, she thought, no tears! And especially no clinging and empty hopes left to burden him.

Finally, she felt prepared to do this and as he fastened his uniform collar she straightened out his Hero of the Soviet Union and as he teasingly polished her newly awarded Order of the Red Banner, he told her, "Comrades Lt. Colonel Galanin and Pilot Major Shanislav will keep you informed and are ready for you to call at any time." She smiled, said, "Oh I won't bother them, too much!" and laughed. She drew him close and said, *"Do svidaniya,"* kissed him and held him for a moment. Looking in his eye she rubbed his head. Oh, one more kiss she thought and gave him one to remember. As she turned and left she threw over her shoulder her parting comment. "Bring that Bear back with no fur missing or he'll never let you forget it!"

Closing the door she walked straight as a ram-rod to her waiting car where she broke down and sobbed until she had herself under control. She could not be seen entering the new lab building she now commanded in this state. Her driver knew the reason for this very uncharacteristic outburst and as he opened the door for her he saluted and said, "He'll be back before you know it, comrade Major. He is our best and bravest!" She nodded and gripped his arm in thanks and entered the building to carry on.

Chapter 23

The chute rigging hanger at Monino Air Base outside of Moscow was surrounded by GRU troops with orders to shoot to kill anyone within 15 meters of the hangar walls. Inside a small group of intense comrades focused on the huge map mounted on the rigging table. Dmitry had assembled his key team members. They included Bear, Chief of Staff Galanin, Piotr, Felix, and Taka. "Comrades," Dmitry began. "This map represents the operational area. You must commit this to memory. This is and will remain the only operational map for this action. It is in the complete care of comrade Lieutenant Colonel Galanin." Galanin nodded and Dmitry continued.

"Comrades, the safety of our beloved *Mockba* (Moscow) and the beginning of our drive to reclaim our Motherland will both be made possible by the success of this plan. We will use GRU *mastroika* to lure the Hitlerites into a devastating trap from which we will spring a counterattack. This mission is the heart and soul of the plan and only three Marshals of the Soviet Union know of its existence along with comrade Stalin. The requirement for security is paramount. We know there are fascist operatives in Moscow relaying word to their troops, they must not have a word, a single word of this plan!" The men solemnly nodded their understanding.

"Tomorrow night comrade Sergeant-Major and I will para drop from an altitude of 80 meters behind German lines in this region. Comrade Major Shanislav will be flying a specially developed Polikarpov rigged for insertion. We will then be a sergeant and private on recon and we will get ourselves captured." The room became very still, even those who already knew the plan were again crushed by the risk their two comrades were taking.

Dmitry continued, "Everything depends on our 'selling', as the Americans say, the fascists on our betrayal of the Motherland and revealing to them the weakness of this sector of our lines. As of today, the 1st Siberian Shock Division is now in camouflaged position to launch a crushing attack against the Hitlerites. These men are tough and ready to strike a blow for Stalin and the Motherland. Comrade General Zhukov, who commanded them in Mongolia, states that they eat nails for breakfast and wash it down with a mix of vodka and fuel which allows them to shit bullets and bombs."

"They are very tough and very dedicated. They will do their job. In addition, comrade Major Shanislav will direct the ground artillery and 'flying infantry' in a crushing bombardment of both the Hitlerite front lines and rear area. The surprise and overwhelming force which has been assembled will drive a wedge through this area of the fascist lines and cause the whole of their forces to withdraw to regroup giving *Mockba* some breathing room. This plan is a good one but we must all do our assignments to perfection for it to succeed."

"While the Sergeant-Major and I are 'captured' Lt. Colonel Galanin will be in overall command. You sergeants will receive twenty good men each from the *razvedchiki* ranks. You will be the skeleton force occupying the weakened sector of our lines. The 1st Siberian understands that comrade Felix Vasilev is to be obeyed in all matters. Lt. Colonel Galanin will remain behind the lines to help direct force response with additional troops. Is that all clear?"

Felix spoke up, "Yes, it is comrade Colonel, but how are you going to get the Hitlerites to attack and how do we treat their recon forces?" "Excellent questions, comrade Sergeant and by the way please wear Lieutenant's insignia for this mission in case someone does not treat Sergeants with the proper respect." Felix nodded and Dmitry continued. "Let me answer your second question first. How should you treat the inevitable fascist recon? Gently but firmly is the method, just how you treat your favorite cow. Let her have her way so she is happy but only within the confines of your field. Let the Germans feel about but do not let them penetrate your front. They must have the sense that the recon was mainly a success. Is that clear?"

Again the team nodded. "Good, because the Sergeant-Major's and my life will depend on it. How will we get them to attack and how will the trap be sprung? I think you will like the details that the Sergeant-Major has cooked up. Comrade, please unveil the *mastroika* plan to the team." As Bear began to speak, eyes widened and pulses quickened. Some punched the air with their fists with visions of the destruction of their hated enemies. Those hated enemies had virtually had their way since entering the Motherland almost six months ago. Still they all quailed at the risk to Dmitry and Bear and swore to themselves to get them back alive. That part of the plan was the most frightening of all.

After the meeting Bear had Taka assist him with the chutes. The low level jump required a perfect chute to bring the jumper down safely. They would be in the air only about 10 seconds and Bear hoped the snow was soft where they were going to land. Taka, who had only done the one night jump and never a low altitude one, was overwhelmed by the details which the Bear rattled off as they prepped the chutes. He could only think that these men were the best of the very best of the Red Army and this gave him faith in their return. They worked on into the night to get everything just right.

Meanwhile Felix and Dmitry went over endless details. The *mastroika* must be complete to function and the trap sprung with precision. It would all be in Felix's capable hands. Dmitry did not tell him that the papers promoting him to Lieutenant, for the successful completion of the mission, were drafted and sitting with the other promotions and commendation recommendations with General Zhukov. Felix did not need any distractions at this moment. After the session they began to assemble the uniforms and weapons that Bear and Dmitry would wear and carry as part of the deception. The day passed quickly and finally the jump off day arrived.

Dmitry handed the letters to Piotr as they began their planning for the actual drop. Piotr was still nervous about accepting them but knew that he would only upset Dmitry by any further comments. He did decide to say a word about him and Natasha. "Dima, I fly after this mission to the Urals to see your sister. I will of course tell her that you are now a great hero after an incredible mission and are safely housed in the Kremlin bomb shelter. I hope that will be the case. I also intend to ask her to marry as soon as possible so we can start work on our family."

Dmitry didn't wait for the end of the sentence but gave Piotr a great hug. "That is for the best, brother. I wish you both all the happiness in the world. I know in my heart that she will accept. Good man, Piotr, good man." With that accomplished, they got down to the drop planning.

One last visit remained for Dmitry. That evening he was shown into Zhukov's office under the Kremlin.

The guards were aghast at the most dismal private in the Red Army being invited to the General's office but obeyed the pass and allowed Dmitry in. His appearance was anything other than soldierly, a dirty, unkempt uniform topped by a sallow complexion of a man who had not shaved in days with the dirtiest lice ridden hair imaginable. At the sight Zhukov slammed the door and made to hug Dmitry. "No, comrade General, these bugs are hell. You don't want them!" "Hell," said the old tough campaigner, "They were my bothers during the Civil War but perhaps you are right. Is everything prepared?"

Dmitry and the General huddled and talked through the plans with Zhukov making a few discreet notes to himself for tasks to be accomplished. The 'broken' mike in his office offered silent guard to the security of the plan. The NKVD would send a fixer but by then it would be too late.

"My son, I am sending you to hell and it breaks my heart. The only faith I have is that you will report to me right here after the success of your mission. I live for that day. I don't pray very much as a good Bolshevik, but I think I must make an exception in this case and ask your parents to intercede with St. George for your protection. Come back, Dima, come back. I need you to help me to win this war. Bless you and that old ratty Bear of yours. Please tell him the same."

"I will tell him, most respected father, and I will come back to you. Hold me in your thoughts," and with that Dmitry threw a salute that belied his ragged appearance. The General said, "Fuck the bugs!" and gave him a powerful hug as he opened the door for him to leave. The guards could only stare dumbfounded at these events as Dmitry exited the bomb shelter. Zhukov looked skyward and his lips moved in the promised prayer.

At 0200 Piotr and Felix met Dmitry and the Bear at the silent, darkened hangar. They carefully got the two men into their chutes and arranged their personal gear. They would drop without weapons or skis due to the extreme complexity of the jump. Piotr would send these down after getting a safe drop signal from them. All was ready. The flight would not last twenty minutes and they would ride the wings of the Polikarpov just the way they had trained for these missions years ago. The jump would be by static line attached to the reinforced struts of the biplane.

Dmitry silently hoped that the reinforcing was enough for the force of the pull on Bear's line. They could not jump simultaneously as the chance of them tangling was too great. The piloting skills required to keep the aircraft level and not lose too much position were supremely challenging. Piotr knew this and the intense concentration written on his face exposed his self-discipline to Dmitry. A final round of hugs and "*Do svidaniya*" all around and Dmitry and Bear took their places on the alternate sides of the PO-2's cockpit and braced for takeoff.

Piotr brought the darkly mottled craft into a gentle altitude gaining spiral. From his peak altitude over the city he would cut his engine and glide them down to the specified 80 meters over the site. Visibility was broken with clouds but at 80 meters all was clear. They were headed for a road intersection well known to them all just inside the German lines. The air was bracing, Dmitry thought at about minus 25 degrees C. Any more bracing and vital body parts might begin to fall off. He glanced over at Piotr just in time to see he and Bear exchange a hand communication that went 'Would you like some wing wagging?' from Piotr and Bear's expressive silent response that conveyed very negative wishes for the pilot's future if he tried it!

Dmitry smiled for the one thousandth time at the behavior of his team members and reflected on his good fortune to be serving with them. The flight was quickly over and in the silence broken only by the howling wind, Piotr looked at Bear and held up one finger, one minute. He checked position and altitude, brought the plane into a gentle curve and set up five fingers which lost one each ten seconds until at the last

one Bear cannon balled off the wing and was clear.
Piotr arced back gently and did the same for Dmitry.
When over the same spot Dmitry cannon balled over
the side and Piotr again arced gently around watching
his altitude. He didn't want to start his engine until a
few miles away.

He saw Bear's light signal and gave one last
rudder push over and dropped their gear and glided for
the German rear west of their position. Another good
Bolshevik said a prayer, restarted his engine, gained
altitude, and headed for Monino.

The tug from the static line was vicious. It
jerked Dmitry hard over as he strove to keep his feet
down as the chute deployed. Counting to six he prepared for impact and right at eight he hit the snow.
Thank god the snow is deep, he thought as he rolled on
landing. He immediately grabbed the chute and began
pulling it in. Bear was just meters away and then the
weapons and skis arrived. Gods, Piotr is good. What a
fucking pilot, dead on position and we're alive! He
whispered to Bear, "OK?" Bear responded with a grunt
as he unpacked skis and weapons. They buried the
chutes and other containers and used their skis to
smooth the snow. Hopefully more snow would arrive
soon. They geared up and got their bearings and began
to ski toward the fascist lines about six klicks away.

With their white camouflage outfits and heavy
white *Ushanka* caps they stood out against the forest
as they knew they would. This was the inept recon patrol of regular troops, not the ultimate stealth of the
razvedchiki. Meant to be discovered, they continued
on for a few klicks and altered course to come in on

the German flank as if they were totally disoriented and going parallel rather than perpendicular to the lines.

As they silently skied they could hear armor moving in the snow and the muffled exhaust of other vehicles. They must not appear too inept so they altered course again. "Good fortune," whispered Dmitry, "Look surprised." At that moment a loud '*Achtung!*" echoed through the forest and Dmitry made a show of slipping and falling just as Bear threw up his hands and dropped his PPsh. A trio of German soldiers approached them with weapons ready. Dmitry made a great show of rolling and flinging his rifle away and slowly gaining his feet only to be shoved down again by one of the grenadiers. "Stay on your butt, dirt!" the German shouted in Russian.

Bear just stood stock still and didn't move as the patrol searched him for weapons, removing his pistol and fighting knife. They then got Dmitry up and searched him but without his rifle he was weaponless. Dmitry took a minute to observe their captors. They were mostly unshaven and did not appear as *ubermensch*. They smelled almost as bad as Dmitry and were also infested with lice. They did not have proper winter gear but appeared to be layered scarecrows with straw appearing in weird locations to try and gain some insulation from the cold. Their boots were almost as large as snowshoes as they were wrapped in straw and then blanket material.

Dmitry noticed the extreme difficulty they had using the bolt action on their Mausers. The oil must be frozen he guessed. They also removed any food that

Dmitry and Bear possessed even though it was just the poorest rations imaginable. This was all as reported by the partisans in the area. These troops were not being supplied in large enough quantity or even the correct supplies for this environment. While looking cowed, Dmitry smiled internally. They were told to remove their skis and hustled along through the snow to the local ranking officer, where they were forced to sit in the snow in the open until daylight.

The *Waffen SS* officer still managed to look sharp despite his troop's appearance. His shaved face was thin but determined as he examined Dmitry and Bear with a sneer. His insignia were camouflaged against Soviet partisans and snipers but there was no question of who was in command. His team of six grenadiers was in a semi-circle with rifles and burp guns trained on the prisoners. A small eye movement launched the sergeant into action as he grabbed a private's Mauser and drove the butt into Dmitry's stomach, as Dmitry doubled over; the sergeant brought the butt up under his chin with enough force to lift Dmitry's long frame off the ground. Dmitry lay in the snow with missing teeth and blood scattered around him, out cold.

The officer turned to Bear and said in Russian, "Your turn unless you have something to say, slime." Bear came to attention and saluted and spoke in German, "*Jawohl Mein Sturmbannfuhrer* (major), I do have something to say." The major eyed Bear suspiciously and opened his white camouflage jacket to see his uniform. Bear was wearing a full sergeant's insignia and his Orders. The major said, "Well, you speak

German. Why are we so fortunate?" "Because, I was assigned to an *SS* unit in Poland when we met in September '39," Bear stated. The officer looked intrigued. "Tell me about Poland." "Not much to tell," Bear replied. "We took our half and you took yours. We were assigned to establish the new border and occupy a line directly linked with the Germans. On our side I did participate in the forest affair."

At this statement the officer's head snapped up and he eyed Bear suspiciously. He brought one of his men forward and put the burp gun against the side of Bear's head. "NKVD?" Bear smiled and spat. "You must be kidding, *Sturmbannfuhrer*. They would shoot me any day just as they would you. I'm what they call the son of a kulak. My parents and most of the family were starved to death in the Ukraine in '32 and that's when I joined the Red Army. They have a nice heavy file on me, don't worry."

Dmitry groaned and rolled onto his side attempting to stand but was still too disoriented to make it. "And this one, what is he?" Bear responded "Oh, he's a stupid Georgian but not so bad. They are loyal like puppies." As Dmitry struggled the officer shouted at him in Georgian. Dmitry responded and fell back into the snow. The officer appeared satisfied with this. "Well, we'll shoot you both in a few minutes, my Russian friend," the officer commented as he lit a cigarette. Bear appeared to shrink in size but found a thin, hollow voice with which to respond. "*Mein Sturmbannfuhrer*, now that we are captured, there is no future for us on the Soviet side. We go to the GULAG or a penal battalion and die anyway. Your offer is therefore a good one but I have another one for you to consider." The officer looked bored to death and his men just smirked. "OK, my Russian friend, what is it?"

Bear continued with a shifty expression on his face. "Perhaps, *Sturmbannfuhrer*, there is a way that we can help you and save ourselves to fight for you. I know that a Russian division is forming in your army. It is being manned by Russians who hate the Soviets and Stalin and would fight to see them defeated. The private and I would like to fight with them. However, I think we can help your cause further. The line in your front is all that stands between you and Red Square. It is thin and inflexible. Wherever you attack, we thin out the line elsewhere to support the threatened sector. As you know this has led to a stalemate. I can show you where to attack that will defeat this maneuver. What do you think?"

The officer controlled his expression very well but Bear saw the tiniest glimmer in his dark eyes. Bear wrung his *ushanka* in his hands and looked desperately at the officer. The Nazi paced and asked, "What is this, a sergeant knows everything about the Soviet line. Are you really a Marshal?" Bear nodded and spoke, "*Nein, Herr Sturmbannfuhrer*, but I have moved about the line very much doing the maneuvers I just described. I know the line for about three or four klicks from the point directly in front of you." The officer studied Bear as he spoke. He drew his pistol and stepped next to Dmitry and hauled him to his feet. Placing the revolver against his head, he said, "Well, we don't need two of you, that's for sure. I'll get rid of this one and we'll go on with the plan."

Bear looked non-committal but stated, "*Sturm-bannfuhrer*, consider, this man can get his comrades to switch sides when you attack. The troops are all Georgian and the officers Russian. They virtually hate each other. The Georgians speak no Russian other than the simplest commands and the officers no Georgian. The unit is ripe for collapse; this piece of shit here can be very helpful to us. You can shoot him afterward or let him also fight for you."

The officer lowered the revolver. He nodded to his men and turned and left. The soldiers kept Dmitry and Bear standing as Dmitry spit out teeth and blood and filled his mouth with snow to try and stem the bleeding. The wait got longer, two hours passed and the Germans rotated to warm themselves at a nearby fire while Bear and Dmitry just froze in place.

The officer returned with his *Standartenfuhrer* (colonel). He in turn questioned Bear, ignoring Dmitry until finished. He then turned to Dmitry and asked, "So, what do you think of your officers?" Dmitry looked frightened and looked at Bear who nodded. "Great leader, they are idiots. They do not even speak our language and are drunk all the time. We Georgians know how to fight and we despise them." The German major translated. Next the colonel asked, "What about Stalin?" "Oh," Dmitry replied "This is a bit more difficult but we must say that he is Georgian but not Georgian. He lives like a Tsar so what is he? We no longer know and really don't care. We just want to go home." The *Standartenfuhrer* nodded and left with the *Sturmbannfuhrer*. "Conduct the recon," he stated as they left to examine maps.

Bear and Dmitry were fed and allowed to warm at the fire. Bear kept up a German conversation with the privates and told them of all the desperation on the Soviet side. He insinuated that the Red Army might stage a coup against the Communists since most soldiers were peasants like him whose families had been destroyed by the collective farm movement in the 1930's. The Germans listened but didn't say much.

The *Sturmbannfuhrer* returned and motioned for Bear to follow. Back at the HQ hut, he motioned to a map spread on the table. Bear immediately walked over and looked and put his finger on their current position which was unmarked. "Well, sergeant, you seem to know your business. What is your name?" Bear responded, "Sergeant Mikhail Nogorov, *Herr Sturmbannfuhrer.*" "Well, sergeant, it looks like you get to live another day. Tonight you will accompany me and my team on a tour of these lines of yours. We will want you to mark units on the map and we will see if they truly exist. First though, what is this field in front of this section of the line?" "Sir, that is not a field but marshland. It is currently frozen through."

What Bear was hiding was that, yes, this area normally would be marshland but it was now flooded marshland and instead of being frozen through the GRU team estimated about three meters of water under one meter of ice. The *Sturmbannfuhrer* continued, "Interesting. So tell me about the line." "Well, it is the weakest in front of the marsh and strongest where the marsh shrinks and trees are the primary cover. However, please remember what I said about moving troops around to threatened areas." "Yes, yes, I have that," the major responded impatiently. "Tell me more about the terrain and the troops. How many troops, arms, armor, artillery, all of it." Bear went into a workman-like recital of the defense in the marsh area always highlighting that the frozen marsh was like a highway.

Soon the major was satisfied and sent for his sergeant and sent Bear back to Dmitry. He told Dmitry, "The recon is tonight. You are too worthless to be of any use but if you do exactly as I say we might just keep you alive." Dmitry shrank and just nodded. With his mouth and jaw swollen beyond proportion he could do little else and they both huddled together for warmth.

Bear was kicked awake at about 2 AM. The clear cold evening was well lit by a full moon. Thank God, Bear thought, it will make the recon a bit tougher. The *Sturmbannfuhrer* and his men were in black with darkened faces. They told Bear to shed his coat and use a German woolen overcoat to darken his large aspect. They then smeared ash onto his face and the *Sturmbannfuhrer* signaled for them to move out. "No speaking from this point. Hand signals only." They all nodded. Bear was next to the sergeant who gave him an evil grin and fingered his fighting knife to bring home the point, run and die.

"Damn, the marsh is lit up like a boulevard!" the major cursed. Indeed, nothing could be more dramatic than the winter moon on the new snow. The glittering surface would show any movement or attempt at probing. The Soviet line was completely silent, seemingly sleeping. Felix had spotted the fascist recon team and took a deep breath at its import. He silently summoned a runner and gave him a note for Lt. Colonel Galanin. The note alerted him to the probe. The import of the German action would be clear to the Lt. Colonel.

The *Sturmbannfuhrer* was disappointed that there would be no closing on the line in this area or probing of the marsh depth. Also, mines were an unknown in the officer's mind. He, of course, did not really trust Bear but had not yet poked any holes in his story. Plus what would be the purpose? Everyone knew they would attack in the next few days. Deception to what end, he wondered. Snapping back into the present he signaled his team to move just behind the marsh bank to the left to probe in the woods.

They continued along the bank and into the forest, slipping easily over the frozen creek which fed the marsh, and pushing closer to the Soviet line. Bear signaled the officer to the possibility of mines. The officer nodded and moved Bear to the front of the line. He signaled one of the enlisted men to give Bear a bayonet which he used to probe the snow ahead of them. Bear expected to find some mines which were hopefully duds, salted into the area and soon his bayonet struck one. He broke off a branch and stuck it next to the mine and moved forward repeating the action as required. Soon they were just yards from the wire and trench system.

The *Sturmbannfuhrer* detailed a man to watch Bear and moved ahead with his sergeant. As Felix had planned they got to the trench after burrowing in the snow under the very inexpertly laid wire and noted the sleeping men. There was no watch. These fucking

Russians are pathetic, the major thought. No guard. They are just plain incompetent as we have proved since entering this god-forsaken mess of a country. He made some mental notes and slipped back into the forest. He still felt uneasy about the marsh but no plan presented itself. He and his sergeant conferred but no possibility emerged.

The recon seemed to confirm Bear's story but it was maddeningly incomplete. Perhaps a snatch might just turn the trick he thought. He and the sergeant headed back towards the line and returned to the thinly manned trench line. Now they saw Felix on guard. Shit and double shit, the major thought. Someone woke up or might have heard them. They dropped the snatch plan and headed back to camp.

On their return the *Sturmbannfuhrer* and his sergeant headed for the command hut. All of the German unit and staff chiefs in the local area were assembled here. They placed the Soviet line on the map and detailed some of the artillery they had seen. No armor was seen but that didn't mean much. The assembled officers tried to get more details out of the two reconnaissance participants but not much more was forthcoming. This was like a stripper at the penultimate G-string, close but not close enough. The frustration in the room was unbelievable.

Finally the general spoke up. "Enough, we have orders to attack. We have a deserter who is dead unless we win. He has laid out the situation for us. There is only a small risk if we use his information over our own. We will use his information but plan for surprises. We attack 24 hours from now. *Sturmbannfuhrer*, I want them made to talk more but not killed; when the time for the attack comes I have a special place for them in the line. Understood?" "*Jawohl, Mein General!*" "Good, let's get down to planning. The operation will be simplistic in the extreme. We will drive forward and end the drive in Red Square. We will send the panzers across the marsh to threaten their line at its weakest point. Hopefully they will draw on other line units to support that drive. Therefore, the bulk of the infantry goes in on the flanks, in the woods. There are mines, so early tonight we begin clearing them. See to it. Finally, I want all of our panzers in the center in two lines, maximum force in a small area."

"Get opinions from Engineering regarding panzer spacing on the ice. Keep them concentrated and break through the line. No artillery fire until the panzers are on the marsh, then devastate the forward Russian line and the panzers should break through with little trouble. Do not stop to mop up infantry but keep going and let the flank attacks blow the fucking Russians to hell. Questions? All right, this is it. This is the final blow that will collapse this whole fucking Bolshevik house of cards. *Der Fuhrer* will know that it was his personal guard that forced the issue and ended this blasted stalemate, the rewards will be immense, maybe even estates in Poland and Russia. Make the blow severe and they will break. I can feel it. *Heil Hitler! Sieg Heil!*" There was further detailed discussion and the plan was set in motion for the next morning at 0500.

It was a long bad day for Bear and Dmitry. Thank god they were only being beaten, Dmitry thought, as for the tenth time he told them all he could gush out of his broken mouth regarding his phony Red Army career. Bear was the same but try as they might the Germans recognized that a simple beating was not really effective against him so they used the carrot and stick. Bear had saved a few tidbits for this moment and soon all parties became bored and just left the two bloodied and swollen Russians in the snow. Bear and Dmitry slept to escape the pain and late that night they were led forward to a waiting Panzer IV and with their hands tied led up onto the tank body for their part in the assault.

Chapter 24

The pre-dawn was frozen, dark, and held little hope for Dmitry and Bear. Their erstwhile 'allies' had a special treatment in store for them if they had lied about the absence of anti-tank mines in the marsh. The center tank, where the armor commander was located, was to be their vehicle. However, instead of being safely inside they were tied to attachment points on the Panzer IV. Bear had been accorded a position of possible survival on the rear of the turret. He was secured to the cable towing apparatus which allowed him to shelter behind the turret. If anything went wrong he was also an easy pistol shot from the tank commander.

Dmitry was obviously considered of lesser importance. The short, squat 75 mm gun of the Panzer IV was designed for anti-personnel action and to this they had looped some ropes over and around and through those lines, binding Dmitry's wrists. If the concussive shock of the cannon firing did not kill him, the spray of machine gun fire from the Soviet lines certainly would. Bear went stoically to his position but when Dmitry saw what they had in store for him, he struggled like a madman. Screaming in Georgian, falling on his knees and begging, he distracted the guards enough that they did not notice the extra coils he gripped as they attached him to the cannon.

Finally, he just collapsed in a nervous distraught heap and figured this was it for him in truth. He could not see Bear or anything else but the forest surrounding the tank positions. The engines whined and struggled to turn over in the below zero atmosphere where the air was heavy with only a darkening future. As they rumbled forward, crushing trees and smashing through drifted snow, Dmitry began to assess escape options and decided that even the extra line he had accumulated would only ensure that as he slid off the tank he would be caught under the treads and crushed into jelly. Holy gods, he thought.

The panzer line moved forward and Dmitry scanned the disposition with interest, if somewhat fatalistically. There were two rows of various Panzer III's and IV's with approximately 15 vehicles in each row. Spacing was wide at about 50 meters apart. Dmitry guessed that this was a safety margin for the marsh ice. He just smiled inwardly. Good luck, he thought. Their front was about a klick wide so this concentrated line was intended to smash though light infantry opposition and open a path for the grenadiers to follow.

Dmitry had no idea regarding air support but he had heard the fascists complaining of their air force's poor showing in recent days since Kesselring and some of his best units had been pulled out. Dmitry pondered the Soviet plan and decided it had a good possibility of success which warmed his, he believed, short lived heart. The line rolled forward onto the marsh and thank god the ice held as they moved toward the Soviet line about two klicks away.

Dmitry could not see Felix huddled forward of the Soviet line in a carefully camouflaged bunker on the edge of the marsh ice. From this spot Felix and his small team were in radio phone contact with Piotr's ground control, Lt. Colonel Galanin, and the commander of the 1st Siberian. Little did the Germans know that their camp had been surrounded with the new sound receptors and their crews had informed Felix of the warm-up of the panzers. Everyone was ready and with the Siberians about a klick behind the Soviet 'line', the response was going to be very rapid. Felix strained through his night glasses to see any sign of the panzers and at that moment they moved onto the marsh ice. His breathing stayed regular but his heart accelerated and returned to normal as he saw the plan coming to fruition.

He signaled Piotr and Galanin. He personally spoke with the Siberian commander and readied all units. His team of eight *razvedchiki* headed by Taka was standing by to perform critical tasks as required. Felix dropped the glasses and said a prayer to the Holy Mother for Dmitry and Bear. He now felt the attacking Soviets didn't need any prayers. They were ready. At that moment the sound crews spotted and alerted him to the infantry movement on the flanks. A very, very cold smile appeared on Felix's lips at this news. He alerted the Siberians.

Now it all depended on the flooded marsh and the aggressiveness of the fascists. As usual the fucking *SS* was in the lead and showing their wonderful arrogance. The infantry was far behind. Perfect, perfect, Felix thought. He turned to the explosives team and raised his clenched fist as the panzers drove onto the explosive laden ice. He watched as the first line gingerly took the marsh and then sped up as the ice held. The second rank showed no hesitation at all as at the prescribed interval they drove onto the ice and it still held.

Felix breathed again. Now the timing was critical. He could not look at the explosives team as he kept the glasses to his eyes to see them reach the firing spot. At just a tick short of that he saw a Soviet soldier tied to the lead tank and his heart burst. It was the Colonel! My Gods, look what they've done. He silently hand signaled Taka to see the scene and act. Felix had to ignore this scene and put Dmitry and Bear out of his mind. He had to focus. The whole attack was orchestrated on his next action. Perhaps a second or two late but with great firmness, he pulled down his clenched fist.

As always with explosives there was that silent moment pregnant with the future and then the marsh in the rear of the two panzer lines erupted. At the same time Soviet artillery began to shell the marsh banks and the German flanks, probing for the infantry. Now the sides of the marsh exploded with the next set of charges and the free ice shelf moved and groaned as if the Motherland herself was throwing off her oppressors. In the split second this took to happen, Taka and his team sprinted for the center tank in perfect camouflage in the still dark winter morning. With all the confusion and German lack of ground support they were not seen. Their mission was to rescue Dmitry. They had not yet seen Bear but as always Bear interceded for himself. Straining at the line attaching him to the tank rear he could just reach the back of the turret hatch where the commander was trying to grasp what was happening as the ground itself began to move and tilt! Bear slammed into the back of the hatch throwing the commander into the tank on top of the driver. The tank immediately did a hard right ninety degree turn at full speed and chewed into its wingman on the right.

Both tanks were locked together but still capable of machine gun and cannon fire. At that moment the tank they had run into began to wildly spray machine gun fire but had no targets. One of Taka's men went down and another was grazed. The *razvedchiki* hit the ice and as the spray moved away they bolted for Dmitry's tank about fifty meters to their front. The tank that Bear had incapacitated got back into the action and fired several wild cannon shots which deafened and burned Dmitry. Not too many more of those and I'll have to hand in my Party card, Dmitry thought. Simultaneously *razvedchiki* swarmed over the tank and tossed grenades into the unsecured hatch. Smoke and screams billowed from the interior. Dmitry felt himself manhandled down the tank side and barely conscious was carried fireman style for the Soviet lines. Taka jubilantly discovered Bear and freed him also.

The ice became a living moving animal. After Taka's signal, the second line of charges just behind the first Panzer line erupted throwing ice and tanks into the air. Immediately the front line began to slide backwards with screaming engines and gears. As panzers began to sink and slide into the water or each other their panicked crews desperately sought to escape. Pre-sighted Maxim heavy machine guns took them down no matter how innovative their escape plan. The armored pride of the *Waffen SS* Division *Das Reich* was disappearing from view into waters well below life supporting temperature. Their amazed commanders could only listen to the hysterical radio reports they were receiving and hurriedly send rescue groups forward.

However, the stunned grenadiers could only stop and stare at the spectacle provided for them in the now black, white, and red mosaic. Soon the work of the ice was done and no living German moved on the ice as the last of the Panzers went to the bottom of the flooded zone. This segment of the battlefield became eerily silent with some of the tanks showing turrets or guns from chaotic angles of repose. Others had simply disappeared into the deeper waters. Even as the elated and stunned Soviets watched, the ice started to re-freeze and seal the German fate.

Taka and his team had no time to observe the fate of the panzers. Moving over the area that had not been demoed they struggled against the wildly bucking ice. They alternately ran or crawled toward the safety of the Soviet bank as the ice began to crack and float even in their area. The moment they broke cover of some up-thrust ice, the Germans on the opposite bank began firing at them. Waving their men on, Taka and Lev turned to spray PPsh rounds on the fascists and satisfyingly saw some go down.

The man carrying Dmitry put him down for greater safety and they all grabbed Dmitry's shoulders and began hauling him over the surrealistic icescape. The other *razvedchiki* assisted Taka and Lev by keeping up a full fusillade of fire to force the Germans' heads down. Bear and his helper used the ice as barricades as they stumbled forward and reached the fake Soviet line. They literally threw Dmitry over the top and into the trench as fascist shells began to explode around them. Taka and the remains of his team fell back leaving two dead on the ice and several wounded. They knew they had to vacate this line for the Soviet rear as fascist artillery would be targeting this area.

The German infantry assault was still going ahead without their armored spearhead. Felix made a brief appearance to hurry them on their way and radioed the Siberians to send stretcher teams to his coordinates. Felix had no time other than to lean over and kiss Dmitry on the forehead and pat his shoulder. He gave Bear a bone breaking hug and Bear solemnly saluted the Lieutenant's insignia Felix was wearing, grinning. They parted and got back to work.

The stretcher teams arrived and loaded Dmitry and the other wounded *razvedchiki* onto the stretchers. As they began to move towards an aid station the air around them erupted with a deep, dark hurrah as the Siberians moved forward. At the same time Piotr led his Il-2's in an ear shattering low level assault on the German artillery. The Battle of Moscow Marsh moved into high gear. All Bear and Taka cared about was getting Dmitry to an aid station so they just watched their brothers move into combat and kept up the pace for the aid station. Taka sent two of the *razvedchiki* forward to get the doctors prepared.

Dmitry's injuries were complex so extra care and effort was required for an effective treatment. Bear and Taka thought he was simultaneously suffering concussion, bleeding from his ears, internal bleeding, burns, and exposure. His pulse was incredibly weak and he surfaced periodically from unconsciousness or called out orders related to the River Vop battle. They soothed him as much as they could and finally got to a forward aid station where the Division's Chief Medical Officer was waiting. A hasty exam confirmed everything that Bear and Taka feared and more. The burns were localized but severe and there was a hidden bullet wound that no one had noticed in his thigh. The surgeon ordered morphine and immediate evacuation to a full hospital.

Taka turned to Bear, "Sergeant-Major I must return to support comrade Sergeant Felix. Can you oversee the return of the comrade Colonel to the hospital?" Bear nodded and stepped towards Taka as the team's attention focused on him. "All of you, *razvedchiki* and you comrade Sergeant Sharadze, you have a comrade for life in the Bear. I thank you for my rescue but I will always honor and protect you for saving the comrade Colonel. He must and will fight again, thanks to you. All Victory to the Red Army! *Spasibo, bolshoj spasibo*, comrades! Good hunting!"

With that he hugged each man in turn and as a Sergeant-Major he saluted and held his salute until Taka returned it. This was the reverse of the usual protocol demonstrating the respect he held for the Georgian. Taka turned and ordered his team back to the fight but each one claimed the honor of kissing Dmitry as they headed back to wreak havoc on the Hitlerites. Bear shook his head, remembering Taka and Sachino as inept and untrained soldiers only six months ago. Now they were some of the best in the whole of the Red Army and even of its elite, the GRU. A truck arrived and Dmitry was loaded in for the drive to the hospital. German shelling followed them down the road but not at the intensity with which it had started the battle. The Bear smiled a very real, very large smile for the first time in weeks and tucked the field blankets tighter around Dmitry as they sped into Moscow. Along the way spirited Red Army units of every type were moving forward under a constant aerial symphony of powerful engines.

Back at the front Felix was relieved to turn command over to Lt. Colonel Galanin at his forward HQ which was still well to the rear of Felix's position. As Felix entered the HQ building Galanin made an announcement which Felix missed as he took off some of the heavy winter clothing and outer boots. As he turned he realized the room was silent and looking up he was startled to see every officer and enlisted man on their feet and saluting, including several Generals. Felix looked around perplexed and suddenly realized they were saluting him! He blushed a bright red and respectfully returned the salute at which time a riot of congratulations and backslapping ensued.

Galanin let it go on for a few moments and finally raised his hands. "Comrades, we have much to do. The enemy fights on. We will get the new Lieutenant very drunk later and initiate those two new stars in the time honored manner. For now I present the Red Army's newest Lieutenant, comrade Felix Vasilev!" Felix looked stunned as the shouting continued but finally everyone got down to work. Galanin and Sachino, who was assisting during his recovery by working in communications, hugged Felix until he almost broke. After some more congratulations, they asked simultaneously, "Bear and the comrade Colonel?" Felix looked them in the eye and responded, "They live. The Bear as always has some fur missing but no real problems. The comrade Colonel is a mess. They have sent him to the major field hospital for treatment." This sobered the two GRU men immensely and they both could only think of Dmitry but returned to their duties. Sachino went back to his radio with tears rolling down his face.

Above these scenes Piotr was simultaneously firing on ground troops and dropping bombs on artillery while directing his 'Flying Infantry' in their assault on the German forces. As the Siberian shock troops began to engage he radioed his comrades that they were to head deeper into fascist air space. The lack of aerial response from the fascists surprised him and he kept admonishing his force to keep a tight lookout. Having rendered the German flank attacks ineffectual at best, he winged the squadron over in search of rear area artillery and supply targets. There was not much armor around as most of it was at the bottom of the marsh.

He just shook his head and smiled at the genius of his friend and future brother-in-law. He tried not to let his mind wander but for a moment it did and a vision of Natasha lived there. This only made him more determined to rid the Motherland of these fucking fascist snakes so life could go on. Soon he saw what he wanted. The day was gray with a fairly high ceiling and there, spread out before him, was the Hitlerite supply dump at Istra. He smiled as he radioed his men in for the attack. Minutes later all that remained of the lifeblood of the panzer armies was flame and dense black smoke. Ammunition and fuel supplies went off with spectacular fireworks and Piotr ordered his men away from the area. They circled back over the battle-field in time to see the charge of the Siberians as they took the fascist grenadiers smartly in the flank.

Soviet artillery had switched to long range bombardment as the 1st Siberian went into action. There were to be no reinforcements for the German infantry futilely trying to launch flank attacks. The Si-berians were directed to the flank of the Germans by Galanin using the team's sound information. First the armor came out of their snow covered camouflaged sites and moved forward. The tank riders climbed on as they barreled down the German flank, undetected, at 30 kph. The T-34's were about to prove their worth as never before. At the specified map coordinates both wings turned inward and burst from the forest onto the German lines. Smashing though the snow at high speed was exhilarating for the Siberian troops. Not on-ly tough but experienced in several years of fighting the Japanese, they were spoiling for this fight.

They loved Zhukov and would do anything for him and the feelings were returned. As they had de-trained in Moscow to march to the front a bit over a week before, he had been at the station to meet them. Standing on a flat-bed truck with folded arms he re-viewed them as they got off the trains for the first time since Siberia. They had not seen him since he led them to victory against the Japanese in Mongolia, which had earned him his promotion. Soon they saw him and the chanting started, "Zhukov, Zhukov, Victory, Victory!"

Zhukov seemed to swell in size from his compact fire-plug frame and returned the chant with a salute. They went wild and their enthusiasm had not lessened.

Now they were secure in the knowledge that he was sending them into the most important fight waged by the Red Army to date and they vowed to make him proud. Their feelings might have been tempered if they knew the demonstration had earned Zhukov a repri-mand from Beria and the NKVD for his 'rightist Bo-napartist' behavior at the train station.

Party politics aside, the nearly full strength di-vision took the Germans in the flank mercilessly. The armor drove though seams in the German forces and isolated them as the tank riders got off and pinned them down with light arms fire. The Shock battalions arrived and using heavy machine guns and field mor-tars, tore the fascist ranks apart. The pent up humilia-tion and sheer heart brokenness of the Red Army un-leashed a tornado of destruction on the German forces. Soon the lead elements of the *Wehrmacht* infantry were broken and running.

The Soviet tanks drove right through their formations, crushing men and vehicles and dispensing cannon and machine gun fire as they went. The tank riders re-mounted and soon the armor was in the German rear. Here the slaughter was even greater as supply units and rehabilitating troops were cleaned up by the ma-rauding Siberians. The tank forces called for forward artillery support to blow open any remaining re-sistance and moved to cut off critical river crossings to surround and exterminate the fascists.

No prisoners were taken until the very end and

even then it was a reluctant Soviet soldier who took prisoners. The Germans were stunned by the ferocity and professionalism of the attack but unfortunately not many survived to warn their leadership about the new Red Army they faced. Several German divisions just vanished from the map and as planned, the German commanders were forced to fall far back to pre-established defensive lines to escape the horrific scenes in the north of the city. This in turn launched a domino effect around the German line until even Guderian in the south was too isolated and had to fall back from Tula. Moscow was saved.

Chapter 25

The truck containing Dmitry and Bear with a nurse and two GRU *razvedchiki* for protection careened through the forest roads surrounding Moscow. Early in the German aerial bombing of Moscow the senior Red Army medical staff had recognized the importance of not centering the field hospitals in the city. With their constant stream of vehicles day and night they would have been an easy target. Additionally, they dispersed the blood collection sites as over two thousand Muscovites, primarily women, were donating blood every day for the fighting men and injured civilians. This all had to be stored at the hospital sites as the demand was great.

Therefore the major hospitals were in deep forest with heavy camouflage over the building and the roads approaching the hospitals. The advantage of some of the newer facilities was immediately apparent as medical advances could be more easily put into operation in facilities designed for those procedures. Dmitry was taken to the best of the facilities in the north of Moscow, now the safest district.

The nurses and orderlies unloaded him and immediately took him past the triage area into a dedicated examination and operation room. Here with modern lighting and wonderfully heated, Dmitry was stripped and a detailed examination begun. Bear was escorted out for his own examination. The newest Colonel in the Red Army's medical staff had been assigned to Dmitry's case and she launched into the examination at high speed but with a professional thoroughness. As head of the newly established Center for Traumatic Battlefield Injuries, comrade Colonel Irina Petrova knew her business and her patient. She had demanded to be here in her own hurricane-like way and no one else would treat Dmitry while she was alive. She had also brought her most modern equipment and sulfa drugs purchased from the Germans by the GRU during the joint occupation of Poland.

She noted with a heavy heart but professional glance the unbalanced eyes and bleeding from nose and ears caused by the concussion from both the beatings and the proximity to the firing of the tank's 75 mm gun. Next she diligently searched for other puncture wounds and dismissed the bullet wound in the thigh as trivial in this situation. She had a nurse clean the wound, apply sulfa and bandages after ascertaining the bullet had gone clear through the thigh. The facial burns were treated with sulfa and a salve.

What steeled her resolve and threw her into high speed was the stomach distention she observed. She quickly realized the swelling was caused by blood from internal bleeding pooling in the abdomen. The only resolution possible was surgery and repair if they could find the damaged sites. She had her team prep themselves and the patient for surgery and turned the room into an operating theater. Her first cut cost her untold strength as she prayed she could find the bleeding and repair it. After three hours she thought she had found and repaired all the contused or punctured organs and with liberal application of sulfa sewed the incisions shut. They moved Dmitry into a recovery room and put him in one of the new oxygen tents to help his body heal and also slow any infection. She gave a staccato series of orders for observation and collapsed asleep in a chair next to his bed.

Ten days later Dmitry was alert and able to move with great slowness. His always tough constitution had pulled him through. Fever had been slight and no apparent infection was observed. His appetite was back and his head bandages were removed. The thigh wound was healing well and only the sutures in his abdomen prevented him from real movement. Irina came by every day after finishing her work, but quickly realized the staff was as devoted to him as she was. They literally tiptoed around him and marveled at the Marshals and Generals who came by to kiss his forehead and just exchange a word or two.

One night at about 0100 NKVD troops burst through the hospital doors and scattered guards and medical staff as a pipe smoking short figure clad in gray was guided to Dmitry's bed side. Putting out the pipe in regard for the oxygen in use, the Supremo himself just stood at the foot of Dmitry's bed and watched him sleep in a drug and oxygen-fed coma. He reached forward and patted Dmitry's foot, nodded and left the room without ever speaking to anyone. Treatment, if possible, improved after that visit.

There was also a constant flow of *razvedchiki* with approximately one million complaints. The room was too cold, the room was too hot. The soup was weak and cold, hotter and stronger was needed! Where is the vodka? How can he recover without vodka? And on and on, finally Irina asked Bear to intercede and after that only Dmitry's team was allowed in. The

GRU had lost another commander, shot at Stalin's orders, so no real senior commander visited Dmitry. Surprisingly Marshal Shaposhnikov, Chief of Staff, who Dmitry had frequently clashed with, took on this assignment. He often came in the early morning hours when he was free because Stalin slept, and sat and reflected on Dmitry.

Finally Irina began to panic slightly as flowers, in winter, began to arrive by the hundreds. It seemed every woman in Moscow was sending flowers and in some cases offers of more substantive reward, to Lenin's savior and now the savior of the city. Even though the NKVD had forbade any publicity regarding the details of the battle, just like in a Russian village, the word of what had really happened spread like wildfire. Bear had to stay at the *Stavka*'s HQ at the Kirov Metro Station to avoid being recognized and mobbed. The legends and stories which Russians deeply love were forming quickly around the event. This was all positive for the city's morale but since Beria and the NKVD were not the heroes they suppressed any official recognition. The victory was attributed to Red fighting forces led by Stalin and his commissars.

In contrast to those false stories, the city's favorite tale was how the Sergeant-Major had transformed into a bear in order to lure the Germans onto the ice where he stomped his mammoth paw and caused the ice to collapse and drown them. This was just like the defeat of the German knights in 1242 on the ice of Lake Peipus by Alexander Nevsky. The city loved it and the story grew with every passing day. Bear did not mind or shrink from individually applied appreciation from some of Moscow's more beautiful young ladies but tried to retain some discretion in the process by using Dmitry's apartment with Irina's permission. He felt he had arrived in the land of sturgeon and honey.

Several weeks later, the time arrived when Irina and the other medical staff felt Dmitry could take the stress of a visit from the *Stavka*. They moved him; indeed he walked at a pace of a meter a minute to a larger room and they made sure everything was spotless. His extensive collection of Orders, wound stripes, and his Order of Lenin and Hero of the Soviet Union were displayed on a pillow next to his head.

The General Staff of the Red Army accompanied by some of the political members of the *Stavka* including Molotov and Beria, entered the room. Zhukov had been the first in and stood next to Dmitry's bed beaming like a proud parent at a school graduation, the very unusual smile illuminating his whole bulldog countenance. Surprisingly Dmitry registered that Rokossovskii along with Galanin, Bear, and Piotr from his team were also present. Dmitry smiled and feebly waved to them all.

Marshal Shaposhnikov stepped forward and read the order from the Presidium of the Soviet Union endorsed by the Supremo, Comrade Stalin, awarding Dmitry a second Hero of the Soviet Union along with various other Orders, more wound stripes, and the stunning news of his promotion to General. Dmitry was completely shaken and only the fact that he was lying down prevented him from fainting.

Zhukov proudly came forward. "As you all

know this is the son of true Bolsheviks killed while fighting for the people of the Soviet Union. I have had the honor of raising him, at comrade Lenin's order, as a son. Before I knew him he had saved comrade Lenin from death by assassination. As I watched this young man I realized that he was not only brave but very intelligent. He has shown that in the service of the Soviet Union for the last twenty years, but now he has saved not one person but millions. His father had counseled him to always defend the people! Comrades, he has done all of that and more."

"Today we honor him for that and as his very proud uncle; I give him my own Hero of the Soviet Union star for his own. Don't worry, nephew, I will get a replacement but it means we will always share the same award number which will bind us together. Secondly, I have no need for these old and worn general's tabs, so honored and beloved nephew, I give them to you to wear in memory of your uncle."

At this the room broke into stomping, clapping, and cheers. Rokossovskii broke through and kissed Dmitry. A corridor was opened and Irina was led forward with flowers and a perhaps more emotional kiss was exchanged. Bear, a Hero of the Soviet Union star on his own chest, was at rigid attention with the whole team saluting. Dmitry broke down in tears and whispered to Irina, "I love you." She gazed deeply into eyes and nodded and responded, "And I you." She broke away as Dmitry struggled to a more upright position.

He gathered himself and tried to speak but no words came. The tears flowed and he looked hopelessly at Bear. A roar sounded in the room as Bear announced, "The comrade General is tired and we should retire, comrades." The *Stavka* stared in awe for a moment at a Sergeant-Major giving them orders but like obedient privates quietly took their leave of Dmitry. Beria left first with a massive scowl that could not be hid and Zhukov shuddered. As always with the NKVD leader a dark shadow seemed to pass through the room.

That did not stop Rokossovskii from again kissing Dmitry and whispering, "St. George himself is pointing to you so your parents can see this moment. We are all so proud of you, comrade General." Dmitry's team lingered a bit longer primarily to tease him over his new rank and need for new uniforms and perhaps a private to carry around his decorations but glances from Irina had them gradually and lovingly take their leave.

However, there was one more honor for Dmitry. A representation of generals and colonels from the 1st Siberian Shock Division came forward and to his honor commissioned him as a Colonel in the Division. This was a signal honor from a group which was never expansive in recognizing others outside of their unit. Dmitry accepted the insignia with emotion and kissed them in regard. The Siberians saluted and exited and finally the room was quiet.

When they were gone Irina took Dmitry's vitals and moved the assorted medals off to a table. As she leaned over listening through her stethoscope to his breathing, he said, "The patient feels cold and somewhat constrained. Can the comrade Doctor assist with that?" With that she replied, "Oh you must be well, so back to duty. No, the comrade Doctor is not going to assist the patient with his animal urges but she will kiss him again and tell him how proud she is of him. Oh Dima, I am so glad you have recovered well. Another week and perhaps special treatment will be in order."

Dmitry just smiled and ruffled her hair which caused her to put on a serious expression and walk over to the mirror in the room to straighten out her hair and replace her blue Medical Staff beret before leaving for the Center. "By the way," she said. "That was very clever getting comrade Marshal Zhukov to promote you so that you would still hold rank over me. As I have just demonstrated it will not work in every case." A soft, lingering kiss followed and Dmitry was left alone with his thoughts.

A week later a summons came from Marshal Zhukov's office for the new general and Bear to report to the Kremlin bunker. As Bear and Dmitry entered the always darkened stairs to the underground command bunker beneath the Kremlin, they noted the infinitely fewer bombing attacks on the city. While still harassing the city the bombing did not reach the intensity of the attacks experienced from August until early December. Now in early January things had quieted down considerably. Zhukov had already launched winter counterattacks against the Germans, driving them further from Moscow. Dmitry assumed that he and Bear had been summoned to participate in the campaign planning for further actions.

Bear seemed to be physically quite flexible but

still a bit black and blue. Dmitry on the other hand still walked with a stiff gait and a slight limp due to the leg wound. His face was still not very pleasant to look at but the swelling and coloration reduced every day. Sunlamp treatments had helped restore some vestige of color and health to his face and he just hoped that he wouldn't frighten any small children. They descended the iron steps and entered the corridor to Zhukov's office at the opposite end from Stalin's 'Little Corner'.

As they moved down the corridor they were surprised to see Major Yedved and an armed NKVD security detail lingering just past Zhukov's office. Although the corridor was narrow Yedved made a point of keeping his back to them. They knocked and entered Zhukov's office. The orderly Sergeant closed the door behind himself as he exited the office with a furtive glance at the two famous fighters. They could hear Zhukov on the phone in the inner office but could not make out the conversation. With the mental equivalent of a shrug the two relaxed and waited for the General.

Zhukov opened the door and they were stunned at his appearance. His face was as red as they had ever seen and a mixture of anger and sadness was written over his countenance. He just stared at them and shook his head. Finally getting control of himself he ushered them in. Dmitry and Bear were wild with anticipation. What could cause such distress in the rigidly controlled temperament of the General? They had both seen him in the moments of deepest danger in combat and not seen anything like this. Their imaginations ran amok with scenarios of fascist victory or Stalin's death.

Finally the General choked out, "Order 270 states....Order 270 states...," and he collapsed into his chair sobbing. Dmitry ran to him. "Comrade General, dearest uncle, what is wrong? How can we help?" Zhukov looked up at Dmitry. "No, Dima, it is I who cannot help you. Please let me talk without interruption." Dmitry and Bear nodded their assent.

The General now stood and looked them both in the eye. "Stalin has ordered that all commanders who surrender be shot. Because of your special case, you are to be turned over to the NKVD for interrogation and assignment in a penal battalion. During your service in the battalion, you will be ordered to perform the most dangerous tasks on that front, unarmed. Only when you are killed or severely wounded will you be accepted back into the honorable company of the Red Army." The Marshal paused as Dmitry and Bear stared at him not understanding why he was quoting something they both knew.

The General continued, "Comrade Beria has asked comrade Stalin why you are not being processed like anyone else would be. He insists that you were captured and must follow the correct protocol." Now Dmitry and Bear stared hard at Zhukov and both experienced a cold feeling penetrating their hearts and minds. Dmitry spoke, "But comrade General, we were not captured. We went voluntarily into capture as part of a plan to save the city, which succeeded beyond all our expectations."

Zhukov kicked his desk and threw the phone against the wall. "Damn it, Dima, I know and I have been arguing with comrade Stalin for an hour. He has also spoken to Marshal Shaposhnikov and asked why the protocol is not being observed. Shaposhnikov and Timoshenko are as distraught as I am. The NKVD is behind this and all Stalin will say is 'we must be fair and apply the order with no prejudice'. This is a plot to destroy you and the Red Army when we are in the middle of a fight for our fucking lives. At any rate I cannot hide from it. I have been unsuccessful. That is why the human worm and his thugs are outside. You are demoted to '*shtrafniki*' and assigned to a penal unit at Leningrad."

Dmitry came to attention and saluted, "Yes, comrade General. I will leave immediately." Now Zhukov was crushed. This man was so loyal, so brave that he saw the plot and took it head on. Zhukov hoped his parents were watching. "No, Dima, you both go." Now Dmitry almost lost self-control. "The Sergeant-Major was operating under my orders. He had no say in the action. I ordered him to surrender."

Zhukov actually smiled, "I knew that would be your position, Dima, but the NKVD has persuaded Stalin that you both go. For that reason I hereby pro-mote the Sergeant-Major to Captain so that you will be assigned to the officers' *shtrafbat* (penal battalion) to-gether. The shortest lived promotion in history. Now we must call Yedved and his cutthroats in but before we do, please give me your Orders and insignia and the most precious HOSU's. I will hold them for your return so that these NKVD snakes will never get to dishonor them."

Dmitry and Bear complied. Bear was crushed by Dmitry removing his general's tabs and almost began to let the rage escape but he held it in. He vowed to personally kill Yedved someday and he also vowed that Dmitry would return to the Kremlin, a general and a hero.

Zhukov opened the door and Yedved and his team started to come in. The General signaled that only Yedved was to enter at which Yedved looked distinctly worried as he eyed Bear's back. "Comrade Major, here are your prisoners," Zhukov explained as he picked up the phone, Stalin's secretary answered and asked them to wait for the Supremo. Zhukov put on the speaker and in a moment Stalin's voice filled the room with its rasping whisper, "Comrade Major, this is your Supremo." Yedved actually came to attention. Stalin continued, "Due to the special nature of this case, there is to be no interrogation or physical protocol of any kind. Is this clear?" Yedved said, "Yes, comrade Supremo." "Good," Stalin replied and hung up.

Zhukov stared at Yedved. "If there is one mark on either of these officers when they arrive in Leningrad, I will have you shot. Is that clear, comrade Major?" Yedved nodded but interjected, "But the Sergeant is not an officer, comrade General." Zhukov pulled out the order promoting Bear and said, "He is now. So beware, and you had better explain that to your thugs and cronies. Any scratch on them and you are dead." Yedved visibly shook. "Yes, comrade General." "Also, they will be transported to Leningrad by plane. I have arranged this. Send whoever you want with them. Please remember, comrade Major, the service these heroes have rendered the Motherland."

Now Yedved smirked and Zhukov's fist shot out, connecting with his jaw. "Comrade, you are on the verge of insubordination and I will not tolerate it!" Yedved shook his head and regained his balance. The hate in his eyes was palatable but Zhukov looked it right back at him. The General continued, "All right, take them to Monino." Zhukov looked Dmitry and Bear in the eye and saluted. Without rank or status as soldiers they were confused on how to respond. Zhukov moved forward and hugged each of them as the NKVD squad entered the room. They saw this and were confused. In a low voice, Yedved gave them new orders on how to treat the prisoners. They all moved into the corridor.

The Red Army staff personnel in the area had seen the NKVD force and assumed Stalin was visiting Zhukov. They came out of their boxlike working rooms to see what was going on. First Yedved exited, and then Dmitry and Bear surrounded by the guards. The staff officers could see that they were without insignia. Something was wrong! An angry buzz started up and down the halls as Zhukov stepped into the corridor.

"Comrade General, what is happening? What is happening?" They asked. Zhukov either would not or could not respond. Soon the cries of "Piss on the NKVD!" started. Then "Fuck the NKVD!" and then most ominously "Kill the bastards, kill the commissars!" The General looked at Yedved as if to say, look what you are causing but Yedved just smiled. This was all obviously part of the plan to purge the Army and most probably Zhukov.

Zhukov raised his hands for silence to prevent his whole staff from being sent to the GULAG or worse. But something else halted their cries. At first they thought it was a failure of the air pressurization system as a low rumble started through the underground complex. Perhaps an ammo dump had been hit in the bombing? No one knew but soon eyes turned towards Bear who evidently was beginning to sing. Yedved and his men also looked astonished as they recognized Bear's deep mountain waterfall of a voice breaking into 'The Red Army is Invincible', the song that was the heart and soul of the Red Army. Dmitry recognized Bear's strategy to save the staff as did Zhukov who joined in.

Zhukov raised his arms and conducted the impromptu choir. The immortal words rang throughout the corridors and echoed up the stairs as the group with Zhukov in the rear climbed into the frigid darkening twilight. Finally the singing stopped and chanting began, "Heroes of the Soviet Union, Heroes of the Red Army!" thundered down the halls. Bear seemed to swell in size at the first linkage in public to his new award. Dmitry smiled and patted his friend on the shoulder. "You deserve this, old friend, you are our best. I am so very sorry you are here." Bear just swelled in size even further and smiling said, "I can think of no better or more honorable place to be, comrade General."

At the top of the stairs the guards came to rigid 'Present Arms' attention, an honor not usually accorded disgraced *shtrafniki*. The voices of the staff were still ringing loud as they all stepped into the frigid

Moscow winter. Dmitry and the General exchanged deep emotive looks. Zhukov then turned to Bear with a look of pleading. Bear gravely nodded and took Dmitry's arm to help him into the waiting truck. The General listened to his staff and watched as the truck drove through the Kremlin Clock gate. As the last rays of the winter sun shone under the clouds, with a war colored hue, the tears freezing on the General's face were transformed to a deep red.

Epilogue

Dmitry slowly walked back to the Washington embassy. His shoulders hunched, his hand incessantly scrubbing his short cut gray bristle. He felt a chill that had nothing to do with the weather. It was in motion. Soon, soon, the world would learn of the Soviet's perfidy and recklessness. Events would spin out of his control. Likely he would die. He fervently hoped he had not ended the world but given it a new chance.

Be sure to be there as Bear and Dmitry's saga continues during the Sieges of Leningrad and Stalingrad in "Red Ice." It only gets worse!

Historical Notes

This is a novel but its intent is to relate a human picture of the reality of the war between the Soviet Union and Nazi Germany. The war was brutal beyond our imagination. We don't really know for sure, but perhaps as many as 30-35 million Soviet military and citizens died. Approximately 75% of German casualties happened on this front. The list of atrocities is endless. Yes, children as young as five years old were used for blood transfusions by the Nazi's. At the same time as they were fighting the Nazi's, Soviet citizens and military were persecuted by their own government. Millions sent to the GULAG's, tens of thousands shot, the endless betrayals. The sheer perseverance and courage of the Russian people is staggering.

Some details: The GRU exists and is still perhaps the largest intelligence agency in the world. Their *razvedchiki* are legend and form the basis for the modern *Spetznatz* forces. The battles in the novel are generally fictional representations of possible events such as the defense on the Vop or fictional retelling of actual battles such as Moscow. The friendship and strain between Rokossovskii and Zhukov is based on historical fact as is Stalin's dialogue in most cases. Yes, the Soviets tortured and killed their heroes. Yes, bread trucks were used to round up the purge victims. Yes, *Order 270* was real. The song *The Red Army is Invincible* is real, and penal battalions are also of the period. Timing of their appearance was moved forward a few months to fit the story line.

Thank you for reading my debut historical novel, <u>Red Tears</u>. I hope you enjoyed it. If you would be so kind as to take a moment and add a review, I would be very grateful. Unfortunately, reviews and referrals are the only ways for a new, self-published author to compete with the big name writers. Your positive reviews will ensure that you get to follow Dima and Bear for three more volumes!